The
Kingdom
of Sand

Farrar, Straus and Giroux

New York

The
Kingdom
of Sand

Andrew
Holleran

Farrar, Straus and Giroux
120 Broadway, New York 10271

Printed in the United States of America
First edition, 2022

Library of Congress Cataloging-in-Publication Data
Names: Holleran, Andrew, author.
Title: The kingdom of sand : a novel / Andrew Holleran.
Description: First edition. | New York : Farrar, Straus and
    Giroux, 2022.
Identifiers: LCCN 2021060839 | ISBN 9780374600969 (hardcover)
Classification: LCC PS3558.O3496 K56 2022 | DDC 813/.54—dc23
LC record available at https://lccn.loc.gov/2021060839

Our books may be purchased in bulk for promotional, educational, or
business use. Please contact your local bookseller or the Macmillan
Corporate and Premium Sales Department at 1-800-221-7945, extension
5442, or by email at MacmillanSpecialMarkets@macmillan.com.

www.fsgbooks.com
www.twitter.com/fsgbooks • www.facebook.com/fsgbooks

1 3 5 7 9 10 8 6 4 2

Keep death daily before your eyes.

—Saint Benedict

The
Kingdom
of Sand

The Dirty Hat

The first touch of winter in North Florida, especially when the cold front triggers a long day of rain, always makes you feel that life is turning inward, that when you get home, there will be someone there. But in my case there wasn't, which was why in December of last year I went back to the video store on Highway 301.

It was the second week of the month, the middle of a cold, gray Thursday afternoon, when I stopped by after not having gone there for a long time. I'd been driving through the sort of fine mist that had me turning the windshield wipers on and off, on and off, since what was on the windshield didn't seem like enough moisture to qualify as rain and yet after a few minutes without the wipers I couldn't see. It was as if I were driving through a cloud. In Florida rain is almost always accompanied by lightning and thunder, but that day the whole world was wet, gray, soft, and gentle, so soft and gentle that it seemed to require some sort of touch, if not tenderness, which was why I decided on my way home from Gainesville to stop at Orange Heights—a place without a single citrus tree, or any elevation whatsoever; an example, I suppose, of what Henry James meant when he called Florida "a fearful fraud" in a letter to a friend.

I was sure no one would be there on such a cold, wet day, though even that, I told myself, would be just fine. Sometimes you go to these places to be alone. But to my surprise, as I put on my turn signal, the white truck I'd been following since Gainesville did the same, and when we came to the video store, it turned into the parking lot. Even more surprising, after we turned off our engines, out of the white truck that had preceded me emerged a tall man whose silver hair, glasses, and neatly pressed blue denim shirt made him look like a prosperous farmer who belonged to the Baptist church we had just passed on our way here, the most conventional paterfamilias one could imagine. Watching him walk by, in fact, made me think of that story by Nathaniel Hawthorne in which Young Goodman Brown goes into the forest at night and finds the leading figures of his community at a bonfire worshipping Satan.

The video store had not been opened for satanic rites—though the people who went to the Baptist church down the road probably thought so; it had been opened for truck drivers on their long haul down to South Florida. That was why it sat on the southwest corner of the intersection of 301 and Highway 26, the east–west state road that connects Gainesville and Putnam Hall.

Roads are to Florida what syringes are to veins—the swiftest means to introduce a foreign element into the body; in this case, humanoids. Build a road, and there goes the forest. Highway 301 was built as a sort of conveyor belt to move visitors to Central and South Florida as fast as possible, one of the first four-lane expressways to do this. That's why for many years whenever I drove to Gainesville on 26 I had to come to a stop at 301 and wait for the light to change. This eventually made the intersection a magnet for businesses: two gas stations, the video arcade, and a fish and tackle store. Yet no intersection could have been less bustling. Even after the video store opened, the crossroads retained its somnolent air, because by that time 301 had been superseded as a major north–south route by two newer highways to the west—441 and I-75. And it was only because those new highways had reduced the traffic on 301 that truck drivers still used the latter, though they never stopped at the video store. What the customers in the video store got instead was the sound of their rigs whooshing by outside the blacked-out window behind which people stood, wondering why truckers didn't stop there anymore.

It wasn't just the lure of I-75 and 441 that made the video store a rather sleepy place, however. Two years after the fish and tackle store closed, the state built an overpass so that people going to and from Gainesville on 26 wouldn't have to stop at 301 at all. Before the overpass one had no choice, which meant that, during the interval created by the red light, one would inevitably count the cars in the parking lot across the highway and, depending on their number, have to consider dropping in—one more choice in a consumer society. But once the overpass was built there was no need to make a decision—instead of stopping at 301 to wait for the light you could drive right over it on the bridge and keep going.

As I glanced down from the overpass, in a state where you rarely see anything from a height, two things never failed to impress me: one, how flat Florida is, and two, how quiet 301 is now. Florida is not an exciting state to drive; there are no mountains, nothing spectacular on the horizon. Years ago a friend from New York who'd decided to drive to Key West with his mother turned back north of Orlando because, he said when he called from a rest stop, "It's just so boring!"

Another friend got no farther than Kissimmee, where he called from the restaurant in which he was having lunch to say it held only two kinds of people: old men in neck braces and teenage girls dressed like prostitutes. Maybe that's just Central Florida. But I understand how the flatness of the state, the absence of any interesting features, does make a drive down to Miami pretty monotonous; the last time I did it I needed an audiobook of Barbara Bush reading her memoir—descriptions of trips abroad after her husband had left the presidency that not only surprised her with their pomp and circumstance but also got me to Fort Lauderdale.

Florida comes to you only when you stop somewhere and get out, preferably near or on a body of water; and then you see its esoteric beauty. Seen from the window of a speeding car it's mostly drab. Looking down from the overpass across 301, however, it wasn't only the flatness that struck me. There is something about an overpass that momentarily detaches you from your life. It's like looking out the window of a Boeing 737 as you're flying somewhere and seeing a private jet streak by below you in the opposite direction.

That's how I felt glancing down at 301 from the overpass. For some reason the trucks looked motionless, like objects in a diorama, a diorama of my life before the overpass was built, when my younger self had to wrestle with stopping at the video store—though I rarely did, even in my thirties. I preferred the boat ramp six miles to the east, where I could meet people in more pleasant surroundings. Video stores like the one on 301, its plate glass windows painted black as if to blot out not just the sunlight but also the judgment of other people, always seemed designed to make you feel that what you were doing there was "dirty." Not the boat ramp.

At the boat ramp you could sit in your car under the live oaks on autumn afternoons watching the squirrels run up and down the tree trunks. You could admire the egrets and blue herons standing along the canal while you waited for the man from Florida Pest Control to drive in—until the police clamped down, that is, and drove away everyone who was not there to fish, which left us with the video store.

The video store was so depressing compared to the boat ramp that even after the latter was off-limits I seldom felt an inclination to stop at Orange Heights, and when I did, whatever pornographic fantasies I walked in with always disintegrated in the sight of the glum and silent men walking up and down the hallways, men so nondescript you would never have suspected them of being homosexual. If aesthetic standards are the foundation of your sexual requirements, I learned, you have restricted yourself to a very small portion of the human race. That was why I was grateful for the overpass—it meant there was no need to debate whether or not to visit a place that I was certain would be a waste of time.

After the overpass was built you had to want to visit the video store, because to get there you now had to take a detour. Driving to Gainesville you had to get off just east of 301 at a vegetable farm where people could pick their own strawberries, proceed to the intersection, and wait for the light to cross. Coming from Gainesville you had to turn off a quarter-mile west of 301 onto a two-lane road that went by a big white Baptist church that over the years had been adding more and more ancillary buildings as the congregation prospered. In both directions one had to go out of one's way, which made visiting the video store a commitment—not something one did on the spur of the moment.

There was, however, one reason I'd stop at Orange Heights on my way home from Gainesville that had nothing to do with sex or loneliness, and that was to listen to the music on the public radio station broadcast from the university, because its signal extended only as far as 301. WUFT-FM, like many public radio stations, had played classical music until the mid-1980s, when it switched to all-talk, which upset so many listeners that the station created a separate frequency, a spin-off for people who could not bear the loss of Beethoven and Brahms. But the signal of this subsidiary station did not go nearly as far as the main frequency; in fact it stopped, more or less, at Orange Heights.

There had always been something frustrating about WUFT-FM when the station played classical music—as if the selections were being chosen by music majors who refused to play masterpieces because they were too popular. When it became all-talk the station was tedious for other reasons. Its few local shows were dumped for syndicated programs that continued even after their moderators were no longer with us. Even after one of the hosts of *Car Talk* died, for example, they kept broadcasting reruns on weekends.

The spin-off station created for classical music presented another problem. If, say, they did select a Brahms symphony while you were still in Gainesville, the minute you crossed 301 it disintegrated in a burst of static. So when some masterpiece of nineteenth-century German music, the only balm, I often think, for being alive, was played, I'd have to make the detour to Orange Heights and listen to the rest of the piece in the parking lot of the video store; and then, when the Brahms or Beethoven or Mozart was over, I'd start the car and drive home, because there was no point in juxtaposing the emotions created by their music with the feelings that greeted me the minute I entered the video arcade.

But one day when Mozart's last piano concerto was on the radio I stopped in the parking lot to listen to the final note and decided to go in. What a mistake! Once inside I stood in my usual corner just inside the entrance and watched the expected assortment of nondescript men walk around until they all gave up and left, at which point a very young man in khaki shorts and a baseball cap came in and they all returned, like buzzards on roadkill. It was the old story: the power of youth and beauty, in this case a student who, when he left, took all the hope and energy with him. There was nothing to do but get in the car, drive across 301, buy pecans for my sister at a roadside stand, and go home. And that was the last time I visited the video store until that cold, wet December day I am speaking of, when I was in such a mood driving back from Gainesville in the mist that even though there was nothing on the radio but some Renaissance dance music involving hautboys and drums that I would have been perfectly happy to have disintegrate into static, I decided to stop at Orange Heights.

The minute I parked and turned off the engine, what struck me was the silence—not just the silence of the intersection, but the deeper stillness animals must feel when they are stalking their prey. There is something primal about cruising. In fact, I was so nervous about going inside that wet day that I remained in my car leafing through a book I'd just taken out of the library in Gainesville even when the man from the white truck passed my windshield.

I did not have to rush; I knew what was waiting for me. The video store consists of a big room lined with racks of pornography and sex toys, a theater in the back where heterosexual porn films are shown, and a small annex for homosexuals off the entrance foyer you can reach without even going into the main room, where the cashier sits on a raised dais supervising his or her domain. That day the cashier was a woman who happened to be standing outside the door smoking a cigarette on her break, smiling graciously at the men going past her like the hostess in a restaurant—a sight so unnerving that I waited till she had finished smoking and gone back inside before I got out of my car. Then, once inside, I walked quickly past the doorway to the big room, entered the gay annex, and paused just inside the doorway to adjust my eyes to the darkness before walking down the narrow corridor lined with video booths to see who if anyone was inside.

I'd been watching so much pornography at home that it seemed to me I needed to see real people having sex. Given the abundance of porn on the Internet, though it sometimes took hours one could always find people with whom one wanted to have sex, and when you did you were given the rare privilege of watching two or more individuals who would never give you the time of day in real life make love to one another while you were, so to speak, in the room. The disadvantage, of course, was that you weren't, and when it was over you hadn't really had sex. You hadn't touched or been touched. The reason I was at the video store that wet December afternoon was that the night before while I watched two men make out in a film, the younger one had turned his face up to the older man in the middle of giving him a blow job and the two of them had begun kissing, and I realized at that moment that the young man was saying to the older one: *I am yours, my body is yours, you can do anything you want with it—anything.* His whole posture, sprawled like an odalisque across the older man's outstretched leg, feeding on his genitals, made the moment when the young one suddenly lifted his head to kiss the older man a gesture of complete abjection, one that said: *I surrender.* Of course, the danger when I got in the car and drove over to the video store was that I'd see no one to whom I wished to submit—and the other problem: Who would want a man my age to surrender in the first place?

Indeed, the idea of touching an actual person was becoming increasingly unimaginable, for not only was I wasting enormous amounts of time watching porn—unless no time that is devoted to erotic matters is wasted—but watching sex on film (where nothing could go wrong) had made me reluctant to have sex in reality, where so much can.

The problem was that my life had acquired an element of sexual frustration unlike anything I'd ever felt before—I'd been feeling almost sick to my stomach, as if I was coming down with the flu. I'd found myself the day before standing at the stove putting on a pot of soup for lunch when I began pushing my groin against the oven door; and when I went over to the kitchen sink, I began to hump it. I need to check into the hospital in Gainesville, I told myself, and ask the nurse to hook me up to an IV—an IV filled with semen. Instead, I was watching movies on my laptop, clicking on one film after the other in search of a scenario (Japanese Businessman, Extreme Grandpa, Motel Hookup, Doctor's Visit) that would give me an orgasm, just the way I'd spent hours at the baths in Jacksonville walking the halls, or sitting in my car at the boat ramp waiting for the Florida Pest Control van to drive in.

There was another problem: my father had spent the final years of his retirement playing solitaire on the very table on the back porch on which I liked to put my laptop when I watched porn. He'd sat there with his back to the lake, drumming his fingertips on the table in an expression of profound boredom, until one day, while I was reading in my bedroom, I heard him call my name and went out, and he said to me, "I cannot raise my right arm." In other words, he'd had a stroke—just a few feet away from the chair in which years later I found myself sitting as I searched for a porn film that was sufficiently well filmed but truly amateur. The only difference between us was that he had played solitaire and I was watching people have sex: a generational decline, I suppose.

Solitaire is just that: a game one plays by oneself. He was waiting for the right card to turn up. I was spending hours searching for a scenario that would lead me to an orgasm, though I could never relax at the table, given what had happened just a few feet from my chair. I'd have to go back into my bedroom, the room in which I'd heard the words that announced what was, eventually, his death, as sudden and life-changing as the apparition of the Archangel Gabriel when he appeared to Mary to announce her pregnancy. But that was just a matter of using my imagination. When faced with actual images on my laptop, I had become aware that the more porn I watched, the more sensitive I was becoming to the slightest thing that would destroy the illusion that I was watching people really having sex. All too often I could see that the men were merely acting—especially when there was no chemistry between them, and the sex seemed to be an athletic exercise in which the actor was trying to strengthen his glutes with thrusts so rapid and forceful they made one think that Americans don't really enjoy sex but only time at the gym. Pleasure seemed to be the last thing on anyone's minds in these movies; it was rare when someone took his time and treated the other person with any sensuality. That was why I found myself searching for films that looked amateurish—for the genuine, the authentic, though now that everyone can film themselves having sex they are so video-savvy that the frequency with which they stop to adjust the camera angle makes one miss the old days when people would pause only to take a hit of poppers. Many nights I'd gone to bed after four or five hours looking for some elusive film I couldn't find, and now, that wet day in December, I was more than normally depressed—not just because I hadn't found that film but because Christmas was coming.

So it was doubly disappointing that afternoon to go into the video store and see that everyone there was as old as I was. How many artificial hips, replaced knees, and pacemakers were in that room I could only imagine—one man just inside the entrance had, evidently, such severe arthritis that the person he'd just had sex with was giving him a hand to help him up. The expressions on the customers' faces were all so blank one could only explain them with old age and weariness, unless it was the experience of having been rejected countless times. Everyone looked like a dog in a pound hoping to be taken home, but with none of the eagerness dogs exhibit in that situation. No barking, no wagging of tails, no jumping up against the wire partition—instead a face from which all emotion, even longing, had been removed. Yet here we were—searching, I suspect, for more than sex could give us. The ancient Greeks thought old men obtained virility by ingesting the semen of young ones. Nowadays you take a multivitamin. So why were these men still coming here? I'd always wondered why an older friend of mine named Earl had gone to the boat ramp in his seventies to "get with," as he put it, someone in the men's room, since it had nothing to do with his having an orgasm. He didn't even bother to unzip his pants. Like Earl, these men at the video store were here for some other reason—habit, loneliness, something they could not name. They made me think of Santayana's definition of fanaticism: redoubling your efforts when the goal is lost. I wasn't even sure why I was there, unless it was the mist drenching the strawberry fields on the other side of 301 in a soft silvery light, the emotions engendered when winter finally arrives in North Florida.

The prosperous farmer I finally spotted in the last cubicle on the right, though he was standing with his back to me, looking down on someone I couldn't see because the farmer was so tall. The only sound in the entire place was something between a whimper and a moan coming from the man on his knees. But that didn't last very long. A few minutes later the farmer gave me a little smile as he passed me on his way to the bathroom. So that's all one has to do, I thought— park your truck, get blown, and leave. The man who'd blown the farmer was a short, shapeless fellow who slinked past me with his head hanging down, rushing to the exit before the farmer could emerge from the bathroom, which made me think: No, that's the secret—not just having a nice cock, but not caring who adores it. And with that I drove home, thinking there could be no greater loneliness than the one

I was feeling as the raindrops splattered on the roof, wondering why the need to touch another human being had to be played out in such a sordid place, in so humiliating a manner.

Nevertheless, I was back the next day. The weather was no longer that gray, misty, wet stuff that had made me so emotional, and I told myself I was stopping off just to see who was there on my way to the gym. Once a week I went to Gainesville for a "spa day," which meant taking a high-interval class in a room full of young women with bouncing ponytails, and then a swim with people my age while the truly decrepit participated in aqua-aerobics on the edge of the pool, peeing, a friend assured me, in the water. After that I planned to have lunch with two old friends, which made me think a stop in Orange Heights might provide me with some amusing small talk. But that wasn't the main reason I turned into the video store on my way west. One of the strange qualities of visiting a place like that is that it has aftereffects. In the same way you can go to bed after watching a porn film without having an orgasm and realize, when you get up the next morning, that you have to find that film before you do anything else, what happened at the video store on one day could very well amount to unfinished business with which you had to deal the next. That's because everyone has a different melting point in these places. Some people are slow, cautious, and risk-averse; they take their time, not only to make sure the situation and object of desire are right but also to overcome their own inhibitions or fear of rejection. The talented, confident few jump right in. So now, twenty-four hours after having realized the farmer would do just fine, a fact I'd been too critical to admit at the time, I was driving back to Orange Heights in the hope that he might be there again. No such luck. When I stopped by to find the handsome Baptist, I found instead the same quintet of egg-shaped men in baggy T-shirts who'd been there the day before. After they left, the only person remaining besides myself was a middle-aged man with dyed blond hair occupying the cubicle where the farmer had stood with his back to me the day before—and when he left there was nothing to do but enter the booth he'd vacated and watch the porn film that was still running, which led me to the lowest form of experience there is in a dirty bookstore: watching porn by yourself.

Of course, watching porn in a place where one is supposed to have actual sex is already depressing; it's then that the pathetic nature of one's fantasies, the depth of one's loneliness, become clear. Had I been home, I'd have watched the movie the previous tenant had selected with no self-consciousness; I'd have been able to enter into the spirit of the thing with no problem. Now it was a mockery of the need that had brought me here, a film that only accentuated my isolation. Of course all my emotions were on edge to begin with because it was two weeks before Christmas, and in one of those strange moments when whatever we are using to distract ourselves from our real worries (e.g., porn) suddenly evaporates—the way we sometimes wake up in the middle of the night and immediately begin thinking about what it is that's really bothering us, even when we didn't know this when we went to bed—so it was that, watching the film on the monitor the previous tenant of this cubicle had abandoned, I ceased to see the figures at all, and in their place was what was actually getting me down: the coming holiday. In seven days I'd have to fly to my sister's up north to spend the week with her family because she didn't want me to be alone. I was doomed. There was nothing standing between me and Christmas 2020 at my sister's but a potluck dinner given by the Gainesville Friendship Alliance, a group of gay men who met at one another's homes every few months for social purposes that had become over the years so elderly that it was in danger of dissolution, my friend Patrick said when I joined him and our friend Luke for lunch in Gainesville at a restaurant on Thirty-Ninth Street after working out at the gym.

"And why can't they get new members?" I said as we sat down on a small patio outside the Gator Growl.

"Because if you were young," said Patrick, "and walked into a GFA dinner and saw people who looked like us, you'd run the other way too."

"Why? How do we look?"

"Like people who have—how shall I put it?" he laughed. "Faded."

The only reason I was shocked that afternoon at being reminded of my age—ten years older than Patrick, two years older than Luke—was that I'd just come from a swim at the gym and was feeling fit and vigorous. But now there it was on the table between us. The reason I had to watch so much porn, the reason I had to go to the video store, the reason I'd not found anyone else in it attractive, and the reason we were having lunch with one another were all the same: we were old.

It was odd, however, how each time we got together a different one of us seemed older than the other two, like a circulating trophy nobody wanted. The last time we'd lunched, at a Cuban restaurant on Thirty-Fourth Street, Luke had looked old to me, walking with a noticeable stoop because of his arthritis. The time before that it had been Patrick, the flesh on his face furrowed, his red hair too long, his eyes those of a thousand-year-old mummy. But today Luke was looking better than Patrick or myself—his short silver hair neatly trimmed, his tanned face set off by a powder-blue shirt and a pair of rimless eyeglasses. He was, I had to admit as we perused our menus, the one who looked most sexually viable. In fact, he was still going to the video store on Highway 301 once a week, he told me, and always had sex there, even if the last man he'd blown, he said, had been wearing a brassiere. He knew, in fact, who the Baptist farmer was; the farmer, he said, had a mole on his left testicle, and the longest prepuce Luke had ever seen. Luke, it occurred to me, was still in the sexual swim of things; Patrick had been in a relationship with a man I knew for so many years I'd lost count.

So there we sat on a dappled patio in Gainesville, Florida, talking, as we increasingly did, about the aches and pains of growing old, which included, that afternoon, their glancing at the floppy hat I always wore on the advice of my dermatologist to prevent skin cancer, a khaki hat I had just put down on the table, revealing inadvertently a stain that ran around the interior of the brim that prompted Luke to observe that my hat looked "dirty."

"It's sweat," I said. "It's the stain that sweat leaves. Remember that detergent ad—'ring around the collar'? It's the hat version of ring around the collar. Only in this case it's ring around the hat."

They started to laugh but the more I thought about it the more ashamed I felt—like so many things in old age, a hat with a sweat stain implied something. I'd been accused of being an old man who didn't take care of himself. There was no point, however, in making excuses. So I changed the subject to the recent death by heart attack of a man who'd chosen Luke as the executor of his estate, a man Luke had known for forty years, a man with whom he'd spoken on the phone every day, a man with whom he'd come to bicker with when they got older so sharply that it was uncomfortable to have lunch with both of them, a man who'd had more sex probably than the three of us put together, a handsome, muscular retired journalist who'd worked for the university and supported a younger hustler the past decade of his life, a hustler who, Luke told us now, had been knocking on the deceased's neighbors' doors to ask for money.

"For what?" said Patrick.

"His drug habit," said Luke. "He's been asking Skip's neighbors for money for drugs. The woman who lives two doors down from Skip asked me this morning why Skip didn't leave Lionel anything in his will—because, she said, he'd 'mentored' him for so long."

"Mentored him!" laughed Patrick.

"That's the word they're comfortable with," Luke said. "I told her that I'd asked Skip the same thing. I said to Skip, 'Leave Lionel a hundred thousand in a trust, so that he can't blow it on drugs.' And Skip said, 'I've already helped him enough!' So Lionel's not in the will."

"Have you ever *met* Lionel?" I said.

"No," said Luke.

"Not in all the years Skip was seeing him?"

"Not once," said Luke, "though I *saw* him the day before Skip did. I was leaving the mall on Thirteenth Street when I spotted this handsome muscle number standing on the curb with his shirt open, and when I looked back he grabbed his crotch. But I kept driving. Skip didn't. He saw Lionel the next day in the same place, pulled over, and said, 'Get in.'"

"And thus began a great romance," said Patrick.

"I don't know if you'd call it a romance," said Luke.

"Well," Patrick said, "they were together for ten years."

"But Skip never let him move in," Luke said. "Of course, Lionel came by so often, the neighbors all thought he lived there. And get this. The woman who asked me why Lionel isn't in the will told me that now Lionel comes up onto their lawn at dinnertime and stands outside the window of the dining room and watches them eat."

"That can't be good for the digestion," Patrick said.

"But you go by Skip's house too," I said.

"I do," said Luke. "I've been looking for Skip's Rolex—which has disappeared."

"Do you think someone stole it?" I said.

"There's no way to know," Luke said. "It could have been anyone—Lionel, the paramedics, the police, anybody who went in there. Who knows? They found Skip on the toilet—the brand-new toilet he'd just paid eight hundred dollars for. I think the day he died he must have thought he needed to take a shit, when in fact it was heart congestion. The two things can feel the same way. He had his heart attack while sitting on his brand-new john."

There was a silence, since neither Patrick nor I knew what to do with that detail.

"Did I tell you," Luke said, "that not only can I not find the Rolex, but Skip left over a million points in his Marriott account that are not transferable?"

"What points?" I said. "What Marriott account?"

"Skip always stayed at a Marriott when he traveled," Luke said, "and they have a sort of frequent-flier program for guests—the more you stay, the more points you get. And the more points, the bigger the discount on your next room. And as you know Skip traveled a lot. He went to San Francisco for the Folsom Street Fair; he went to Miami for the White Party, to New York for the Black Party; he went to Chicago and Washington and Miami for Gay Pride. He was a circuit queen!"

"For which I give him a great deal of credit," I said. "Skip was always able to enjoy life. I think he was in some way the happiest homosexual I knew."

"What does that mean?" said Patrick.

"I mean he had it all. He was handsome, well-built, outgoing, he had a beautiful house, a good job, and he had no guilt whatsoever about being gay. He always had lovers, and lots of friends, gay and straight. He loved his life in Gainesville and he loved to travel. I thought he had a very happy and successful life. I think he actually enjoyed being gay. I mean, he really *liked* going to the White Party."

"He did," said Luke. "And he was racking up points with Marriott when he took all those trips. It got so that the last time Skip stayed in New York it cost him, like, thirty-five dollars a night."

"You must be kidding," said Patrick.

"I'm not! And he died with over a million points that he could not leave to anyone else. Imagine what those are worth!"

Neither Patrick nor I knew what to do with this news either, so we fell silent until it occurred to me to ask if Skip had ever gone to the video store on 301.

"Are you kidding?" said Luke. "We both went, at least twice a week. Skip used to drive by my house to see if my car was in the carport before he went—because he didn't want to go if I was there. I'd be sitting on the porch talking on the phone, and I'd look up and see Skip drive by—always in the baseball cap, the baseball cap he never took off—to see if my car was in the carport. We had a rule. If Skip's car was in the video store parking lot when I got there, I had to wait twenty minutes before going in, and vice versa. As you know, it was hard to compete with Skip. Everybody wanted him, and he wasn't shy. So he got everyone he went after."

"Skip was everyone's idea of Daddy," said Patrick.

"That's right," said Luke. "And when he was younger, he was everyone's idea of Son. I mean, did you see the photos of him when he was in his twenties that they used at his memorial? He could have been on TV! He was that good-looking. But back to the video store," he said as he lifted a roll to his lips. "I've cut back on my visits—mainly because it has the problem that all those places do."

"And what's that?" said Patrick.

"Too many cock-suckers," he said, biting a piece off his roll, "and not enough cock."

We fell silent at that too, as Luke began eating his soup and a handsome young man on a bicycle came onto the patio and stopped a few feet away from our table. He was so good-looking I nodded subtly in his direction so that Luke would turn around and look at him, but before Luke could the young man said something I didn't hear, for not only do I wear a floppy hat to prevent skin cancers and disguise my hair loss, but I am also now nearly deaf—particularly when listening to Patrick, who speaks in so low a voice I can only compare it to Jackie Kennedy's when she gave a tour of the White House to Edward R. Murrow on CBS. That's why I missed most of the exchange that was going on between Patrick and the handsome young man until the latter raised his voice and said, "And when would that be?" to which Patrick replied, "Never," whereupon the young man yelled in an even louder voice, "You asshole!" at which point I realized the whole exchange had been a request for money.

After a few more insults, the angry young man rode off across the parking lot and stopped at a white car parked by a fence, a white car out of which three big, burly men in civilian clothes got and flashed their badges, at which point I realized the young man had just had the bad luck to go up to an unmarked car in which police officers were sitting.

"I suspect he's homeless," said Luke, turning back from the scene.

"And he just tried to panhandle the cops," Patrick said.

Whereupon I was moved to ask, "How many homeless men do you think there are in Gainesville?"

"About eight hundred," said Patrick. "And now that it's getting cold they're moving into town from their camp on the south side. Have you ever been? There's litter everywhere. They shit on the ground, and then they put some small article of clothing over it to hide the turd. There are so many places for them to get off the street. Instead they crap on the sidewalk and leave a paper napkin or handkerchief on top of their bowel movement."

"That's mental illness," I said.

"I agree," said Patrick.

I was thinking that this angry young man was good-looking enough to earn money hustling—but thought I'd better not voice that idea, since Patrick had set up a shelter for the homeless near the bus station. The trouble with Patrick, I thought as we sat sipping our drinks, was that he was so good he made you feel bad, and so intelligent he gave you the impression he knew what you were going to say before you said it. But I couldn't blame him for being competent, charitable, and smart—a combination that is seldom endearing, when you spend your hours watching porn. Indeed, when he excused himself and went into the restaurant to get another lemon slice for his glass of water, I took the opportunity to say to Luke, "Did you know that Patrick helped get that social service facility for the homeless out by the bus station started? And that he mentors people? And that he's doing an oral history of Gainesville, interviewing gay people before they croak? And he's on the board of the Gay Pride Center, and the Natural History Museum, and he went to the hospital every day his sister was there with that strange skin disease to make sure she was getting good care—and picked me up after I had a biopsy on my right eyelid, which I couldn't have had if Patrick hadn't agreed to do that, since they won't release you after anesthesia if you have no one to drive you home, which is the central problem of my life at this point—I have no one to drive me home—which I think is unfair to people who live alone, but that's the rule. He does things for people we don't even know about. He does what the Church calls corporeal acts of mercy—which makes sense, because he went to St. Patrick's, right down the street, when he was growing up, though I think he's an atheist at this point. But he really does try to help people in practical ways. He's like a priest—a good priest."

Even so, I did not say when Patrick returned to our table

that the look that came over him every now and then—the eyes of a thousand-year-old mummy—was that of a prelate who's seen so much disgusting human behavior that he wishes God would send another flood and wipe human beings off the planet. Instead, when Patrick started to talk again about the homeless after his return with a fresh lemon slice, I waited till he'd finished and then I said, "Enough of all that! Let's talk about sex!"

The moment Luke learned I planned to stop at the video store on my way home, he made me promise to e-mail him an account of what happened. I told him nothing would happen, though Luke always had sex when he went, even if the last time it was with a man wearing a brassiere.

"The ironic thing is that I shouldn't have to go to the video store," I said, "because there are a lot more homosexuals in my town than I used to think."

"What makes you say that?" said Luke.

"Well, lately I've been looking at the sex ads on craigslist. Have you seen these ads on craigslist for 'panty boys,' these photographs of big butts in lace underwear with their assholes pushed right up against the camera lens? The ads from my town look like a textbook for proctologists—one asshole after another in close-up. Why does anyone think that's attractive?"

"Because they're narcissists," said Patrick. "They think their butts are hot."

"So what are you doing for Christmas?" I finally said, blurting out what was really bothering me.

"Staying home," they said in unison.

"I wish I could," I said. "But I have to go to my sister's. She feels sorry for me because I'm alone and she doesn't want me to spend Christmas by myself. But I'd love to spend Christmas by myself. It would be so relaxing."

"Then tell her you're not coming," said Patrick, with that look on his face that he got when proposing an obvious solution people were too stupid to take.

"I can't," I said. "I feel it would mean I was repudiating the family—and she's all I've got. She's still the person I put on those forms when they ask who to contact in case of emergency. I don't know what I'll do when she dies. At least she'll die with her family. I'm going to die alone. Have you heard of this Japanese term for people who die alone in their apartments and the body is not discovered for several days?"

"*Kodokushi*," said Patrick. "Lonely deaths. Is that what you're worried about?"

"Yes," I said. "And not just me—I worry about my friends, who are now scattered around the country. We're all wondering whether we should move into assisted living now or wait awhile. Whenever my friends don't answer the phone I assume they've croaked. That's, I guess, why I keep going to my sister's. She's family, though the weird thing is, she knows I don't want to come. But she thinks it would be worse for me if I didn't."

"Christmas triggers women's territorial imperative," said Patrick. "They think it's their responsibility—their turf. My sister wanted me to come to her house at Christmas even after I met George, and I told her no. She said, 'But you have to come home for Christmas!' and I said, 'I *am* home.'" He laughed, and cocked his head and looked at me with a twinkle in his eye. "It's very simple," he said. "Just say no."

"You and Nancy Reagan," I said, hoping he would drop the subject.

Instead, they both picked up the theme of my being alone and insisted I go to the GFA potluck on Saturday night. They gave me directions to a house on the west side of Gainesville. But I knew I didn't have the courage to walk into a room full of men my age with a bag of jalapeño potato chips, pretending that we were going to find love or even companionship with one another at this point. Who were we kidding? And so we went inside and paid our bills.

I was feeling so lonely that when we stood outside the restaurant to say goodbye I wanted to hug both of them, but they were standing there with a posture that deflected such an impulse, so I returned instead to the question that was increasingly on my mind.

"Skip died at home," I said, "on his own toilet. But do you ever wonder where you'll kick the bucket? I mean, you and I, Luke, live alone, so if we have a stroke or heart attack it may very well happen when there's nobody else around, which means we may lie there on the floor for some time before anybody discovers us, *if* anybody discovers us. We'll be *kodokushi*—which could happen to you too, Patrick, because you spend time down here without George."

"I agree," said Patrick. "In fact, the man who lived in the unit next to mine just died. He was ninety-three, a Dutchman who retired as an engineering professor at the university. They discovered his body when he didn't show up for physical therapy. His son's here now. He flew in from Amsterdam, and he told me to take whatever books I wanted from his father's library."

"And what did you take?" I said.

"The memoirs of Chateaubriand," he said. "I've always wanted to read them—they go from the French Revolution to Napoleon. Napoleon died on St. Helena," he added, "but they exhumed his corpse and reburied him in Paris in Les Invalides."

"And where will you be buried?" Luke asked.

"In Les Invalides," said Patrick.

"You told me you were going to be buried in that ecological cemetery," I said.

"What ecological cemetery?" said Luke.

"The one on Paynes Prairie," said Patrick. "They don't bury you in a coffin, they just put you in the ground so you can decay along with all the dead leaves and branches and squirrels and snakes. We're all biodegradable, you know."

He looked at us with a smile.

"But who's going to *put* you in the ecological cemetery?" I said. "I mean, who's going to find your body? That's the question."

"You mean now that we're old queens who never had kids so there's no one to be with us when we kick the bucket?" said Patrick.

"That's right," I said.

"You mean the main reason parents are upset when children tell them that they're gay—that they'll be all alone when they're old?'"

"That's just a stereotype," said Luke.

"I wish," I said. "I can't even get an appointment with a gerontologist. Did I tell you that my neighbor the retired doctor goes to a gerontologist he raves about so much I decided to go to him myself—but when I called I was told he's not taking any new patients."

"None of the good ones are," said Patrick. "That's the problem—everybody wants the good ones. It was like auditioning at the Met to get my doctor. I had to make friends with the receptionist, I had to write a letter, I had to go down and make a pitch."

"Well, what can I do," I said, "except wait till one of his current patients dies, which presumably will open up a slot. But how do I know when that happens?"

"Call the receptionist every day," said Luke, "to see if anyone's croaked."

"Don't be ridiculous," I said. "I can't do that. But I have decided to go through all the papers in my house. And rewrite my will, and get rid of the old porn magazines I keep in a garbage bag in my closet—in other words, make everything shipshape so when I die I'm not a burden on my nephew. He's the executor of my estate. I've decided to devote the next two or four years to getting ready for the next event—because it is the next event, and we have to make our deaths as smooth as possible for our survivors, we have to minimize the stress and inconvenience. It's only polite. I just read a letter an eighty-something woman in San Francisco wrote to *The New Yorker*. She said the most valuable thing she's leaving her children is the name of the woman who, when they've taken what they want, will get rid of all the rest. There are people who do that, you know, for a fee. Human buzzards."

"You should move to the Village," said Patrick.

The Village—not to be confused with the Villages, a large retirement community north of Ocala that has not just the highest concentration of old people in the state but also the highest rate of venereal disease—is an adult assisted-living establishment on the west side of Gainesville, a reasonably pleasant collection of dorm-like buildings centered on a body of water that looks more like a chemical retention pond than a lake on which three ducks that the residents like to feed paddle back and forth all day, leaving their feathers floating behind them on the oily water. Patrick had taken me there one day; we visited his sister in her one-bedroom apartment whose balcony view was so charming it softened my antipathy to the idea of moving there—till Patrick told me, in a burst of enthusiasm, that he already knew which pieces of furniture in my house would work in my new place ("You could put the red chair here!") and the bubble burst. And now, here he was again, urging me to move there. But there was no point in going on with the conversation, it was too depressing, so with no more ado I said goodbye and set off to the video store. As I drove I kept thinking of a line in that song that Streisand sings about a house not being a home when no one's living there, which is what was waiting for me, and that reminded me of the story about Rudolf Nureyev when he went back to Russia and an old babushka asked him where his home was now and Nureyev said, "What's home?" and she replied, "Where someone waits for you." Leave it to a babushka, I thought. Pow! Bang! Right between the eyes!

The weather was no longer that cold gray mist or the light rain that had made me want to stop at Orange Heights to be touched two days before. I was making the detour this time not for sex but simply to see who might be hanging around. What was hanging around when I arrived were the same egg-shaped men in loose T-shirts, wearing such glum expressions I didn't stay. There was nothing I could do to stop Christmas from coming, I told myself. Patrick was staying in Gainesville with his partner because he'd had the courage to say "No"—with the same decisiveness that had enabled him to say "Never" to the panhandler's request for money. Luke had an elderly aunt in town he'd spend the day with. I was doomed. The earth was going to spin; one day was going to succeed the next; I was floating on a river of Time to a dock at which I'd have to get out and deal with the natives. Standing in the video arcade watching the egg-shaped men walk by was not going to stop Christmas. So I left. But that brief quarter hour inside had made me feel, as it always did, "dirty." So when I got home the first thing I did was wash my hat.

The Endless Cantaloupe

Toward the end of their lives my parents ate nothing but ice cream—though my father liked to put peanut butter on top of his. There was no point in remonstrating with them. I felt the way the doctor did when he told the woman who complained that her hospitalized husband's request for a pastrami sandwich was not very healthful that "at ninety-four, he can eat what he wants!" That was it: my parents had reached the stage where there was no point in worrying about their diet. Let them eat cake, I thought. At a certain point, you learn in a nursing home, they don't care what kind of food the patient is eating—just that they're eating something. I was grateful, as I watched my mother consume her little packet of ice cream, that she was getting any nutrition at all.

But at the same time it worried me, because we grow up with certain nutritional ideals; as children what you're supposed to eat is a huge matter. You are told to drink milk because it will make your bones strong, to eat spinach or broccoli because it's good for you. Just about everything said about food in a middle-class house is couched in moral terms. "There are starving people in India who would be glad to have what you've left on your plate," my mother would say to me. And: "Do you know how much this meal would cost in a restaurant?" And: "You are not leaving this table until you've finished your peas."

When I was seven, I stopped eating altogether; I sat at the dinner table long after the rest of my family had left because I was not allowed to get down off the chair till I'd finished. It got so bad my mother took me to a doctor. But food—like showers—appalled me. I suspect that for many children food is still no pleasure. We have to eat when we are small, and we are supposed to eat certain things and not others, because we are being prepared—for Life.

But when Life is behind you, you can eat whatever you want because you're on your way out. My father would fix the most outlandish meals the last year of his life, when he was depressed over my mother's incarceration in a nursing home: a big bowl of ice cream with two slabs of peanut butter slathered on the top, four fried eggs and a rasher of bacon every morning. In fact my father was a very good cook. He came from a small town in Ohio, where they ate vegetables from their own gardens, and lots of meat. My father never ate with an eye out for cholesterol. I was sure he was risking his life as clearly as a man playing Russian roulette when I'd watch him prepare, every morning, a breakfast that consisted of those four fried eggs, hash brown potatoes, and a rasher of bacon or sausage. I was living then in New York with a copy of *Let's Eat Right to Keep Fit* by Adelle Davis on my kitchen table, making milkshakes of brewer's yeast and blackstrap molasses, eating sardines and liver. But I wasn't about to tell my father what to do. So I watched him digging his own grave in silence as he prepared those feasts of fatty acids, and when he reached his eighties (old enough, I suppose, to prove the breakfasts had had no deleterious effect), I was not about to chastise him if he chose ice cream and peanut butter for dinner. His wife had been taken away from him after she fell and had to be put in a nursing home, a situation that so upset him he could not even bring himself to visit her, or even take much pleasure in the fact that I brought her home on weekends. When she was home it didn't lift his spirits the way I thought it would, and when she was not there, he sank even further. The only time he came alive after my mother's fall was when he had to do his taxes; having worked as an accountant most of his life, there must have been something calming about numbers—as opposed to the chaos of life itself. But that was it. One Thanksgiving he prepared his usual splendid feast for the three of us and then, in the middle of it, it dawned on me that he was nowhere in sight, so I went out into the living room and found him sitting in his favorite chair, smoking a cigarette in the dark; and when I asked him why he wasn't eating with us, he said, "Oh . . ." and then, after a pause, as if there was no point in searching for better words, "I'm depressed," a statement to which I had no answer. There was no answer for the situation we were in. So I kept my mouth shut.

Watching him eat breakfast, however, it was hard to bite my tongue. My father enjoyed his breakfast (which he often ate for dinner as well) so much that when he finished eating he would tilt his plate and lick the remaining egg yolk off it, a sight that made me think of that drawing by Goya of Saturn devouring his children. (Hadn't he sent me to college so I could make such connections?) It made me wonder what childhood lesson of "waste not, want not," what Depression-era habits of frugality, were surfacing at this late date in his life. Before licking he would first clean his plate with repeated passes of his fork over the porcelain, pressing it down forcefully so that the tines would pick up every crumb, and then, finally, he'd put his tongue directly on the surface, which at this point could only contain the thinnest smear of egg yolk and bacon. He'd lick and lick the plate, then put it down, as if he had done nothing unusual at all, and look around, like a dog or cat that has finished its meal.

Yet my father so far as I knew had never been deprived. He came from a family of prosperous German Americans; his father had worked as a bookkeeper for a lumber company and then started a lumber business of his own, though I think its failure induced a sort of nervous breakdown that may have involved a heart condition as well, which put him to bed for a long time, and caused him to withdraw from business altogether. No one in the family ever told me what happened. It seems astonishing to me how much I was not told about my father's past, as if it was none of my business, or irrelevant to my life. But then that is the fate of children—they are brought onstage in the middle of an opera whose libretto they have never read and whose language they don't even know. When my grandfather died in his mid-fifties, my father was still an adolescent, but I'm not sure what effect this event had on him, or whether the scarlet fever he had as a child or anything in his past could "explain" him. I learned only later that he had worked on farms as a young man before moving to Chicago, where he studied to be an accountant, because he wanted to earn money, which he did.

My sister claimed my father was the only person in our family who knew how to spend money. He was so generous, such a good provider, in fact, a man of such quiet authority, that even when he sat there licking the plate at the age of eighty-four, it did not diminish his dignity in the slightest.

And it certainly did not indicate mental derangement; all his faculties were intact.

As were his courtesy and sense of privacy. At a certain point during my mother's incarceration in the nursing home, my father began getting up in the middle of the night to watch whatever was on TV. I'd return from the baths in Jacksonville at three in the morning and find him sitting in the den, but he never asked where I had been; he assumed I'd gone to a bar or nightclub, I suppose, in order to take my own mind off what was depressing him even more than me. Without my mother, it was alarmingly clear, our home was not a home. The two of us were lost. We simply said hello to each other—like traveling salesmen in a hotel, or soldiers stationed in the same barracks while waiting to be shipped out—and I went to bed, leaving him up in the sepulchral light emanating from the television. It was a measure of his generosity—of letting me do what I wished—that he never even inquired where I had been.

Then one day, in the second year of my mother's paralysis, he was doing his taxes on the porch while I lay on my bed reading and I heard him call my name; I put down the book, went out to see what he wanted, and found him sitting at the table on which he had played endless games of solitaire in his bathrobe the last ten years of his life with his back to the lake, so bored he'd drum his fingers against the table-top while contemplating his next play. "I can't move my right arm," he said in a perfectly normal voice. My first instinct was to get him to bed. He was a big man and it was not easy moving him from the chair on the porch to his bedroom, but we managed, though once he was on his back, he refused to tell me the name of his doctor, because he knew what would happen if he did: he'd end up at the same place my mother was in Gainesville—city of hospitals, nursing homes, and crematoria—in other words, a sort of concentration camp.

He was right. Two weeks later, after a stay in the hospital, he was living down the hall from my mother, in such despair he did not even brighten up when I wheeled her in to visit him. But then my father had never shown emotion in front of me unless he lost his temper. It was a neighbor of ours who told me that he'd found my father with his head resting on the table like a second-grader during rest period when he visited him at the nursing home, whereupon my father had looked up only long enough to tell our neighbor he was going to get out of this place any way he could, which he did by dying a week later.

"If a job's worth doing, it's worth doing well" was one of the few pieces of advice I remember him ever giving me. The only other statements of philosophy were "Good golf is easy golf"—an adage that is more applicable to life than one might think—and the admonition that one should never "cheat your feet"—i.e., buy ill-fitting shoes to save money. My father was a determined, disciplined businessman. He did whatever he set out to do, and once dying was the task he had set for himself, he accomplished it quickly. He was out of that nursing home in about a week; his wife lingered another eight years.

My mother, in my brother-in-law's opinion, was afraid to die—something, I thought at the time, and still do, that anyone with an ounce of sense is—even though she would say quite calmly, from time to time, "I want to die," something I could only listen to without replying, since I was not about to help her do that. Instead, she lived almost another decade. Like my father, however, what she wanted to eat changed. I knew we were coming to the end when she lost interest in everything but ice cream—though I was relieved whenever my mother ate that; it meant she cared about something. Nothing in fact makes anyone who loves someone who is sick happier than to see the loved one eating. It means that person wants to remain on earth. But at a certain point even ice cream lost its allure for her, and by the time she stopped eating I'd learned that this is a natural way the body shuts itself down. Food, after all, is fuel, the fuel we throw into the little furnace in our chests, burning constantly to keep us going. No fuel, no combustion, no combustion, no life. Stop feeding the fire, and your life goes out.

At least my mother never had to have a feeding tube— that object of universal distaste, even, or especially, in nursing homes. She was killed by a series of strokes. Some membrane or vein gave way in her brain, and her body began convulsing, like a machine that shudders after you shut the engine off, on the way back to the nursing home in the car, though she was still alive when I put her back to bed in her room. By then she had a room to herself, I'm not sure why; I suppose she was nobody's ideal of a roommate at that point, though she could not have been quieter. She was not doing much with her days but lying there with her eyes closed, not even watching the television that, like food, had been for so many years a sign of her interest in life.

I wasn't there to see her die. By then I'd had more than I could stand. After driving her back the day she had convulsions in the back seat of the car, I returned home and went to bed, where I waited a few hours after waking the next morning before returning to the nursing home, and when I did, I learned it was over.

When I walked in she was still in bed, the sheet pulled up to her neck; I forget what she was wearing, whether she was dressed in street clothes the way she always was when I came to take her out, or if she was in one of those thin cotton hospital gowns that tie at the neck. I simply remember the room being clean and empty, and the television being off. It was so quiet there was nothing to do but sit beside the bed, where I began smoothing her hair for some reason, pressing it down over and over, as if trying to massage away a headache. My next memory is of going out into the hall to talk to her doctor while my mother lay there, visible over his shoulder through the doorway. He told me how he'd never forgotten the story she'd told him about the way she fell and broke her neck: standing on the stairs when her grandchildren were running toward her to embrace her. Startled, I said nothing, though this wasn't the way it had happened at all—my mother had risen in the middle of the night to pee, and tripped on a rolled-up rug. She had told the doctor this version, I presumed, because it made the accident less meaningless, more touching, or expressed her ideal: that she was loved by her descendants.

That my mother had not felt loved made no sense, though I could not forget the night she'd sat on the stairs of my sister's house one Thanksgiving, the same stairs on which she had placed the accident for her doctor, saying as she wept after one cocktail too many, "Nobody loves me, nobody loves me." It must have been something from her childhood, growing up in a family of seven children where it was probably quite easy to feel ignored. I can't say. But the next thing I knew I was sitting with my sister in a room at the funeral home, our mother laid out on a table beside us, quite unable to appreciate the fact that not only did we love her, but we were both bawling at the sight of her corpse, though I cannot recall what she was wearing there either—the hospital gown, the pale blue patterned thing, or something else. I do remember how different she looked, how cold and white. Death had already started to alter the color of her skin from flesh to marble. The cessation of her heart had taken away from her the circulating blood, the élan vital, that animates human beings; she was shutting down, the way a tree dies limb by limb till there's not a green leaf on it, the way she'd told me to fall asleep when I was a child by relaxing my extremities one by one. My sister and I were finally living the scene our mother had used to tease us when we were small— with a somewhat macabre sense of humor, it seems to me, but one that never failed to have an effect. "You know, I'm not going to be around forever," she'd say. And now that was true. It was the worst sight I'd ever seen.

She was beyond ice cream at that point. Ice cream: so American. Ice cream: the one thing Europeans will concede to us in the realm of food. Ice cream: at the fair the U.S. Army in Heidelberg put on every summer, it was ice cream the Germans would come to gobble, just as we American soldiers went to their bars and *gasthauses* to drink beer. I myself never eat it, unless a host serves the stuff, because I don't want to put on weight. But I love ice cream. Who doesn't? For a while I ate fat-free ice cream, defending its pleasures to people who said it was pointless. Fat-free ice cream was, I thought when it first came out, yet one more American miracle. You could eat all you wanted and not put on weight. Of course, you were getting so much sugar that that wasn't true, and eventually I stopped. Like so many Americans, I have always been a puritan about my diet—unlike my father, I saw it in moral terms.

I thought, I guess, that if you ate healthfully there was no particular reason you should ever have to die—for the same reason you could keep your car running forever as long as you changed the oil every three thousand miles. After my mother died I continued to care for the car and myself with the same conscientiousness I'd always shown. I did not make the spinach lasagna she'd liked on weekends—it reminded me too much of her—but there were other healthful recipes. Instead of ice cream, for instance, I'd buy cantaloupes for dessert—though halfway through, I'd tire of eating them, even when I'd added fresh lime juice, and finish the enormous melons only because I considered it a sin to throw food away. My breakfast was the opposite of my father's—whole-grain cereal, skim milk, and fruit—and I drank alcohol only after reading that people who consume red wine with their meals have less heart disease. But I eschewed the roast beefs and steaks my father had served us, the hash brown potatoes, and the delicious custard he would carry across the street to the neighbors when they were sick. And it was only when a friend told me that if you eat just two tablespoons of peanut butter a day, no more, you won't gain weight that I returned to one of my favorite foods from childhood. But otherwise I rarely ate for pleasure, I ate because broccoli had indoles that were thought to deter cancer, and cantaloupes were good for the bowels.

What I was maintaining my bowels for, however, I was not so sure as the years went on and I remained in my parents' house, in part because I had no wife and children of my own and considered my parents, and the memory of them, my main relationship. Though they were dead they still seemed to be in the rooms they'd once inhabited. Eventually my grief diminished, but whenever I found myself eating out of boredom, when I was not really hungry, I would recall that my mother had been fed food for years when she probably had no appetite at all, and the thought of her eating in the nursing home, of her being kept alive when she probably felt she was of no earthly use to anyone, would make me put away the snack. I continued to eat what I thought was good for me: broccoli and beans, whole grains, fish, greens, and fruit, including cantaloupes from South Florida that were sold on the roadside up here and were so large it took forever to finish them. You could always dice the cantaloupe and put the chunks into a bowl, I discovered, add some pitted cherries or blueberries, and drench it all in lemon or lime juice—but even then I had to make myself keep eating till the giant cantaloupe was gone, and only the knowledge that they were full of vitamins would make me buy yet another.

Of course, by then I was eating all my meals alone—not recommended for good health—and even the glass of red wine did not make up for the absence of table companions. My parents had given dinner parties when they were alive. Guests loved the grapefruit sections soaked in crème de menthe with which my father began, and the Waldorf salads, and perfectly cooked roast beef. But when I had friends over to eat they were gay men like myself, and the sight of them around the table made me think of sailors in a seamen's home, or homeless men in a shelter. The one Thanksgiving I made dinner for friends, following my father's example, I simply missed my parents and waited for everyone to leave. Food for me now was just fuel—something one threw down one's gullet while reading a book or listening to the radio; I could scarcely imagine cooking for taste or pleasure, as my sister did.

But I was still a sucker for the list of foods that supposedly increase longevity (Swiss chard, mustard greens, blueberries, and still, decades after Adelle Davis, those old standbys, sardines). I believed somehow in the absurd idea that if you ate right you could live indefinitely. Even when, a decade after my mother's death, I began getting skin cancers, all I could think was: How could this be, given all the broccoli I've eaten? It must be loneliness, I concluded, the lack of a person to live for other than myself, since we are also told that health is psychosomatic. Meanwhile the little boxes of tea taken from the gift basket a woman had sent after my mother's death sat in the cupboard along with my father's bottles of Scotch, and in the cheese box in the refrigerator the little triangles of Boursin from the same funeral present, which I would not permit myself to eat, and in the freezer my father's last carton of Breyer's vanilla ice cream, turned yellow and hard as a stone.

It was then I began eating out with my friend Earl at a local restaurant—just to be in a room filled with other people at mealtime. I always had the same thing: the turkey wrap (more healthful than the barbecued pork), but that wasn't what I went there for; it was the chance to glance at the other diners, mostly families, in the booths around me, eating the fried onion rings and garlic bread I would not touch.

One day an old man in town who had lived with his wife

for over fifty years in a little cottage by the lake was cooking lunch when his wife had a heart attack; she died a few hours later in the hospital, and when he got back to their house, the potato he'd been boiling for her was still in the pan on the stove. I've always wondered if he ate it. I still do.

The Kingdom of Sand

Of the four roads leading out of this town only one looks the way it did forty years ago—and even that, the road to Florahome, is starting to show the small, unmistakable signs that it will end up the way the others have: the forest cut down to build a public storage facility, a Family Dollar, a gas station, a mini-mart, a housing development. Though the place my father retired to in 1961 is what the real estate agents like to call "centrally located," that means you must drive about an hour to get anywhere. An hour to the northeast is Jacksonville; two hours to the south is Orlando; thirty minutes to the west is Gainesville; an hour to the east is St. Augustine. What lies between these points is a web of small towns, located on average about seven miles from one another: Hawthorne, Lamont, Simmons, Interlachen, Florahome, Carrabelle, Madison, Lawtey, Macclenny, Grandin, and Brooker.

"Is it lazy—or does it just look lazy?" a friend from Boston asked years ago when she stopped to have lunch on her drive south. "Both," I said. One of the great appeals of Florida has always been the sense that the minute you get here you have permission to collapse. When my sister came down to visit it was always fun to watch her hit the Wall. On the way in from the airport in Gainesville she'd be chattering with manic energy—insisting we stop at the farmer's stand near 301 to buy strawberries or collard greens, asking for news about the neighbors, observing changes in the scene going by the car window. Then, half an hour after arriving at the house, I'd look over and see her stretched out on the porch sofa, her lips parted, head back, as if chloroformed, wiped out by the sheer nothingness, the silence.

The sounds I associate with Florida used to be: the whistle of the train from Palatka that ran through town at night on its way to Atlanta; the squirrels and raccoons running across the roof as I lay in my bed waiting to fall asleep; my parents breathing in their beds across the hall; and—that most Florida of all sounds—the drone of a small plane crossing the sky in the middle of the afternoon. But only two of these were left after my parents died and the train tracks were torn up and converted to an asphalt trail on which people can now walk and bicycle all the way to Palatka—theoretically.

Palatka is forty minutes' drive to the east; Gainesville, half an hour to the west. Palatka is an old town on the St. Johns River that for some reason has remained pretty much the way it always was. Gainesville has not. Gainesville is the main thing, the Paris, the Athens, of North Central Florida. That's because it's the home of the University of Florida, and used to have a wonderful bookstore, and still has gyms and an excellent public library. That's the reason one goes to Gainesville: to get a book you can't find anywhere else. The other reason is to see a doctor: the dermatologists, dentists, ophthalmologists, orthopedists, and audiologists who make Gainesville a boomtown in the American medical-industrial complex. Its hospitals are huge and state-of-the-art; Gainesville is where the astronauts are sent if anything goes wrong. Gainesville is the place you go to get your taxes done, eyes examined, teeth cleaned, skin checked. Gainesville is the planet to whose gravitational pull people in the small towns around it are all subject. It's where we know we'll probably be taken when we die—which is why having to put my mother in a nursing home there, and having to take my father into the hospital the day he had his stroke, seemed like such a defeat. There's no way around it: Gainesville gets you in the end.

There is an adult assisted-living place in this town, but what exactly they offer has never been clear to me. For years I was under the impression that it was like Penney Farms, a retirement community half an hour to the east—where for many years the only people admitted were retired missionaries. But I think that rule has been relaxed, along with so much else about Christianity. A young woman I met at the gym who works there once told me, when I asked what the night shift at Lake of the Palms could possibly be like, that residents get out of bed in the middle of the night thinking they are in their own home and fall. Knowing that there is a night shift at Lake of the Palms makes me think I might go there instead of Gainesville when I need to, though I haven't made the effort to tour the place or make inquiries. As Freud said, nobody believes in his own death. For some reason, one thinks one is going to live forever. In a small town, one thinks that Time is not even passing.

The mother of a friend who grew up in Gainesville used to write the date of purchase on the bottom of everything she bought, and whenever she picked up some object she said it was always a surprise to see how much time had gone by. That can happen anywhere, of course, but it seems to happen more easily in Florida—even though North Florida has four seasons and trees lose their leaves in both spring and fall. Much of this part of Florida, in fact, looks prehistoric. There's a prairie south of Grandin that resembles the painted background the museum in Gainesville uses for its diorama of dinosaurs—a flat golden plain with pine hammocks breaking up the sea of grass—and in the garden I still find shells that must date back to a time when the ocean covered the state, though we are sixty miles from the sea.

When my father settled here the town was just a faded summer resort for people in Jacksonville, fifty-three miles to the east, a place where families sent their children for summer camp so they could swim and water-ski. Nobody water-skis anymore; the very idea summons up a vanished America, the one that made movies about mermaids played by Esther Williams, and built Cypress Gardens downstate so that tourists sitting on bleachers could watch human pyramids go by on water skis holding the rope handle that connected them to the speedboat in one hand and a flag in the other. When my father retired, all the lakes in town were high. People skied at five o'clock, after the daily thunderstorm, when the lake was smooth as glass and every pine tree, including the cones, was reflected on the surface of the motionless dark water. We'd ski from the Big Lake down a chain of smaller lakes that were all connected by narrow channels lined with weeds in which we'd been warned not to fall because they were full of water moccasins. The lakes were so high there was water beneath the pilings of the pier at the public beach, and the pier still looked just like the photograph of it on a postcard in the five-and-dime store uptown.

The only other postcards they sold in 1961 showed a woman standing in a bikini beside an alligator with its jaws wide open, and a more generic card that was used for California as well as Florida that featured a little old lady in a lawn chair surrounded by strapping young men in red Speedos above the phrase "Having the time of my life!"

There was something forlorn and faded even then, however, about the pier at the public beach, the paint peeling off the walls, the concrete shuffleboard court half-covered with sand, the moss hanging from the live oaks through which one glimpsed the lake. It looked like a set for the Moon Lake Casino—the one where Blanche's husband shoots himself in *A Streetcar Named Desire* after she discovers his sexual secret.

One reason for this may have been the fact that we'd arrived at the end of one decade and the beginning of another. Whatever the explanation, as popular as it had been in the fifties, nobody was using the pier in 1961. The concrete terraces lined with square concrete tables and benches were as empty as a restaurant accused of food poisoning. Across from the public beach was a white clapboard inn to which people had once driven miles to have dinner on Sunday afternoons, a place where the football team from the University of Florida would spend the night before a game to ensure some sort of monastic bonding. But there had been a fire that gutted the building, after which it simply sat there for years. Rumor had it a man in Gainesville who owned the inn was using it as a tax write-off—a man who ended up a patient in the nursing home in which my mother lived for almost a decade. One day while pushing her down the hall in a wheelchair I saw the name on a door—Mr. Skirpal—and thought: That's the man who owns the inn! It was like finding the Wizard of Oz.

For most of the sixties the inn, like the town itself, seemed to be suspended in Time and Space: no one was fixing it up, and no one was tearing it down; a perfect emblem of our new home. But it created a certain atmosphere. In front of the inn the road dipped down into a shallow ravine, and for a minute the rotting inn was on your left, a grove of old live oaks on your right. But that did not last very long. The man who owned the land next to the public beach sold it, the live oaks were cut down, and two new houses were put up in their place: my first lesson in private property—that everything you look at in Florida, even the woods whose beauty you take for granted, is owned by someone, and that person can sell what he owns when he wants, and the person who buys it can do what he wants with what he's bought.

A few years later a child on a church outing drowned at the public beach and lawyers for the town council made sure that fences and warning signs absolving the town of responsibility for anyone swimming there without a lifeguard were posted, and what remained of the grove of live oaks was enclosed with a metal fence, and then some women built a playground made entirely of old railroad ties that looked like a medieval fortress and was mentioned on the television news as an example of grassroots volunteerism, and then, not long after the five-and-dime stopped selling the postcard of the pier, the pier itself was painted and cleaned up, the burned-out inn torn down, and the town began to change as people from Jacksonville who did not want their children exposed to drugs in the public schools began moving here.

In 1961, however, the town was still little more than the intersection of two highways, presided over by a silver water tank on which the graduating class would paint its year. The town had one drive-in movie theater, one grocery store, and one homosexual, a senior in high school who started coming over to my parents' house at cocktail hour to regale them with local gossip while they worried that he was too young to be sipping a martini until he explained, "My mother's from New Orleans!" and that was that.

We never asked why my father chose this place for his final years; it was a question so taboo no one dared. Years later I tried to understand his dilemma. He'd not lived in the United States for decades. He was returning after thirty years in the tropics spent working at an American oil refinery, and he and my mother must have concluded two things: there was no way to reproduce the life they'd led in the Caribbean, and no point in returning to the snow and ice of the Midwest, and because South Florida probably seemed too crowded, they stopped one day in this little town on a lake to have lunch with a woman my mother had grown up with in Chicago and after lunch they looked at a house that had just been built for an insurance executive who'd been transferred to Jacksonville before he and his wife could move into their new home and bought it.

Perhaps they were just tired of traveling, or thought this place would do as well as any other. After all—I'd learn years later when I was wondering myself where to go—it's almost impossible to be wholly rational about something like that. How does one choose one particular spot to occupy out of a country as vast and varied as the United States? Or, now that Americans are retiring to Central and South America, the globe itself? As Turgenev said: a good man will end up not knowing where to live.

Still, their choice shocked us; my sister said it was the worst mistake they'd ever made. When I flew down from school for the first time to see my parents in their new home the man in the seat next to mine was wearing a cowboy hat, and as the plane started to descend over the solid dark green tree canopy stretching west as far as the eye could see I made some remark to the effect that I hadn't realized that Florida was still so forested, and the man in the cowboy hat replied that most people had no idea that the primary industries in the state before World War Two were timber and cattle. Even in 1961 there was something unspoiled about Florida. As we got closer to the old Imeson Airport in Jacksonville the tree canopy gave way to marshes laced with winding rivulets on whose gray water the sun blinked on and off as we flew over them, and finally, as we landed, the tree canopy turned into individual pines, open fields, and cows. When I stepped out of the airport even the air seemed devoid of energy or scent, and my father, a heretofore conservative businessman who had worn a suit and tie to work every day, was waiting for me in yellow slacks, raspberry-colored shirt, white shoes, and matching belt.

On the drive home from the airport, which took about ninety minutes, I had trouble keeping up the conversation. I had trouble making small talk with my father in the best of times, but after half an hour I could not think of another thing to say. I'd started talking excitedly about what the man on the plane had told me about Florida, but soon my words petered out under the spell of the flat, monotonous landscape. The cardboard signs advertising boiled peanuts made me want to ask why anyone would want to boil a peanut, but my father would not have known. The scrawny cattle, old motels, and walls of pine trees were the landscape of the literature I was studying in school: the prewar South, though it might as well have been the steppes of Russia. Even when we reached the aptly named town of Starke—ruined, as so many have been, by a four-lane expressway run through its heart—I was told that we still had twelve miles to go, and by the time we finally rolled down a dirt road through a grove of live oaks draped in Spanish moss to my parents' new home I felt a gothic element had entered the scene. It was night, and even though at night most things look better—even their white concrete block ranch house with its four faux–Spanish Colonial lanterns—I could not believe it was this building into which all their possessions, their associations with the past, the lives they'd led till now, had been crammed.

Worse, when the car came to a stop my mother, who was still inside the house, stood up and glanced out the window and then back at what I suspected was a television set I could not see, a television set she would watch for years and years, as if to make up for the time she had not had one in the trop-ics. A bad sign, I thought, as she came out to greet me—that even my arrival could not compete with whatever was on the tube. Entering the house I felt obliged, as visitors do, to bring some cheer, to evince some pleasure in being there. But what I instantly realized instead was that everything had changed—not just the place we lived, but our lives and our relationships with one another. The latter had all been based on that island in the Caribbean; with that gone, we were different people. In fact, it seemed to me, we were total strangers.

My father seemed the least altered of the three of us, but that was because he was a calm man who always kept to his routine—which meant going to bed soon after our arrival. That left my mother and me sitting up talking in the fluorescent light of the den like two people stranded in an airport. All the furniture around us was new, as was the arrangement of the objects my parents had brought with them from the tropics: the vases and carved chests, the paintings and figurines my mother had accumulated during thirty years in a duty-free port, displayed on shelves and tables in the living room like objects in a museum. Their arrangement had been supervised by an interior decorator associated with the furniture store in Jacksonville from which they'd bought their new furniture. And since this story is about the things we accumulate during a lifetime but cannot bear to part with before we die, I think I would not be exaggerating to say that I felt these objects had already assumed some sort of claim on me. Arranged in new combinations, displayed in a different setting from the one in which I'd last seen them, they had a power over me they'd never had before: they were all that remained of our former lives.

Once they were installed, however, I don't think my mother gave them a single thought; the only claim they had on her was her worry when the cleaning lady washed the figurines in soap and water that one might be broken. Her real interest lay elsewhere. As soon as I was up the next morning my mother took me out to show me the clothesline strung between two tall pine trees, which she declared was now her greatest pleasure: hanging a wash outdoors. My father went off to play golf every day at the little nine-hole course just outside of town. At five they had cocktails and watched *The Mike Douglas Show* or, as the years passed, *Donahue*. Neither one expressed any interest in the lake, or the motorboat that had come with the house, though they did say they hoped it would make their children and grandchildren come visit them. The idea that they thought their offspring needed an inducement to visit startled me; it seemed incumbent upon us to visit them wherever they chose to settle, and whether or not they had a boat. But such are the insecurities of growing old. My sister was already married with children of her own when they made this move—and I was away at school.

Those first years I flew down to Florida on Eastern Airlines; the plane stopped in Charleston, where I was surprised to see palm trees when I stepped out of the plane to get some air. In summer I tried to find a project that would take me elsewhere: three months living with a family in Mexico City to learn Spanish, a drive across Europe with two classmates in a rented Citroën with sleeping bags. When I got back from the latter I gushed so rapturously about the cathedrals and chateaux and museums and castles that my mother, after listening silently as she smoked a cigarette in a high-backed red chair in the living room, said something to me when I paused for breath that was so cutting that while I cannot remember what it was, within seconds I was on my knees on the carpet sobbing. Thus do mothers clip their sons' pretentious wings. We were not in Paris, she seemed to be reminding me; we were living in a small town in Florida where there was nothing to do but get in the car and drive to a shopping mall, where, the commercial on a radio station at that time said, Belk-Lindsey was "a shopper's paradise!"

Soon after arriving they bought a cinnamon-colored convertible with beige leather seats and set out to see the country from which they'd been exiled for three decades, my father at the wheel in a herringbone cap, my mother beside him in her nutria stole. Off they drove with a thermos of martinis to visit friends and grandchildren. When they returned they made friends, with whom they alternated hosting games of poker. At first they seemed to like their new life. My father played golf and worked in the yard. My mother hung clothes out on the line between two pine trees and went to church on Sunday morning.

The church, surrounded by sand as soft as you find at the beach, was made of unpainted concrete blocks; through the open windows you could hear the blackbirds chattering in the trees. I was so reserved I disliked having to shake hands at the Sign of Peace with the people around me wherever I was, and when my mother lingered on the steps after Mass to talk to her new neighbors I fled to the car and sat there waiting for her in a state of subdued fury. What on earth, I wanted to know, were we doing here?

Her first Sunday my mother put on her best—a silk dress, a flowered hat, a white cashmere coat—but the moment she got home she put them in the closet in a zippered bag full of mothballs and never used them again. The following Sunday she wore a pantsuit she had purchased at Belk-Lindsey. There was no reason to dress up anymore. The Catholic Church considered the town a missionary post, according to the young Irish priest who came over for cocktails, after a few of which he recited Shakespeare by heart, a parish assigned to priests who'd spent their lives working in places like Africa but were now, like my father, retired. Our favorite priest, a white-haired Irishman who brought my mother Communion every Saturday when she was an invalid, would expire on the golf course in St. Augustine while teeing off on the ninth hole.

Each time I returned to visit, my father looked more like an ice cream cone; each time we came out of Mass my mother paused again on the steps to talk to her fellow parishioners and I fled to the car. As I sat inside the stuffy automobile whose electronic windows I could not lower without the key, looking at the scene under glass, I knew only one thing. My sister was right. Moving here had been the biggest mistake they'd ever made.

This never seemed clearer than at the dinner parties my parents gave. It seemed to me they were putting on a show for people who could not possibly appreciate the refinements of the entertainment—the grapefruit sections soaked in crème de menthe my father served at the beginning of the dinner, the Bénédictine and Courvoisier brought out at the end. Nothing is sadder than a host proud of his cordials who turns to the guests to ask what they would like and sees on their faces that they have no idea what a liqueur is. The sight of those beautiful bottles with nineteenth-century script on the labels, the Drambuie and crème de menthe that summoned up monasteries in Europe, vineyards and castles, seemed to baffle the guests. My parents, I decided, were casting pearls before swine. That was one reason I always excused myself as soon as I could after dinner and went to my room to sip a different liqueur: the bitter knowledge of how far we'd fallen by moving to this godforsaken town—like the teacher in that story by Chekhov who leaves Moscow to live in a village where she thinks she can bring culture to its muddy streets and ends up sinking into the slop herself.

At the entrance of our driveway there was a lamppost on which hung a piece of wood with the family's name carved on it; I could see it from the bed on which I lay reading after excusing myself after dinner. One evening, as the guests grew merry on my father's liquor in the living room, I looked out the window and saw one of the invited—a retired schoolteacher from Pennsylvania—saying good night to my parents in the drive. They then returned to their guests while I watched the woman get into her car and back right up into the lamppost, which to my surprise bent over to the ground as if it were made of licorice. As the tipsy guest drove off, unaware of what she'd done, I started laughing—at the flimsiness of the lamppost, the resemblance of what had just happened to a cartoon, our attempt to start life over in this place. The next morning I went out and put the beautiful bottles of liqueur—green and gold and amber—back into the cabinet and then, like a butler, emptied the ashtrays, cleaned the tables, and examined the rugs for cigarette burns. Then I went outside and pushed the lamppost, which had simply tilted in the soft prehistoric sand, back into place, where on dark nights its light illuminated the name of our family, registering the three of us, at home within, a cozy unit.

I supposed I'd have been happier if all the possessions my mother had acquired in the tropics had been put into the vault of the bank uptown along with the bottles of liqueur, never to be touched again, but only viewed, like the crown jewels of the British royal family. The fact that my parents were actually using these possessions to entertain people of such little sophistication seemed to me merely punishment for having been so happy in a previous life. It was not surprising that people were awed by the display when they visited the house for the first time. As the years passed, alas, newer items began to infiltrate the place. Eventually the magazine rack my father purchased for his *Wall Street Journal* and *Barron's*, the plastic chairs, the wall calendar from a ball-bearing company in which he had invested, the vibrating belt that supposedly took off weight, the back scratcher, the dehumidifier—things sold on television—began to form a separate generation of objects, of inexpensive plastic gadgets that this country is always inventing: night-lights, Dust-busters, telephone covers, an artificial Christmas tree with a revolving colored light.

I hated having to go back down to Florida for Christmas—especially after leaving school and starting life on my own. What was I going back to? A drive-in movie theater whose last movie before it closed was *Lawrence of Arabia*; a grocery store with two refrigerated cases filled with ice cream sandwiches, its concrete floor strewn with sand; an old clapboard inn that had been gutted by a fire; a decrepit pier on pilings above a receding lake; a grid of sandy streets on which some people from Pennsylvania had built small stucco houses when they founded the community in the 1920s. There was nothing to do at night but lie in bed reading while listening for the whistle of the old freight train, the dog barking down the street, the squirrels and raccoons racing across the roof, the sound of my parents breathing across the hall that made me think of the ship my mother had taken me on when we traveled to New York, when she lay on the bunk bed beneath mine, telling me that the way to fall asleep was to relax my entire body, starting with my fingers and toes. Unfortunately, we were not on a ship in the middle of the ocean—though I might as well have been. Ten years after my parents had retired, I was the only person my age on our street who had not moved away and married. I was the only member of my generation walking out in a navy-blue cashmere sweater with his father's scalloped potatoes to the community park where the neighbors gathered a few days before Christmas to build a bonfire and share a meal. The reason was simple: I was not about to marry and start a family of my own.

Years later the daughter of a neighbor who'd flown to Florida from San Francisco to take care of her dying father, a retired air-conditioning salesman who lived across the street from us who had prostate cancer, remarked to me with breezy nonchalance as we took a walk one day, "Everybody here knows you're gay, you know." Gee, no, I wanted to say, I didn't. But I went on pretending anyway. Walking out with my father's casserole to the Christmas party, I was still the dutiful son, unlike all the other boys my age on that street who'd moved away and already started families of their own. Having to return at Christmas—which is, after all, the celebration of a baby—made me so depressed that I tried thinking up excuses that would absolve me from having to make the trip, anything that got me out of going back to Florida, which felt, for so many reasons, so much like returning to a prison that it seemed right that the actual penitentiary in which the serial killer Ted Bundy was incarcerated was just twenty miles away.

By that point I'd stopped trying to lighten the drive home from the airport with my father with conversation. We simply drove in silence. I even began taking a bus from Jacksonville to Starke to reduce the distance he had to drive to pick me up—till Greyhound discontinued the route. One thing remained the same, however. The boredom of the place had made of my mother such a devotee of television that I knew she would not come out to greet me if my arrival coincided with a dramatic moment on *Donahue*.

There was never a fire in the fireplace when it got cold, because when we tried to have one the living room filled up with smoke. But it was very pleasant in December—the reason, I suppose, for Florida's popularity. But it was not just that; it was good to be home. The scent that greeted me when I walked into the house at Christmastime, a mélange of the Pine-Sol and Lemon Pledge the cleaning lady used every other week on the furniture, warmed my heart; the gleam of white terrazzo floors, the comfort of the house. By Christmas the camellias my father planted were in bloom, the kumquat covered with bright golden fruit, the poinsettias red, the lake a silver-blue. The camellias that fell from the bough decomposed on the ground in the same shape they had on the branch, while in the sky above, the fantail of a jet caught the last rays of sunset, a sunset so luminous the bands of color seemed to be submerged beneath a layer of ice. At night the slender scimitar of a new moon floated high above the live oaks, and as I lay in bed listening to the freight train rumbling through town I wondered how I could ever have not wanted to come back.

Nevertheless, the fact that for many years I was still

carrying the casserole to the Christmas party in my cashmere sweater, the only unmarried child my age on that street turning up each year, was a source of deep embarrassment. The communal cheer the neighbors exuded, standing around the bonfire in the cold night, with whiskey and beer in hand, all of them part of the Great Chain of Being, made me feel like a fraud. I had nothing in common with them; I was not going to reproduce. I had stopped wearing a suit and tie to church, but after Mass nothing had changed: my mother stood on the steps talking to people, while I fled to the airless car.

After Christmas a wonderful peace descended on the town; the humiliation of the annual Christmas party was behind me. No one ever asked how long I was going to stay. In New York I was still working as an office temp, typing up reports on American attitudes toward Speedo bathing suits at ad agencies or proofreading loan agreements at law firms in Midtown office buildings late at night—there was no reason to go back to Manhattan. That way I witnessed the other seasons. In March the yard turned into a coral reef composed entirely of azaleas, camellias, and dogwood. In April the reef crumbled into a fine white dust that settled on the hedge like talcum powder after a car went down our dirt road. In May every Wednesday the widow across the street who brought us a tin of homemade rum balls at Christmas waited in a green pantsuit outside her house to be picked up for bridge at the Women's Club by her best friend. Then, just when everything was so parched that even the azaleas had started to droop, there was the sound of thunder and the daily monsoon arrived.

Lightning in the seventies, it seems to me, was more dramatic than it is today. Mrs. McAfee across the street would go into her closet and close the door, sit on the floor, and play solitaire until it stopped, while my father went out onto the back porch to sit in one of the folding chairs and watch, as if he were at the theater. My mother, who told us not to use the telephone or the shower because we might be electrocuted, stood behind the louvers of the front door crying to my father, "Get in here now, you fool! Why are you doing this to me?" while he sat and watched the sheets of rain cascade into the driveway, relieved momentarily of the depression into which the idleness of his retirement had degenerated.

Once it got so hot that a ceiling fan was no longer enough to let one fall asleep at night, my father turned on the central air-conditioning—like the bishop blessing the shrimp fleet in Tarpon Springs. The house changed character from a breezy tent to a shadowy cave. During the day the lamps were lighted, the curtains and shades all drawn. The only sound was the air issuing from the vents along the baseboards, like that of a patient on a ventilator. Our household god was the inventor of the thing that makes modern Florida habitable, which must be why, I discovered one day while taking a tour of the Capitol in Washington, one of the two statues representing the state in its rotunda is of the man who invented air-conditioning.

There always seemed to be a congressional hearing of some sort on TV during those years; the reason didn't matter. Together we watched the funeral of JFK, the riots at the Democratic convention, the Watergate hearings, all of it presided over by Walter Cronkite. In between these historical events there was the low clink of the golf ball hitting the pin as my parents sat in the shadowed den, watching yet another PGA tournament and, every four years, the gymnastics and platform diving at the Olympics that transfixed me. In the meantime the peninsula on which we lived, a hunk of Florida swamp that a man named Mr. Peters had divided up into lots shortly before he died, experienced a building boom. Some of the new people worked at the mine that the Dupont Corporation owned outside town, where they dredged up the sand to extract a mineral used in house paint; others for a smaller company that was mining sand itself off Highway 21. The rest were retired couples.

And just about then, as if to prove to the latter that Florida is indeed a fearful fraud, a drought began, a drought so severe that the Big Lake separated into several bodies of water cut off from one another by dry land on which trees began to grow. As we drove back from Gainesville there would be rain all the way, and then, a few miles from home, the pavement was dry. Someone on the town council got a grant from the federal government to build drainage ponds and culverts all over town to facilitate runoff during storms, but—as if our hubris had angered the gods—it stopped raining altogether. My father decided to cut down our big pines because it was thought they drew lightning; and the common park that had been a thicket of palmettos and grapevines when we arrived, a remnant of unspoiled Florida, was cleared by the neighbors because they said palmettos harbored snakes, though it seemed to me it was because people needed an outlet for their energy. My father grew so bored he began drinking, so much my mother threatened to leave him. By that time the train tracks that ran through town had been ripped up and converted to a bike trail, the nightly whistle was gone, and shortly afterward a shopping mall was built outside of town, along with a Hardee's, a Burger King, and a McDonald's, not to mention a karate school, a computer store, and a health food shop, because so many people from Jacksonville had moved to town.

My parents had long since traded in their convertible— too jaunty, too young—for a Chevrolet Caprice so big one could have hung a chandelier from the roof. Trips to Chicago shrank to trips to the grocery store and the golf course on the edge of town. Florida was where they lived, where I kept coming back, though nobody asked me questions anymore about what I was doing. One day, when I was sitting in the back seat of the car as we were waiting for a railroad train to go by on our way to the mall, my mother turned back to me and said, apropos of something I forget, "You *are* a separate person, you know," but I felt I wasn't. I couldn't get away from them, which is why I kept coming back to Florida.

Change is an omen of death, Santayana says in a book I can no longer find. It started, I see now, when my father's favorite neighbor, a retired high school janitor, came down with pneumonia and died. Before very long my father became everybody's favorite pallbearer. Another couple moved to assisted living in Jacksonville without even saying goodbye because, we learned later, one of them had begun to show signs of dementia. Mrs. Price took a cruise and returned with a respiratory illness that put her in the hospital, and then the grave two weeks later. It used to be "See Naples and Die"—now it's Alaska. The widow across the street who played bridge at the Women's Club and brought us a tin of homemade rum balls every Christmas vanished without a word of goodbye because her closest friend, another widow, had decided it was time for them to move into a home in Jacksonville. And then the childhood friend my mother had stopped to have lunch with the day they were searching for a place to live expired after a struggle with cancer. And Mr. Sullivan, the banker from New Jersey who lived down the street, became so depressed in his retirement that when he walked around the park every day beside his wife—six times equaled a mile—the blue eyes behind his glasses were glistening with tears even when he smiled and said hello.

Not long after that the Sullivans went back to New Jersey. The reason for such a move was always the same: to be near the children. The handsome Irish priest who loved to quote Shakespeare after a few drinks had long since been assigned another, more remote parish in western Florida, and the young homosexual who hung around with rich widows my mother's age turned into an alcoholic real estate agent a few years after graduating from the University of Florida. One winter when I was living in New York he called me from his hotel and asked if I could recommend places to go, but I was so afraid that if I gave him what he wanted it would acknowledge the homosexuality we had in common that I recommended some jazz spots in the Village, which were obviously not what he was looking for. But I could not take the risk. He drank; he gossiped; he was going back to Florida. Shortly after returning, in fact, he fell apart. After spray-painting obscenities on one of his favorite hostesses' cars he was banished, as in medieval times, from the county by a local judge, and after that moved up the coast to manage an antiques store on St. Simons Island, where he died in his forties of diabetes.

The only time my parents came to visit me in New York I showed them nothing of my private life. The things we did were so touristic that one day my mother asked me, when we went to a diner for lunch, to choose a song from the juke-box so she could know what sort of music I liked. It was her way of trying to understand my generation—her way of trying to understand me—that knowledge I kept from them so unfairly because I could not imagine sharing the truth with them. I perused the selections, knowing all along that the sort of music I liked could be found only in dance clubs downtown at four in the morning in a crowd of homosexuals, and chose a song by Carole King: "It's Too Late."

Leaving Florida, nevertheless, I always felt regret; though when I found myself back in New York my mother's voice on the telephone seemed so shrunken and small, I vowed that I would never waste time in that town again. How could I? I was not responsible for her happiness; she wanted me to live, and life was wasted every day I was there. Look how the noiseless spider, the relentless metronome, the secret thief, had staked their claim on even these two people, these once glamorous parents who had turned into a pair of country mice. Indeed, I'd made a firm decision that there was no reason to waste another moment of my life in that dismal town, even on visits, when one day in September I picked up the phone and learned that my mother, a week after slipping in the shower on a ship going up the coast of Alaska, had fallen at my sister's and broken her neck.

The next day I flew north to live with my sister and her

family till our mother had finished with rehabilitation, and then flew back with her in a wheelchair to Florida.

By the time I went back to Florida with my mother the neighborhood had changed. People who lived on the street had died, many of them taken away—weeping as they were driven off—just before that happened to the places their children lived so the children could take care of them, although that meant they ended up in communities where they knew no one but their offspring. A decade later, after my mother died, there was only one set of the original neighbors left— the McAfees, a couple who lived across the street in a house designed by a local architect overlooking what had once been the Big Lake. It was her second marriage; her first husband had been a wealthy man from Atlanta whose philandering she could no longer stand. Mr. McAfee had retired as the personnel director of the subsidiary Dupont operated outside of town. After retiring he continued his work in human services, going around to all the new neighbors, knocking on their doors, and welcoming them. His wife continued to play solitaire in her closet during thunderstorms, and once cable television was installed, she started collecting dolls she found on the Home Shopping Network. The UPS truck was pulling up before their house every day, it seemed, until she began to fail and was moved to a nursing home near town that today is a puppy shelter—a small establishment with only six beds that I'd rejected for my mother because I assumed it couldn't offer sufficient care. But that was not the reason I didn't visit Mrs. McAfee there. Having spent time in another nursing home, the one in which my mother was installed after her return to Florida, had made visiting one not easier, but harder. I was like doctors and nurses after they retire: they're in no mood to give you sympathy for your medical problems. Nor could I bear the idea of seeing this woman—so fastidious she wore jewelry when walking her dog—in a hospital gown; instead I watched her husband's car go down the street every day on his way to visit his wife with the Lhasa Apso to which they were both so devoted yapping on his shoulder.

One evening while driving home from a visit to his wife, the medicine my neighbor was taking to suppress hiccups made him so drowsy he fell asleep and lost control of the car, which left the road, continued airborne for a short distance, and then landed on top of someone's mailbox. Neither my neighbor nor the dog was injured, and Mrs. McAfee died without ever knowing that her Oldsmobile had been totaled.

My neighbor seemed to take the loss of both his wife and their Oldsmobile with equanimity. When, however, he told me a year later that the dog had died, he wept. He could scarcely mention the dog's name six months after this event without crying. It was the dog's death, I think, that led Mr. McAfee to say he was "ready to go now anytime the good Lord wants." Instead his son came down from Maine to get him. My neighbor sent his offspring back to Maine alone, but compromised by putting his house up for sale, and went back to work pulling weeds. I took comfort in the fact that houses took forever to sell here, because I didn't want to lose him; after my mother died I'd had enough of change. I continued to walk across the dirt road between our houses almost every day to visit him: the last vestige of the old neighborhood. Time seemed to stop. Life, after all these deaths, had resumed a certain order. It was a dry spring. One day succeeded another. I liked coming back from my nightly walk and seeing, at the end of the drive, the lighted window of my bedroom, a perfect place to read, and then turn off the lamp and lie there listening to the patter of animal feet on the roof.

When I finally went up onto the roof one day to inspect it I could see Mr. McAfee kneeling on his lawn, pulling weeds under a conical straw hat, as patient as a farmer in a rice paddy. What I could not identify were the animal droppings scattered on the roof. The roof was in bad shape—plants were growing out of cracks in the tar and gravel; dead branches broken off the live oaks lay strewn across the shingles. The entire roof obviously needed to be patched or replaced. Yet I did nothing about it—because I had no desire to go through the commotion that involved. When it rained I simply lay on my bed watching stains spread on the ceiling like Rorschach tests.

One day not long after he'd put his house up for sale I went over to visit Mr. McAfee and found him sorting through albums of old photographs. He was sifting through the accumulation of fifty years of life in Florida. Some of the snapshots were of the neighborhood boys when we were adolescents who lived to water-ski. I did not tell him I'd idolized his son; I simply looked at the photographs of the two of us holding slalom skis in some far-off America that no longer existed, the one where water-skiers sent up arcs of water that caught the setting sun each time they swerved to recross the wake. That same day I told him I was thinking about building a fence between my yard and that of my neighbor on the east side, a relative newcomer who while I was away on a trip, I was convinced, had come onto my property and trimmed the lower branches of a magnolia tree, a tree I'd planted years ago to blot out the sight of his new house, thereby obscuring his view of the lake. When I asked the man sifting through photographs if he thought a fence was a good idea he replied without looking up, "Well, that depends on how long you plan to stay in Florida."

No answer could have shocked me more—the idea that one day I'd leave, that Florida was not forever. At that point I had only one friend left in town, a retired accountant named Earl who lived by himself with three dogs and a roomful of opera records, but I could not imagine leaving. People are always telling you to "move on," however, and there was my neighbor sorting photographs in preparation for a move to Maine, so when a friend in Washington called a few weeks later to ask if I would help him teach a course, I accepted the offer and made arrangements to leave town.

The morning I left I went over to say goodbye to Mr. McAfee. I was not worried about being gone for several months; I knew he would watch the house.

In novels—at least in nineteenth-century novels—people lock up houses, go away, travel for years, and then return. There's something romantic about the way the manor is shut up, so that the protagonists can wander through the Far East and come home several years later, because their house, like some ancient tree, will always be there, the roof covered with leaves the oaks are shedding in the autumn sunlight. The servants rush out to greet them; the hero hears that the woman he loves is still unmarried; the plot resumes.

I wasn't sure if you could leave a house that way in the twenty-first century, or at any time in history outside a novel. But it seemed to me that since there was little if any crime on the street I lived on, the chances of someone breaking in were small, and with Mr. McAfee weeding across the street every day it would be like having a watchman. I could not do what Mr. McAfee was doing. Instead, the day before I flew north, I went up on the roof to take a look at everything.

The roof was a fascinating vantage point; halfway up the five-hundred-year-old live oak around which the house had been built I could look down on the neighborhood, the yard, the dirt road that ran around the community park and the other houses, as if none of it had anything to do with me. The roof, a week after raking it, was so littered with fresh leaves, branches, and feces that it made me think of Saint Jerome's vindictive wisecrack about the Roman temples that Christianity had emptied—temples of the gods, he wrote, "where now only bats and owls reside." The gods had been my parents; now they were gone, and raccoon, cat, and squirrel droppings lay scattered across the tar paper. Across the street I could see my neighbor kneeling on his lawn, pulling dollarweed out under a straw hat: eternal Florida. Mr. McAfee had promised to keep an eye on the place while I was gone. So the next day I said goodbye to my neighbor and had Earl drive me to the Jacksonville airport, where I flew north to Washington to take up residence in a stranger's house.

Hurricane Weather

When I met Earl I was forty-one and he was sixty-two, which is why I thought that going to the boat ramp where we met must have been for him a sort of hobby, a habit he'd developed when going to dirty movie theaters in South Florida, something he did not want to give up even in old age, not because he needed sex but because it got him out of the house—like the games of golf my father used to play until his legs would no longer support him.

There was a real movie theater in Starke, twelve miles away, that we sometimes went to after we became friends, the old-fashioned kind with a ticket window right on the street where you bought your ticket as you stood on the sidewalk and a concession stand in the lobby where you could buy candy bars and popcorn—a theater that had inexplicably survived the age of the Cineplex and still for some reason got first-run films, though mainly those directed toward teenage boys, which meant that it was there we saw Harry Potter and some of the Batman movies whose soundtracks were so violent they shook us literally in our seats, till Earl stopped going because, he said, he found the audience so restless and noisy, which meant he'd become used to watching movies on his television by himself at home.

Earl didn't even have an antenna—or he had one that didn't work well. Like so many people who have the money to replace something but stick with whatever they have, he lived for years with a set that was by no means up-to-date but transmitted a sufficient number of channels (two or three) for him to be content. His speakers and record player were state-of-the-art; he had the very best of those. But the television in front of which he spent so much time he didn't bother to replace, though it was quite old; and it was there I used to go over in the evenings, to watch a movie or some episode of *Masterpiece Theatre* on Sunday nights.

When Earl retired after three and a half decades teaching accounting at a community college in South Florida, he had so many opera records and books that he needed a house with room for them, but even after he found that, there was still not enough space on the shelves for them all. His new home was a long, low ranch house built halfway up the slope between the lake and the paved two-lane highway that goes through town. It belonged to a series of houses that had been built along the lakeshore in the forties and fifties. The town itself went back a bit further. It had been founded in the twenties by people from Pennsylvania when North Florida was still an open range on which cattle were allowed to graze wherever they wandered and most of the highways were dirt. The houses of these original settlers, small stucco cottages that remind me for some reason of Los Angeles, were so diminutive that their little porte cocheres, tiny porches, scalloped walls, and urns seemed built for people who were shorter than succeeding generations, or who at least needed far less space. Earl's, however, was a large, modern house on what had to be at least two or three lots.

In the yard was a grove of camellias the previous owner had planted that ran from the sidewalk down the slope to the lake, some old sago palms, several live oaks, a dogwood that grew inexplicably in the open sun, and a guest cottage separated by a brick patio from the main residence. It was a long house, which Earl used only the tips of—the kitchen on the west end, the music room on the east. The dining room between the two never held a dinner party, so far as I know. It was filled instead with waist-high stacks of books that Earl had intended to read when he retired. Next to that was a living room in which I never saw much living; as unused as a front parlor, it was furnished with antiques he'd bought or inherited from a neighbor of his in South Florida, an old woman who'd married into, or was descended from, a distinguished New England family, I forget which. She was, I gathered, one of the reasons he had left South Florida. They'd lived across a stairwell from one another for so many years that when she told him one day that she had decided to move to an assisted-living place in Lauderdale Lakes the ground shifted beneath his feet. One of those casual relationships that reveal themselves to be, when they are removed, not so casual after all was ending. In other words, the life he'd known was over; he couldn't imagine living there without her across the breezeway, and the fact that he would now have to get used to a new neighbor seemed out of the question. They had been, he realized, married in some way—perfect neighbors—a widow and a bachelor who both loved music, books, and fine furniture. For a moment he considered moving to Lauderdale Lakes with her, but then he decided to make a break for it instead—one last chapter in another place—so he drove north, and after visiting several of the little towns that surround Gainesville, he found this one—this house, I should say, because it had enough space for his books and records and antiques.

That was all I guess he wanted, since most of the house was rather ignored. In the living room was a fireplace that was never used, and an olive-green wall-to-wall carpet that he did not bother to replace, even though it had a few chunks missing, as if a dog had taken a bite, which made visible the vomit-colored foam rubber underneath. There was an enclosed porch that ran almost the length of the living room on the side facing the lake, but not only did he never use it, he also didn't bother to put furniture out there; it was simply another book repository. Nor did he seem to have any interest in the lake. The only time he looked at it was when he was washing dishes in the kitchen, where the window above the sink provided a view of the water, increasingly far away as the drought that began not long after he moved here deepened.

The one room that he did use, the room in which he spent almost all his time, had originally been I suspect the master bedroom but had been transformed by Earl into a music and movie library. The shelves covering the walls were packed with long-playing records. There were books and stacks of DVDs on the floor, and a little table at the end of the room with a big typewriter on it that he used to register the titles of his movies on small white cards that he put into a little file box in alphabetical order, a sort of cinematic card catalog. The music-and-movie room looked out onto a small wooden deck, and beyond that, the lake; but as long as I went there, I never saw Earl once open the vertical blinds that covered the sliding glass doors that led outside. It was as if Nature did not exist; only Art. There was a small room across the hall in which he'd stored the paintings he'd bought at estate sales in South Florida, and a bathroom behind the high-backed chair in which I used to sit watching TV with him, a bathroom used so rarely that the first time I went in there I should not have been surprised to find it full of dead cockroaches strewn across the tiles or lying on their backs in the bathtub, a cockroach cemetery where for some reason they all had gone to die, the way people around here all seem to take their last breath in the hospital in Gainesville, a town twenty-three miles away.

Earl's first years in town were as active as my parents' when my father retired to this town in rural Florida for reasons my sister and I never understood. Like them, he took trips. One was a drive to Indiana, where he'd obtained his doctorate in accounting, another to Virginia to visit battlefields of the Civil War (the subject of so many of the books he read), another a trip to New Hampshire, where he'd spent a summer working in a hotel with his cousin when they were in college. Then there were shorter drives to South Florida to see his brother, who still lived in the town in which they'd grown up. And then the trips began to dwindle, as my parents' had, till Earl's itinerary shrank to visiting his cousin in Gainesville, or eating at a fish restaurant he liked in Lake City, or cruising the boat ramp in Madison six miles away. At the boat ramp he would read a book while waiting in his car for someone to drive in; even after the police tried to rid the place of homosexuals, that's what he'd say he was doing if the officer inquired: reading. Meanwhile, because we both went to the boat ramp, we became friends.

Most homosexuals in small towns don't want to know each other; it threatens the closet in which they are living. The first time I realized another man in my town was gay I felt I'd run into the only other human being in the Arctic

Circle, but I was soon given to understand that what we had in common was not going to be the basis of a friendship— rather the opposite. So I behaved the same way.

With Earl it was very different—we became friends at the boat ramp immediately. Not only did we both live in the same town, but we both liked to read and listen to classical music. When I began visiting him it was like visiting one of my aunts in Ohio; he had the same dignity, the same slow-moving, slightly formal calm. The only eccentric thing about him was a habit of shaving his head once a year because he believed it encouraged hair growth. Otherwise, he was conventional. I could count on certain things when I visited Earl: a cup of tea, a musical recording, a discussion of a book, not to mention what had gone on the day before at the boat ramp. He was the only person in town with whom I felt I could be myself. Before very long we were like two women I'd known when I was still in my twenties: two widows who'd grown up in Jacksonville, gone to the same boarding school, married, lost their husbands, and retired to our little town, where they played bridge at the Women's Club every week until one of them decided it was time to move to a nursing home, which they did in unison, because one was not about to live in this town without the other.

That's how I thought of the two of us—as Gertrude and Belle—especially because by the time I was going to the boat ramp I knew almost nobody else in town, even though I'd been coming and going here for almost fifty years. Everyone I knew had died or moved away. I'd only started living in the town full-time in 1983, when a fall rendered my mother an invalid. My mother said two contradictory things when I came back for good. The first she said in a completely neutral tone, as if commenting on someone she hardly knew, one afternoon as I was putting her to bed: "You'll never leave me. Your conscience won't let you." The second, which came much later, betrayed her own: "I'm holding you back." But the truth was she was holding me back from nothing at that point—and when she died years later I'd become so used to life in a small town that I could not imagine moving back to New York. So I stayed.

And then, after my mother died, I made a vow: to remain in her house until everyone on the street who had felt sorry for her during her long period of invalidism had themselves kicked the bucket—a desire for revenge that made no sense, since her accident and subsequent paralysis were not their fault, and they had been extremely kind to her. Yet that was how I felt. The other reason was that I didn't know how to disperse her effects—the things she'd collected living with my father in a duty-free port in the Caribbean for thirty years: the porcelain and silver, the figurines and vases, the Delft and Copenhagen and Wedgwood and Georg Jensen. A friend up north viewed both explanations with contempt. He told me there were people one could pay to dispose of such things; he told me I was staying because the property taxes were low and my parents had paid cash for the place in 1961. Whatever the reason, I could not think of a thing to say when, a week after my mother's death, I ran into one of her friends at the post office and she exclaimed, "I thought you'd be gone the next day!" Instead, I was still here when that woman died twenty years later.

Earl never asked why I'd stayed in town, though my friend Clark told me not long after my mother died to "get out now, while you can, and don't look back!" The reason was simple: he, in the face of the same circumstances, had not. I met Clark in the Ambush, a bar in Gainesville I'd stop at on my way back from the nursing home after having dinner with my mother. Following dinner we would watch *Jeopardy!* and then I'd arrange her in bed—she didn't want the blanket to be too close to her chin—and then go to the Ambush, where I'd spend time watching pool players who were so drunk I never understood how they could stand up, much less hit the eight ball with unerring accuracy when the moment came. Clark, like me, had lived in New York, though he'd moved to San Francisco when his mother began to fail, and he came back to Crystal River, the small town in which he'd grown up on the Gulf Coast. Now he lived in Gainesville, a big, bearded hippie who spent his days driving around North Central Florida photographing old beauty parlors and attending estate sales. Clark hadn't gone back; he'd stayed. And yet his advice to me after my mother died was instant and heartfelt: "Get out now, while you can!"

"Your mother didn't expect you to watch her figurines for the rest of your life," he said in a voice flooded with scorn. But that's what I seemed to be doing. Clark and I, moreover, were not the only people who'd moved down to Florida to care for ailing parents and then found themselves unable to go back, people whose contact with small-town life, or inability to abandon a house that had been in the family for years, had rendered them unable to sell it even when they did go north, a house on which they continued to pay the property taxes every year, though there was nobody living in it—like the architect I met once at a party in Washington who stared into space searching for words when I asked him why he hadn't sold his father's house near Tampa.

"You think you're hanging on to something," Clark said one day when he stopped by our house on his way to some beauty parlor in McIntosh, "but there's nothing here—not even on this street. None of the neighbors you have now are going to stay around forever. And they're not going to tell you when they go—you're just going to see a 'For Sale' sign outside the house. One day they'll move to North Carolina without a word. Nobody stays in Florida. You'll be left high and dry—the way I was in Crystal River. And when you need help, what'll you do? When you've had your stroke and you're lying on the floor wishing you could crawl over to the phone to dial 911!" he said. "Those figurines aren't going to do it for you. Thirty years from now you'll be living alone, with nobody to rely on, certainly not the neighbors, who'll have no idea who you are at that point. And you won't know their names. There's only one thing you can count on—one of these days a tiny blood vessel in your brain is going to give way when you are all by yourself!"

There was a reason Clark's nickname was Cassandra.

My father's stroke was, actually, on my mind—because most of us assume we're going to die of whatever killed our parents. But I ignored Cassandra's warning. I liked the idea of keeping the same post office box, the same bedroom with the same books I'd had to read in high school lined up in the headboard of my bed, in a little compartment whose sliding door I merely had to push back to pull out my well-worn paperbacks of *Hamlet* and *The Great Gatsby*. I liked never having to write the alumni magazine to say I had a new address, never having to switch banks or have to ask my dentist to forward my records to a new town. I wanted to stay in one dear, perpetual place. I wanted to watch what happened to it over Time.

Then, too, there was a voice telling me, despite Clark, that when I got old the house would make perfect sense; I'd once read in a local paper the obituary of a woman who said, when she moved to a nearby town in 1922, that she took one look at Hawthorne and knew, "This is where I want to die." That's why it was so ironic that just a few weeks before my mother fell I remember standing at the kitchen sink in New York one day thinking that I should not even go down to Florida anymore for visits because it was such a waste of time; the town was so boring.

That opinion never changed, actually, which is why one of the main reasons I got to know Earl was that he could drive me to the airport. My father had driven me to and from the airport in Jacksonville, and after he died Earl took his place, till one day when I was waiting to be picked up he phoned to say he was feeling too sick to make the drive, upon which I called a car service and barely made my flight. It was a reminder that one cannot depend on anyone, even, perhaps especially, a friend. After that, hiring a car was the only way I could get to Jacksonville, although doing so cost almost as much as the plane ticket itself, and I felt so awkward being driven to the airport in a black town car by a man in a suit and tie half my age that I could not enjoy the service. So I developed a new plan. Earl had no problem driving me to the airport in Gainesville, which was only thirty minutes away, and there I could rent a car to drive to the Jacksonville airport the next day. On my return, I'd reverse the process: I'd rent a car at the Jacksonville airport, drive home, and the next morning Earl would follow me into Gainesville, where I'd return the vehicle, and he would drive us both back to town, usually to a tape of opera arias he'd made.

This worked for quite a while, so that I was able to go back and forth between Florida and Washington, where I kept an apartment, every six weeks or so, although when the woman at the Enterprise desk in Jacksonville reading the form I'd filled out one day to rent a car remarked in a pleasant voice that it must be nice to live in two places, I blurted without thinking, "Not really—you end up living in neither one."

But by that time I could not imagine giving up my geographic bigamy, and I counted on Earl to drive me to the airport the way my father had. My father had become so bored in retirement that he liked having to pick me up, I think; it gave him something to do, like filling out his taxes. I wanted to think the same was true of Earl, though I still made an effort to bring him something for his pains—a brochure from a lecture at the Sackler Gallery (because he'd once lived in Iran), or the handout from a series of classic movies at the Library of Congress (a subject he loved), or a *Smithsonian* magazine with an article on Persepolis—the way my father had brought me Hardy Boys books when I was sick with a cold in fifth grade. Indeed, I told myself, after my mother died, that I'd take care of Earl when he needed help—like the niece in the story who everyone assumes will finally live her own life after the aunt she's been caring for dies, but moves instead to the house of another aunt and starts taking care of her. I might be useful to Earl when the time came, I told myself, after which I could then leave town for good—if only because I wouldn't have anyone to take me to the airport to escape it.

When I compared my having stayed in Florida to a movie that we watched one night at Earl's—*Psycho*—Earl just smiled. "I hardly think your house is the Bates Motel," he said, "and so far as I know your mother's body isn't in a rocking chair in the cellar. You don't even have a cellar!" But she was still in the collection of figurines and vases that looked to me whenever I glanced at it like an altar of some sort. The walls of my parents' house were white, but behind the handsome piece of furniture a neighbor built for my mother our first year here—a series of shelves rising above a long cabinet with louvered doors—the wall was painted a pale pink to set off the figurines and vases, and it was this flushed emanation that greeted me whenever I walked in—as if day was always dawning at that end of the room, for these porcelain figures, at least. For that reason alone I sensed my mother was still in the house.

It was Earl who believed in ghosts—one of those eccentricities at which one could only smile, given his intelligence and erudition—but I was the one living with them. The whole town was full of people who were gone, whereas Earl had moved here only recently. I was the one who remembered the dead when I took my nightly walk past houses and driveways and mailboxes that had once been owned by someone I knew, or had merely seen around town, but the only person left was Earl, reading in his music room, listening to Gladys Swarthout sing Schubert, or watching *Are You Being Served?* as I passed his house on my way home.

Earl had no past in this town; none of its citizens had he

survived. He'd spent his life elsewhere. When he walked his dogs up and down Palmview Drive he didn't have to think of people who'd disappeared. He knew only the present. I remembered so many people—not just the young man who'd gone on to become an air force general, who'd been an altar boy when I was not much older than he, but the way the light reflected by the bronze paten he held beneath the lips of the parishioners being given Communion played over his face, the way water casts a leafy pattern on the underside of a dock. I remembered the nun who'd left her community to take care of her elderly mother and worked in the library on Saturdays after her mother died; the two sisters with whom my parents had played poker; the old man who'd lived with his parents until they died and then supported himself mowing people's lawns until he was so bent over and arthritic he could not stand up straight when he walked uptown, the only figure on the sidewalk. Of the present I knew much less. It was Earl who told me there were two lesbians living four houses down from him, across the street from a handsome man in another house who rented a room out to young men who were always so good-looking it raised suspicions, the way the staff at the nursery uptown did because they all seemed to have been chosen for their looks. It was Earl who kept tabs on the young schoolteacher who was living in one of the two rental cottages that were so close to the sidewalk one could look in when one walked by and see what the occupant was watching on TV. The schoolteacher had put up lace curtains, Earl informed me one evening when I ran into him on my walk, as if that clinched the question of his sexual orientation, though two months after that the teacher got married and moved out. But Earl did not walk past Bess's house and remember her playing solitaire in a wig and muu-muu on a TV table on the porch as she listened quietly to her guests before laying down the law on whatever subject they were discussing. Nor did he know that Bess had lived to ninety-two, confined to her bed just a few days before she sat up one morning as her maid was washing her face, gasped, fell back, and died in a room whose window I always glanced at when I went by, though it was her kitchen I looked into because I felt she was still standing at the sink washing a dish while she looked out to see who was walking by—me, forty years later.

Earl's house was full of associations, I presume, inspired by things he'd acquired over the course of a lifetime and brought from South Florida, but nobody he knew had ever occupied the rooms in which he now lived. Nor was he populating it with new memories. I never saw another person in the living or the dining room. They were full of books. The master bedroom was now a music room. The bedroom in which my parents had slept, on the other hand, looked exactly as it had when they slept there. When I left the comforters on it looked as if they were still alive; only when I stripped the beds did it look as if they'd died. Either way I'd wake up in the night and think: Listen, there's no one across the hall, nobody breathing, you're all alone in this house, admit it.

But I could not. It had taken me years before I'd allow overnight guests to sleep in their beds, and I still felt I was being impious when I did, uneasy when I passed the doorway and saw my visitors' luggage, their hair dryers and books and T-shirts strewn across a mattress that was to me an altar, glad when they were gone to have the room restored to the shrine in which I kept the curtains drawn and the furniture exactly as it was when my parents had been alive.

Earl had his antiques; I had all their possessions, undisturbed—the clothes in their closet, my mother's gowns, the madras shirts my father had bought long after he'd gotten so old that they were too beautiful for his wizened face, the package of Pall Mall cigarettes he had left in the refrigerator; all of their liquor, my mother's bottles of perfume, a picture of her own mother in a red high-necked dress, looking Victorian in a small oval golden frame set between a crystal statue of the Virgin Mary and a bottle of Chanel No. 5. Even I could see that I'd made their bedroom into a temple, which was why it made sense, whenever I left on a trip, to kneel down just inside the door and pray for them; and whenever I came back, to kneel down in the same spot and greet them with another prayer—and why having houseguests always made me slightly nervous till they were gone, when I could restore the bedroom in which they'd slept.

Yet all that actually remained of these people were the contents of two white jars in a louvered cabinet in the living room that looked as if they had once contained cold cream but held instead a heap of gray ash mixed with small chunks of bone on whose disposal my sister and I could not agree. The local cemetery, a patch of parched grass and turkey oaks surrounded by a metal fence on the edge of town, was so bleak we could not imagine interring them there, especially when the town's sole connection to them was merely that it was the last place they had lived. So they remained in the house, behind the louvered doors of a cabinet whose upper shelves displayed the vases and figurines and trays inlaid with Brazilian butterfly wings that my mother had accumulated while living in the Caribbean, objects that were so impossible to imagine dispersing via a garage sale to the homes of other people in town that they were as much a reason for my remaining there as the ashes. In other words, I didn't know how to, or couldn't bring myself to, break up the house; so my parents remained what undertakers call "shelf people." They lived in a tomb filled with the things they had enjoyed while alive and might want in the afterlife, like the objects buried with the pharaohs, even if my parents had not been mummified, but cremated—and I could not even be sure that the ashes in those two white jars were their remains after reading somewhere that funeral homes just scrape the ashes out of the crematorium and there is no guarantee that the ones you get belonged to your loved ones.

Those were the ways in which the house seemed haunted—even if I did not believe in ghosts the way Earl did. Earl's parents had died years ago and he rarely spoke of them; I, on the other hand, was still living with mine. In the living room, my father's favorite chair exercised such a power I never even thought of sitting there, or asking anyone else to, and when I dusted it off I felt as if I'd dusted him; and my mother's shelves of figurines—the Royal Doulton and Copenhagen representations of an elephant, a crab, a deer, a small boy, dogs, young women in nineteenth-century gowns—I left just where they were. It would have been unthinkable to put the things my mother had collected on a table in the driveway and attach a price to each one over which

I'd haggle with whoever came by, and I could not pass them on to the next generation because my sister had told me that her children had no interest in them whatsoever. Even the car I kept driving, long after the window on the driver's side ceased responding to the button that made it go up and down, long after the radio stopped working, long after I had to take it to the auto repair shop to have something else replaced almost every month, simply because it was the car I'd taken my mother home in on weekends during the decade she lived in a nursing home, the car on whose back seat I'd prop her up behind two pillows, two pillows that did not prevent her from rolling off when I had to come to a sudden stop, upon which I'd pull over to the side of the road and find her lying facedown on the floor of the automobile, though she never complained. Even accidents were a break in her routine, the routine in which she had been trapped by the injury to her spinal cord, after an operation that illustrates better than any the insane desire of our medical profession to keep people alive no matter what. At no time did my mother laugh more sincerely than when someone slipped and fell in front of her, so that rolling off the back seat of the car when I had to jam on the brakes was no big deal. The reason was simple: she was so bored, so helpless, that even falling off the seat was an adventure. The only problem was that I couldn't see the reality behind this: that by being a faithful son who arrived at her nursing home exactly when he said he would (Tuesdays and Thursdays at five for dinner, Saturdays at eleven to take her home for the weekend), I'd eliminated any possibility of surprise, or change, in her life—a life in which I picked her up every Saturday morning and drove her home in the same car, the car in which she began dying with a series of small strokes; a car that I realized, when I finally replaced it with a new one, had been holding me here as much as the tray inlaid with the wings of Brazilian butterflies and the package of Pall Malls in the refrigerator.

How long the dead take to die! Some people don't even want to accept the fact that there has been a death—as if such an event were unimaginable—like Andy Warhol, who told no one that his mother had expired for months after the event. I can't recall what Earl said to me when my own expired—how long it was before I even mentioned it, for that matter. In fact, I have no memory of knowing Earl when she was alive, though surely I must have. I certainly don't remember him coming to the small memorial service we held at the Catholic church.

Once that event was over, however, attended by the few people still alive who'd known her, I was surprised by how easy it was to live selectively in the house, ignoring my parents' presence when I had to, recognizing it during my departures and arrivals, maintaining the illusion that there was still someone there, even if, when I went to bed, I could no longer hear them breathing in the bedroom across the hall, and even if, as the years passed, when I came home from a trip, unlocked the front door, and went inside, I could almost hear the house saying, "*You* again? Still coming back! For *what*?"

The first night I brought someone from the boat ramp back to the house he asked, when I turned on a lamp that revealed a framed photograph of my parents and me taken the day we attended the opening of a new savings and loan in town, "Are these your folks?"

"Yes," I said.

And then I added: "But they're away on a trip."

Some trip, I thought as I led him down the hall to my bedroom—the one you never come back from.

The photograph was of the three of us in 1975: my father with the false teeth he'd foolishly decided to get so that he would not have to deal with dentists anymore, my mother with one of those elaborate permanents women seemed to like after a certain age, and me with the dark mustache popular among male homosexuals in New York City at that time. I hadn't intended to lie about it; I just didn't want the man I'd met at the boat ramp to feel sorry for me. There was something shameful in my mind about living by oneself. Imagine the families with children who could use this place, I'd think, who could fill its rooms with noise and laughter. That was why I didn't even want repairmen coming in after my mother died, why I let the leak in the roof draw carpenter ants, why I let mildew stain the walls, and hedges grow too high, and the wall of the carport rot away under the onslaught of raindrops bouncing off the gas tank. That was why when I returned from a trip late one night and the shadows on the white wall of the house cast by the Spanish moss were swaying with the wind, I thought of one of those film noirs Earl and I liked to watch, films in which the hero is about to discover a dead body—in this case my own. It was not till I became as old as Earl that I didn't mind letting the air-conditioner repairman in the door, because by then I felt the social shame was gone, since a lot of old people end up by themselves; one assumes the people they loved and who loved them have died off, it's part of the natural course of life, and living alone when you're old doesn't mean you haven't been loved; most people, including lifelong couples, get stranded when one dies before the other. The media love those stories in which the husband dies only hours after the wife.

Halloween, however, was a problem; I dreaded the possibility that a mother and her kids would knock on the door, a fate I'd try to avoid by turning out all the lights and hiding in a walk-in closet in my parents' bedroom, where I'd sit on the floor and read a book by flashlight. Earl found this ridiculous. "That's like the Jews in ancient Egypt," he said, "hoping the Angel of Death will pass by!" Exactly. Of course, I was overreacting. But I was not about to embarrass myself or horrify the children by being the only person in the house. Children know; they recognize eccentricity, loneliness, immediately. But that didn't frighten Earl. He simply found it annoying—to be taken away from his television to deal with trick-or-treaters. He'd buy candy and get ready for visitors, though he was always relieved, I could tell the next day, when he told me that nobody had showed up, and he was left with bags of M&Ms on the kitchen counter that he could now eat himself. In his case it wasn't a question of shame; it was having a sweet tooth. But either way, within a very few years our houses became for some reason places not to stop on that gayest of nights; just as I wanted, though I couldn't help but complain. "We're like convicted sex offenders, confined to our homes."

"But you don't want anyone to stop by!" he said.

That was true; I was running a motel with no desire for a customer, like Norman Bates in *Psycho*. Earl, on the other hand, never worried about publicity, though he did have his phone number changed after someone at the boat ramp who'd taken a dislike to him started calling to say he was going to tell his neighbors the awful truth, a harassment that stopped only when Earl got a new number. I, however, was preoccupied with the possibility. For instance, I had two sets of T-shirts, one plain, one printed with logos that advertised gay art exhibits, archives, and bookstores. The latter were what I slept in at night but never wore outside my bedroom, till one morning I awoke so late that I had to jump out of bed, pull on a pair of shorts, and bicycle as fast as I could uptown to get to my yoga class and the minute I entered the gym a man looked at me with such a strange expression that it was only when I'd assumed the lotus position on my mat before the mirrored wall that I realized I was still wearing the T-shirt that said *Key West Gay Arts Festival*. Fortunately, the rest of the class was meditating with their eyes closed, which gave me enough time to remove the shirt and put it back on inside-out so that the logo was invisible. "A close call," I told Earl, who did not share my fear—which was why he didn't even mind being questioned by the police when he sat in his car at the boat ramp waiting for someone to drive in. Earl seemed happy with life in a small town whose quiet I found as sinister as it was soothing—happy fussing over his dogs, happy watching the squirrels dart around the bird feeder he'd put up outside his kitchen window, happy listening to Gladys Swarthout sing "An die Musik," happy inviting me over to watch Claudette Colbert in *The Egg and I*.

Halloween, alas, was the only time there was anything even slightly campy about our town. The community was conservative and Christian. There were, within and outside

the town limits, a total of twenty-seven churches—one reason Earl had settled here, I suspect. He liked the Protestant
atmosphere, the one in which he'd grown up. He'd stopped
attending church when he became too hard of hearing to appreciate the sermon, but he still read the Bible. And though
he missed seeing the families in the pews, he was still connected to family life. The cousin in Gainesville, a man his
age with whom he'd drive around looking for antiques or
spend an afternoon listening to opera records, was homosexual, but he had married and had four sons with whom Earl
would eat Thanksgiving and Christmas dinners. His older
brother in South Florida, who still lived in the town in which
they'd grown up, would stop by once a year on his way to
Kentucky to check on property he owned there. There was
even a woman who lived in a town twelve miles away whom
Earl had dated when they were at the University of Florida,
a woman who shared his love of chamber music, whom he
would take out to dinner at a seafood restaurant in Lake City.
A sister who lived in California he never spoke about. They'd
had a falling-out, I gathered, over the price of a plane ticket
that would have taken one or the other to a reunion, and her
two grown children, his niece and nephew, not only had little
to do with him, Earl told me, but called him "Uncle GB," the
letters standing for "Gay Boy."

Growing old, they say, is not for sissies, and neither is
living alone, but after my father died I was alone during the
week, and after my mother died I was alone every moment.
Before that happened, however, it was as if the Oedipal complex had come true in some awful way. Both Earl and Clark
had lost their mothers; I had mine to myself, a mother I could
dress and bathe, the way a child takes care of a doll. In fact,

I'd never experienced an emotion like the love I felt when soaping my mother's body as she sat under the shower in a folding chair, her head bowed beneath the stream of water.

That must have been why I felt superior to Earl, I have to admit, when my mother was alive; I had a life less lonely than his. He lived by himself; I didn't, not quite. I don't know what Earl did on Saturday mornings, or whether the weekends meant anything to him at all, other than the fact that the boat ramp was off-limits because there were too many fishermen. But when I went to Gainesville on Saturday to take my mother home for the weekend I was acquiring a family. Pushing her down the corridor past the other old women lined up in wheelchairs, wheelchairs that were going nowhere, I felt guilty to be parading her past people we were leaving behind. But it was very important to me that she not be one of that faceless cluster around the television set in a room across from the nurses' station. I didn't want her to be one of those. I didn't want my mother to even look old. One Saturday, after dressing her to go out, I removed the blouse I'd chosen, because, I said, "It makes you look like a little old lady," and she replied, "But that's what I am."

I didn't think so. In my mind my mother was not like the others. The other women on the corridor did not have sons or relatives coming to get them. My mother had me. On Saturday mornings Lochinvar arrived to free the princess in the tower. And, as in a fairy tale, soon after our arrival home she always fell into a deep sleep—a sleep she couldn't achieve in the nursing home, she said (a form of insomnia I did not want to even try to imagine). Then, late Saturday afternoon, she would awaken when the priest came to hear her confession and give her Communion, at which point I always left the room. That was another difference: Earl was a Methodist; we were Catholics.

The priest for most of those years, the ruddy-faced Irishman with snow-white hair, had spent most of his career at missions in Africa. Our parish was, I assumed, a reward for his long years of service, which is how so many people conceive of Florida. He liked to tell jokes that did not stop as I walked him to his car. When he dropped dead of a heart attack while playing golf in St. Augustine the church could not contain the crowd that came for his memorial Mass. The bishop said the deceased had been "a priest's priest," someone who came to warn him that a priest in another small North Florida parish was feeling isolated and depressed, a man who went up frequently to Brooklyn to stay with a nephew who was battling cancer, a pastor who had visited countless people like my mother, which was how he became such a fixed part of our weekends, which began, really, after I walked him to his car and returned to the house and we settled into an evening at home. Because I subscribed to cable TV then, there were always shows to watch. Life in the United States, it seemed to me, boiled down to having someone to watch television with—though Earl, whom I did not speak to on the weekends, apparently had no problem watching it by himself. Earl watched television into the wee hours; my mother and I quit around eleven.

My mother would sometimes say, when we were home, going up and down the driveway under the big live oak, "I want to die," but she said it in such a way that it was not a complaint, merely a statement of fact; and when she did know, I'm now convinced, that she was about to do just that, she asked me to let her come home for good. But I could not imagine having her all the time, if only because she had to be moved every two hours during the night to prevent bed-sores, but also because I did not want the vacuity of my own life exposed to her. On weekends I'd get phone calls from friends in New York and California, friends I'd made in the bars and baths during the seventies, after which she would ask, "Who was that?" and I would say, "Just a friend," until she asked one day, "Why are they all men?," a question I was not about to answer any more than I could imagine having her home all the time, spending every day and night with her in the same room. Instead I pointed out the difficulties of bringing her home for good—and let the topic drop.

My mother, who'd grown up in Chicago, wanted two things before she died—to see snow, and to come home—neither of which I granted her. By the time she died I had stopped thinking that she would ever expire, but now that she had there was no reason to drive into Gainesville on Saturday mornings anymore; on Saturday mornings I awoke now to a long, dull day that began with oatmeal, blueberries, and NPR, the national news that always included a sermonette on race that Scott Simon would give in the voice of a man in a funeral parlor, followed by the peppy voices of two men who hosted *Car Talk*. Saturday was now a long, dreary day punctuated by a phone call from an old friend in California whom I'd hear ask in a very loud voice, when I picked up, "Will this weekend never *end*?," a question that a friend of his, a retired dancer who'd been in *A Chorus Line*, used to ask before he killed himself at sixty rather than see his legs deteriorate. Saturday could only be relieved by one thing: a call from Earl asking me down for a movie that evening. Otherwise, I was on my own.

Of course, when you live alone in the interior of Florida you're never really alone; you live with cockroaches, spiders, wasps, bees, chiggers, raccoons, mosquitoes, rabbits, deer, buzzards, egrets, herons, woodpeckers, owls, frogs, snakes, silverfish, carpenter ants, and lizards. For weeks after my mother died they were the only other creatures in my life.

My mother had always had a man from Florida Pest Control come once a month and spray the perimeter of the house, but I let that service go, along with the cleaning woman who came every other week, because the sound of her rinsing the marbles in the soap dish in my bathroom drove me crazy—and so I began to share my solitude with various amphibians and reptiles. Earl took an inordinate delight in two species: dogs and squirrels. My favorites were more various. Frogs I'd find huddling inside the mailbox that never closed tightly, beautiful green tree frogs that got into the house as well, frogs I began to identify with when I found them trapped inside the house because they didn't know how to get out. Often I'd come into the hall after getting up in the morning to find one sitting in the foyer facing the front door, like a dog or cat letting you know it wants to go out, whereupon I'd open the door and watch it hop outside. Other times it was too late. Like the lizards that entered through gaps in the screens, once the frogs got inside they faced a certain death from starvation and thirst. One morning I found a frog perched on one of the glass louvers of the door to the back porch, looking out toward the garden it could not reach, but since it was already dead, I left it there because it so perfectly exemplified my own predicament.

The living frogs I found enclosed in dust balls so thick they couldn't move, because I'd neither swept nor vacuumed the floor in years, frogs I'd take outside and drench with a glass of water that converted the dust ball into a thick and soggy goo that I would anchor to the ground with my flip-flop so the frog could struggle free, at which point I'd think as it hopped off into the jungle of that immortal line from Henry James's novel *The Ambassadors*, in which the protagonist, on realizing one evening in Paris that he's wasted his entire life, advises a young man: *Live, live all you can, it's a mistake not to!*

One day, while driving to Gainesville, I was surprised to see a frog on the windshield, a frog that had evidently perched there when the car was still in the carport but now found itself raked by fifty-mile-an-hour headwinds as I drove down Highway 26, its universe utterly destroyed—like my mother when she tripped on the rug and broke her neck. She could not be repaired, but I thought I could make amends to the frog. Instead, when I stopped to let it hop off the windshield into the grass beside the highway, I realized, after resuming my journey, that I'd left it in an open field, which meant it had no protection from the sun and would therefore die. In other words, I had condemned the frog to death through my carelessness, though by the time this dawned on me it was too late to go back, because how would I ever find it?

In this way the demarcation between the indoors and outdoors at the house began to blur, which made Earl's house seem so much more orderly than mine, another reason I liked going there, though I don't believe he ever had a cleaning lady either, and I never found him with mop or rag in hand.

How Earl lived with the bathroom off the music room

that was a cockroach cemetery could only have one explanation: he never opened the door. But my cockroaches would not remain in the areas I had conceded them. When warm weather started, and I went to the kitchen during one of those bouts of insomnia that make going to bed in old age such an unpredictable journey and turned on the light, I would see them running around the counters on which, during the day, I prepared food. Sometimes they were sitting or standing, whatever one calls it, in the middle of the hall, just like a cat, as if they liked having the run of the house. The fact that these insects, so versatile, so quick, so able to fly off a countertop when one forgot they had wings, so able to disappear into almost invisible cracks between the dishwasher and the cabinet, living God knew where during the day, existing on God knew what, were roaming my kitchen and lounging in the hallway when I slept was not something I wanted to think about.

Only staying away on a long trip seemed to reduce their numbers; when I got back from a month up north I'd always find them lying on their backs on the terrazzo floor, some of them still wriggling their legs helplessly. But I could not kill them. My mother had made fun of me when I was small for being averse to squashing bugs, but some reverence for life, which as a child was instinctive, made me think that I had no right to destroy anything I could not make myself, including a cockroach. "But you eat animals!" Earl said when I mentioned this. This was true, and some people eat roaches. But I was too squeamish to step on them, though occasionally when I got up in the middle of the night to pee I would hear a crisp little crack when I put my foot down and realize I had done just that. To do this intentionally, however, was beyond my powers. When I found them in the sink I'd turn on the faucet so they'd be swept into the drain, where they'd try to keep from slipping to oblivion by climbing back up and fighting for life no matter how hard I ran the faucet, making them seem almost heroic. Still, I hated them. I hated their feelers, their legs, their wings, which I'd find when I came back from a trip, strewn like rose petals across the floor. I hated their lightness and ability to hide.

Earl's cockroaches were all confined to a single unused bathroom off his music room; how he kept the rest of the house free of them I do not know. My own were out of control, because I was suspicious of pesticides. The worst scenario was finding them on their backs and concluding they were dead only to have them come back to life the instant I swept them into the dustpan. Nevertheless, I always tried to eject them from the house with their lives intact—for the same reason I took pains to usher outdoors the lizards and frogs that had become trapped inside the house—so they could go on living, especially the lizards, so beautiful and graceful when alive, so rigid and desiccated when dead.

And then there was, as in a fable of Saint Francis, the lesson of the earthworms. There was nothing more startling than running the tip of a shovel along the edge of the driveway to neaten the border only to expose a mass of earthworms twisting in agony in the open air and light, as shocked, no doubt, as the frog on the windshield of my car on its way to Gainesville. Even worse, some days I'd come out of the house and find them curled up on the cold terrazzo of the back porch, like whales that had beached themselves or swum up a shallow inlet where they would die. On such occasions I would slide a dead leaf underneath the worm and carry it over to the little hedge of boxwood and leaf litter, where, I presumed, it would find something to eat and someplace to hide, the two things we all need to go on living. But the morning after moving the worms (on whose labors all of agriculture, and therefore human civilization, is based) to the boxwood hedge I'd find them back on the porch, like whales that had swum up the same fatal inlet again, till finally it dawned on me: they had crawled up there to die—until a friend informed me that earthworms breathe through tiny holes in their skin and they were only fleeing the rain. And so I stopped interfering—though many times I found them on the porch when there had been not a drop from the sky.

I refused to use pesticides because I was convinced they all ended up in the lake. Earl used pesticides with abandon and treated his yard with such brutality I could not see how he could be homosexual—having his yard man chop his azalea hedge nearly to its roots, or cut down big trees at the slightest excuse, while I was letting oaks grow up near the house against all advice, letting ferns and cherry laurels and pine cone lilies take over the yard, simply because they wanted to be there. Earl and I were opposites when it came to our yards. He saw his in practical terms: obstacles to lawn mowing. My fantasy was that one day I'd come home and find the house so covered in vegetation I would not be able to find the doorway. That was why I kept bringing things home to add to the already thick hedge I'd planted years before between our yard and the house next door: the desire to camouflage my own existence.

Hiding in my house at this point was, however, unnecessary. Nobody cared. Earl lived in one of a string of houses on a slope above the Big Lake, beside the highway that ran through town, on which there was always some sort of traffic going by. I lived on a peninsula whose only road was a cul-de-sac that circled a communal park before returning to the highway. Over the years my end of the street had become a sort of necrotic tissue; half the houses were unoccupied, and therefore dead, for all intents and purposes. One was part of a dispute over the settlement in a divorce in Virginia, though it had been sitting empty for almost a decade. The house next to mine was almost as vacant. It belonged to a man who was living in the same nursing home in which my mother had been installed. His adult daughters, who lived elsewhere, came and went. The house would be dark for weeks; then I'd look over and see the lights on, or hear the barking of their little dogs, and on Sunday morning there'd be heaps of trash put out on the street—things from the past they'd decided to get rid of. But that was my only contact with the women. One of them was a physical therapist in Gainesville; the other taught school in Jacksonville; a third had moved to Orlando. They'd come back to have the floors refinished or to simply spend the weekend going through their closets.

This went on for so long that at a certain point I assumed their father had died. But no, he was still alive, I'd learn when I spoke to them. He was still in the nursing home, in some kind of limbo, neither alive nor dead; a man about whom Earl sometimes inquired when we were chatting before we started the movie because they had both gone to the Methodist church before Earl's hearing deteriorated.

Earl at least was still in his own house, driving his own car, walking his own dogs, a friend with whom I could listen to music, discuss books, and pick blueberries every spring.

Depending on what the winter had been like, in May or June we'd drive over to one of the farms west of town where you could pick your own. The one we liked most belonged to a married couple in their mid-forties whose acreage lay between Madison and Highway 301, a couple so big, blond, and handsome they looked like one of those old Flemish paintings of Adam and Eve after they've been banished from the Garden of Eden. They had two Labradors Earl always fussed over, after which we would set out into the rows of blueberry bushes, each of us carrying two plastic pails, a big one by hand, a small one dangling on a cord around our necks. Since May's too early for storms we could take our time without worrying about lightning. Even so, the buckets we brought back differed. Mine were always full of twigs, leaves, and spiders because I pulled the berries off impatiently in clumps, as if a storm was coming, whereas Earl picked them patiently one by one, so that when his were weighed there was very little detritus in his bucket, and none of those pale pink berries that look pretty but are unripe.

Picking blueberries with Earl was, I thought, like our friendship, a perfect combination of solitude and companionship—standing in a row of bushes so tall we could not see one another, yet knowing the other was just a few rows away. Everything slows down when you pick berries, especially if, like Earl, you try to pick each berry individually rather than rake your hand down a branch and knock them all off at once. One berry at a time returns you to the Middle Ages. The occasional bird or dragonfly that landed on a bush, the rare car going by the wall of pinewoods enclosing the farm, the distant voices of some family on an outing from Gainesville were the only distractions. The season was often so long one could pick more than once, until the bushes were depleted, usually by the time the harvest had moved up the Eastern Seaboard all the way to Maine. But until then picking blueberries, weighing the fruit, talking to the owner of the farm, was a bucolic dream—a dream that allowed us to gorge on blueberries for weeks and go back sometimes in July for one more harvest.

Otherwise, my friendship with Earl, during those years, consisted mostly of phone calls—to alert one another to some sale at the grocery store, or a new bag boy, or something that had happened at the boat ramp (a police raid, a fight). We rarely went to the boat ramp at the same time, and when we did, we sat in our separate cars, alone. We would never have competed for the same person. I wasn't even sure why Earl went, since as far as I knew, he had no interest in having an orgasm; he just facilitated other people's. It never occurred to me that he was impotent; I assume he was doing it for the pleasure of giving pleasure. Whatever the reason, our visits to the boat ramp were not the basis for our friendship. Movies were. After my mother died I'd had the cable television in my house disconnected because I'd decided I could spend my time more profitably reading, but on Sunday nights I could always go to Earl's to watch Miss Marple solve another crime.

The television was in the music room, where, before we started whatever film we planned to watch, my host would insist I listen to some aria, or song by Schubert, or even a hymn. Earl's musical tastes were eclectic; he liked country as well as classical, gospel as well as opera. On Sunday morning he listened to a program that featured hymns on the Christian radio station. Wagner was his favorite composer, but had Earl never made a tape of opera music for me to listen to in my car I'd have never heard the sextet from *Lucia di Lammermoor,* or "Casta Diva," or "Va, Pensiero." He liked so many different kinds of music that going over there amounted to an education, which led me to suggest more than once that he contact the university in Gainesville and teach, but he never did.

He had already taught. His career in education had begun in the fifties at a high school in a small town on Lake Okeechobee so dull that the only salvation was to pile into a car with two other teachers every weekend and drive to Miami to attend the opera. But even as a professor of accounting later on at a junior college in North Miami he'd despaired of the teaching profession, or rather the student body. People had no manners anymore, he said, and no respect for authority.

When my parents moved to Florida I was certain that people in North Florida were stupid; it took me years to realize that the population in Florida is so fluid that there are as many northerners here as southerners, and that even if they are southerners, they are not stupid, and even if they live in a small town, it does not mean they are less intelligent than people in a city; it just means they have chosen life on a smaller scale, which may mean a difference in sophistication but not in that native shrewdness, that basic intelligence, with which human beings navigate life. Earl had grown up in a small town in South Florida, when the towns north of Miami were still just farming communities, but he'd gone to the university in Gainesville, and, after entering the army just when the Second World War was ending, he'd taken a job with the State Department and after that obtained a doctorate at the University of Indiana.

His years in the foreign service, though only three, seemed to supply a large part of his memory bank; after posts in London and Tehran, he'd come home by circumnavigating the globe, which was why there were, scattered through his house, inlaid boxes, brass vases, and carved chests he'd bought in Isfahan and Jakarta and New Delhi. The other happy time in his life, it seemed, had coincided with his getting a doctorate at the midwestern university he spoke of with as much fondness as he did Tehran, when tales of mosques and bazaars gave way to tales of toilets in the university library, though what the degree led to—teaching accounting at a community college in Miami—was not something he missed at all. Anyone who taught, Earl said with surprising vehemence one evening, was a fool. He was happy to have left teaching behind, and now, among his dogs, his books, his records, his tapes, his antiques, his paintings and objects from the Middle and Far East, he seemed content to be doing just what he was doing: reading history, listening to opera, watching movies, and walking the dogs.

When he came north his last poodle had just died, but over a period of a year three new dogs had come to him, two abandoned at rest areas on the interstate, and one that wandered into his yard one day through the hedge. The latter, a hound, had been so mistreated she would not even touch her supper while he was in the room. Six weeks later she was eating out of his hand. The dogs brought a certain purpose to his life; he walked them twice a day; he took them frequently to the vet's for shots and checkups, and found their habits and temperaments a source of constant interest, amusement, and irritation, the latter most noticeable on my walks at night when I would come upon him cursing loudly while all three dogs strained to run off in different directions as he pulled on their leashes, like someone driving a troika through the snow, which patches of sand in Florida resemble on moonlit nights.

On moonlit nights our town must have resembled the one in which Earl had grown up—where nobody even locked his door—but Pompano Beach had become so urban after World War Two that when the widow across the stairwell announced she was moving to a senior living facility in Lauderdale Lakes, he'd gotten in his car and driven to North Florida looking for a small community like the one in which he was raised. My father had done the same thing—and, I suspect, the woman who said that the minute she saw Hawthorne, she knew that was where she wanted to die. I don't know if that's what Earl had in mind; I think it was just because the house was big enough for his books and records, which were so numerous that his first year in it he spent his spare time creating a file catalog for the records and DVDs of movies on the shelves of the library, arranged by title and artist.

This meant I could request any movie that came to mind and he would simply look it up in one of his little file boxes by flipping through the alphabetically arranged three-by-fives that reminded me of an old-fashioned card catalog in a library. The only thing I could not watch at Earl's, for some reason, was the Oscars. Perhaps it was simply because he no longer saw new releases. Or perhaps he had no interest in the sensibility of contemporary films. But when I found myself in Florida on that night I'd have to restrain myself from telephoning him.

The music room was like a library: a library of music and movies. There was a sliding glass door at the end of the room that would have given us a beautiful view of what remained of the lake beyond the branches of two moss-hung live oaks on his lawn, but Earl kept the vertical blinds closed all the time, no matter how beautiful the weather. The music room was like a theater one reaches after walking through a city on a cold, slushy winter day; it shut everything out. The north wall was a bookcase lined with volumes of film and opera history. At the foot of our chairs were encyclopedias in which we could look up whatever film we'd just seen, or the actors in it, to get their credits. One encyclopedia of actors was for the living; the other, for the dead. The west wall held bookcases filled with record albums, all of them obsolete at this point, though vinyl was making a comeback, I assured him. Behind and to the left of the chair I sat in was the door to the bathroom he never used, proof of which was provided the first time I asked to use it and found the tiles littered with dead cockroaches. Why they had chosen this room to die in I did not know; perhaps because it was never used, or because they'd crawled up through the drain in the shower, since they were in the bathtub too. Whatever the reason, it was a cockroach graveyard I forgot was there as we sat in our chairs listening to Marilyn Horne sing lieder, or watching Ingrid Bergman's mother-in-law poison her in *Notorious* till she was so weak she could not lift her head from the pillow, much less get out of bed and leave the house, which was, I did not tell Earl, more or less how I felt about living in that town.

When friends from Earl's days at the university in Indiana stopped by on their way to South Florida for the winter, he put them up in the guest cottage. "The worst part about guests," he liked to say, "is that you have to clean." His best friend lived in New York, a classmate from college who would call once a week and perform what Earl called "a monologue I have to sit and listen to"—something I occasionally interrupted when I dropped in. But he rarely visited. Earl seemed to have ended up the way I had: alone in a town in which we knew almost no one, our friends scattered across the country.

When I introduced Clark to Earl the first thing Clark said as we drove away was, "That man is clinically depressed," but it seemed to me that Earl was quite content, even if living by oneself in a house in a small town with dogs might seem lonesome to some people. Though one never knows the level of unhappiness with which a person is willing to live, it seemed to be just what he wanted. If I thought of myself as Ingrid Bergman growing weaker every day in a mansion overlooking Rio de Janeiro, I thought of Earl as Miss Marple, knitting in her cottage in the Cotswolds. He didn't seem to mind being alone at all. After a certain age, he told me one day, love was out of the question. "You may find someone in your twenties or thirties," he said, "but after that, it's not very likely." That must be why, I thought, he contented himself with the boat ramp.

Earl and Clark had one thing in common, however; both were that rara avis, a native Floridian, which made me, the immigrant, regard them with a certain respect. He was, furthermore, "a small-town aristocrat"—like Clark. Earl's father had served on the state agricultural commission; Clark's father had been in the legislature. Perhaps that was one rea-son Earl seemed suited to this town. He had no doubt about his place in it. His reserve reminded me more of New En-gland than the South, two regions that, separated by the Civil War, we forget were settled by the same English and Scots-Irish stock. He was garrulous but formal, down-to-earth but aristocratic, someone whose dignified manners I ascribed to a previous era, as vanished as his hometown, like the demeanor of my father's sisters, German Americans in small towns in Ohio who moved more slowly perhaps than I liked when I was a child but had a great dignity. Of course, some of Earl's demeanor might also have been ex-plained by the fact that he was old. Whatever the reason, he always remained calm when the police questioned him at the boat ramp. He even went down on occasional Sat-urday nights, I was amazed to learn, to a notorious biker bar in the next town, a place not even Clark would enter, a place where a man had been beaten to death with pool cues, but where Earl would sit calmly at the bar nursing a beer as he watched the game, like an Englishman in his pub, while the bikers swarmed around him. In short, Earl was confi-dent in a way I was not, calm and unsurprised by whatever life had to throw at us, though occasionally that included things that would trigger his temper, while I lived in a state of constant nervous apprehension. I think that was the rea-son I asked so many questions—to know as much as possi-ble about a situation was to guard oneself against it. Earl's old-fashioned manners, on the other hand, guaranteed that I need never fear an intrusion or request; indeed, he seemed utterly indifferent to whatever I was doing in between our visits. It would not have occurred to him to inquire.

That meant I could ask Earl anything I liked but he would never ask me anything even slightly personal, though he was aware of my needs and ready to help. One summer while I was away a pipe beneath the kitchen sink in my house burst, and when I got back weeks later there was water in the living room and patches of mold floating like lily pads on top, and I had to move away so that the house could be dried out. The moment Earl learned I was living in a motel in Gainesville he offered me the guest cottage, where I made sure to interrupt his life as little as possible, eating at a local restaurant we sometimes went to together. But when I got a cold one week and could not go out, he brought me dinner on a tray every evening, which reminded me of the time I was sick with a cold in fifth grade and every day my father brought me a new Hardy Boys book when he came home from work. But there was no way to repay his kindness; all I could do when I got well was take him out to our favorite barbecue restaurant, where a meal never cost more than fifteen dollars for the two of us, and the only real pleasure of the place was looking at the people in the other booths.

I never argued with Earl, not only because, like my father, he had a temper, but because no issue we might debate was worth our friendship. His political opinions were not mine; he subscribed to newspapers like *The Washington Times*, whose articles he would sometimes cut out and give me to read. He was convinced Hillary Clinton was a lesbian. He thought Barack Obama was the worst president in American history. He refused to vote for anything that would raise taxes, even though our town needed a sewer system. Once when we were faced with a gubernatorial election in which neither candidate was appealing—the Republican had run a company accused of defrauding Medicare; the Democrat seemed like a party hack—he announced he was going to vote for the former, because, he said, "I'd rather have a crook than an idealist. At least the crook won't be able to steal as much as the idealist would give away." On a personal level he was what his fellow Methodists would consider a complete contradiction: a devout Christian who'd only had sex with other men. This did not keep him from judging others. He did not approve of his neighbors' daughters because they brought boys back to the cottage they occupied behind the main residence. He would not even go to a restaurant because one of them was a waitress there, and he despised her father, whose vehicles clogged the driveway between their houses, though he did admire the wife. About the family next door he was like a teacher grading students: the neighbors' son was "painfully shy but sweet," the eldest daughter "lovely," and the two middle daughters "absolute tramps." The irony, of course, was that I had met Earl in the toilet of a boat ramp where men went to have sex with one another; some people had even accused him of hogging the john, though in a competitive environment like the boat ramp almost everyone was said to have done that at some point.

The door of Earl's refrigerator was plastered with photographs he'd cut out of magazines: Ronald Reagan, puppies, children holding flowers, and other sentimental images, including a handsome young father lying with his little son on his chest in a hammock—the last one reminiscent of the pictures my roommate in New York had taped to the refrigerator before he killed himself, either because he'd learned he was HIV positive or because his best friend had just died of

AIDS, I never knew. My roommate's display featured a quote from Saint John: "In the twilight of life there is only love." In the twilight of Earl's life there were movies, opera, and books, though he was surely more religious in the conventional sense than my roommate in Manhattan had been. I knew no one besides Earl who had set out to reread the Bible from beginning to end, the way one would a favorite novel.

Inside the refrigerator covered with images of dogs, fatherhood, and Ronald Reagan was evidence of Earl's interest in staying alive at whatever age: jars of wheat germ, brewer's yeast, and extract of saw palmetto he took for his prostate. For someone so sedentary he was quite health-conscious. To begin with he had the sound constitution of someone who grows up if not on, then connected to a farm. His only disability was some sort of nausea that would come over him when the weather changed; he had learned over the years to recognize the signs that it was nigh, whereupon he would cut up some of the gingerroot he kept in his refrigerator, and if he was lucky that would forestall the attack. Otherwise he'd simply have to go to bed and lie down, sometimes for several days, until it vanished. But that wasn't the reason that when I walked by Earl's house at night it sometimes looked like a tomb, that it seemed to me that he had buried himself alive like the man in the story by Edgar Allan Poe. It was simply that he was proceeding into a time of life I was not looking forward to, because he was twenty years older than I—the tyranny of numbers.

I'm talking about the twenty years, the two decades I would presumably have that he would not—the ultimate unfairness: people's different positions in Time. It upset me when in his late seventies he began talking of moving to an adult assisted-living facility. Though there seemed to be nothing wrong with him, the idea, presumably, was to plan for the time when there would be. But I didn't want to hear about it. It even made me nervous when I learned he'd begun giving his books away to the library in Gainesville for their annual book sale, and I got especially upset when he asked me one day if there was anything in the house I wanted— like a Buddhist at the end of his life detaching himself from earthly things. All I had ever asked for were plants from his yard—ferns, four-o'clocks, seeds from his sago palms. I did not want to hear that he intended to leave me a brass lamp I'd admired. Even more alarming one fall was the news I heard from a handyman he employed who was sometimes working in the carport when I went over to visit that Earl had actually chosen a rest home near Lake City, where a cousin of his lived, a move that would have been the equivalent of death, since I'd learned over the years that when a friend in one of these small towns in North Florida moves even ten miles away, they might as well have moved to Alaska.

To my relief Earl went nowhere, I relaxed, and we resumed our shared loneliness together. I spent Christmas at my sister's. I'm not sure what Earl did—I never thought about it. I imagine he had a peaceful day, reading and walking the dogs; I went north. On Memorial Day and Labor Day I waited for the long weekends to be over while the neighbors across the street threw parties whose guests' cars blocked my driveway. On Thanksgiving I simply cooked the traditional meal and ate it by myself. Halloween I spent in the closet reading by flashlight. Oscar night—which to me was the most festive of all—I had to wait for the results the next morning, since Earl did not observe that one. July Fourth we spent apart. Since the fireworks went up from the public beach, there was no need to get together; we had an equally good view from our own yards.

When my mother was alive, I'd push her wheelchair across the street to the bluff from which our neighbors' houses had a better view of what remained of the Big Lake. Pushing a wheelchair through sand was a challenge, but when we got to the neighbor's lawn we had our reward: everyone came up and made a fuss over her. After she died, I'd go over by myself, but secretly. I'd wait till nine o'clock to leave the house and walk over to the end of the bluff, where it was so dark I could stand unseen by the guests my neighbor had invited over. Like all July Fourth displays, the fireworks began in a tentative fashion—like the deaths of people when you are still young. By the finale, all hell would break loose—the way, in old age, everyone you know or love seems to come down with something at once. These last fireworks would explode on top of one another in a sort of orgasm—and then, when the individual flames had spiraled down to the earth and there was nothing but wisps of smoke rising into the air, the darkness you get only in a small town in the country would return. July Fourth was over. The guests along the bluff would begin to go home, and I'd go back to the house without having spoken to a soul, though I lingered behind the hedge to listen to the sound of their voices receding as they returned to their vehicles. And then, after the slamming of car doors, everyone would drive off . . . and leave the world to darkness and to me.

But I have no idea what Earl did on that night. He certainly didn't read "Elegy Written in a Country Churchyard," as I did after getting home. Days went by when I did not hear from or speak to him. That's why I was always glad to come upon Earl on my nightly walk, straining at the leashes on which his dogs were pulling him, like Charlton Heston on his chariot in *Ben Hur*; and I was always happy when the dogs stopped to greet me while Earl and I exchanged news, though our subjects tended to be confined to the UPS deliveryman, or a sale on ice cream at the grocery store, or a new person who'd moved into the rental cottages down the street.

One can make a life around almost any set of circumstances, and even though I'd returned to Florida because my mother had been condemned to immobility I found the years when she was alive quite happy—dinner beside her bed on Tuesdays and Thursdays as we watched *Jeopardy!*, a stop at the Ambush or the boat ramp on my way home, a visit from the priest each Saturday when he came to give Communion, drives around a part of Florida where forests still alternated with pecan groves, blueberry farms, and little lakes, dropping in on Earl on my way back from the post office, when he would inevitably insist I stay for tea. Tea gave Earl a chance to take down from the cabinet two mugs decorated with the figures of Adam and Eve whose private parts were revealed when the hot water caused the ceramic leaves that covered them to move aside, inducing laughter in both host and guest. At such moments I felt completely content; I'd hidden myself away from life and everything that made it brutal.

Peace and quiet, however, breed their own forms of anxiety. Without a TV I listened to the radio, if only to hear the human voice, which on NPR was always used to recite a litany of what was wrong with the country and the world, so downbeat that I'd get very upset sometimes; but when

I raised some of the issues that *All Things Considered* kept serving up every day—the things that made the future of the planet look so dim—Earl refused to be upset. He'd simply say, "Well, I won't be around to see it." It was, in a sense, a shrugging of responsibility, a kind of giving up, but I could not come up with any other solution. If one could not imagine Florida, or the planet, in a hundred years, what comfort was there but that one wouldn't be around to deal with the mess? Even the race problem in the United States, Earl said, would eventually be solved—"by intermarriage." After that was settled he pressed the Play button so we could watch Eleanor Powell dance with her dog in *Lady Be Good*.

Those were cozy evenings in that pine-paneled library: Earl and his dogs, and, on the TV table in front of our high-backed chairs, a bowl of soup or piece of pie. One would not have wanted to be anywhere else. By the time Barack Obama became president I'd seen more films with Bette Davis and Barbara Stanwyck than I'd known existed, not to mention vehicles for Marjorie Main, Claudette Colbert, Jean Arthur, Irene Dunne, Ava Gardner, Dame Edith Evans, Greer Garson, and Myrna Loy. Earl had been going to the movies before I was born; he even liked silent films. In fact, the only thing catholic about him was his taste in cinema: I disliked silent movies, but he insisted I see *Wings*, not to mention westerns and war pictures I'd rather not have watched. He introduced me not only to a series of movies starring Ann Sothern as a character named Maisie but also to the oeuvre of an actress named Joan Leslie, who made—I learned after consulting the encyclopedia Earl left by the chair—*The Great Mr. Nobody* with Eddie Albert; *The Wagons Roll at*

Night with Humphrey Bogart; *The Male Animal* with Henry Fonda; *The Hard Way* with Ida Lupino; *The Sky's the Limit* with Fred Astaire; *Thank Your Lucky Stars* with Eddie Cantor; and *Cinderella Jones* with Robert Alda, none of which I'd heard of. Of course, we watched the classics too, from *The Awful Truth* to *Roman Holiday*, from *High Noon* to *She Done Him Wrong*, interspersed with Hitchcock's *Notorious*, *The 39 Steps*, *North by Northwest*, *The Man Who Knew Too Much*, *Vertigo*, *The Lady Vanishes*, *To Catch a Thief*. Some evenings, before the movie, he'd insist I watch a segment from one of his favorite television programs: *Antiques Roadshow*, *Live from Lincoln Center*, *Keeping Up Appearances*, or *Are You Being Served?*, whose effeminate British salesman especially tickled him.

Whether we watched a movie always depended on his health: when he was having one of his periodic attacks of nausea, I did not hear from him; when he got better he'd phone to ask if I wanted to come over, though as he aged, I found myself waiting longer and longer at the kitchen door for him to let me in, watching him walk slowly down the long length of the house with his cane. In fact, sometimes during the movie I would turn to say something and find him sound asleep in the adjacent chair. When that happened I generally got up and left. But although I worried that he'd be embarrassed at nodding off in front of me, when he called the next day there was not a hint of that; he'd just apologize for having taken a nap and ask me down for another movie.

By the time Earl was in his eighties and I was in my sixties there were evenings when I walked home from the movie wondering if my interest in him was not slightly sadistic:

watching what happened when old age gets its claws in you, or at least puts you to sleep in your chair, like a man overcome with carbon monoxide in a closed garage. I was even reading a book at the time called *How We Die*; its theme was that death is a part of the life cycle whose final act almost always robs us of any dignity, and that all we can control is what we do with our lives—a common philosophy that has never seemed to me to counter what is still an appalling insult. Often when I walked out to the end of my driveway to put the yard trash out on the street for pickup I'd see a couple who lived at the other end of the street coming toward me on one of the twice-daily walks they took around the little park our houses surrounded. The man was a doctor who had just retired from a hospital in Jacksonville; he carried a gadget that counted the number of times he, his wife, and their son circumnavigated the park, which they did till they'd completed fourteen laps, which equaled two miles.

The doctor looked back on the career to which he'd devoted his life with no more satisfaction than Earl had gotten from teaching. When I asked him if his career had turned out to be what he thought it would be when he studied medicine, he said, "Not at all." The amount of paperwork, of bureaucratic tedium, had increased to the point that practicing medicine had ceased to be a pleasure; he'd spent more time working on patients' charts than he had seeing patients. But what he regretted most were the so-called heroic measures taken at the end of life, the resuscitations—pounding on people's chests, breaking their ribs, shocking them with electricity; there was even a machine that compressed the chest, like something in a factory—measures so repugnant that he'd often asked the families in ICU to come in and witness what the staff was doing at their behest, because almost always the families said, "Stop, no more!" But the most curious thing he told me was that when the corpse was being wheeled down to the morgue after the resuscitation had been called off and the nurses and doctors were joking with one another to relieve the tension, there would almost always be a final emission of gas from the deceased's body, which they called the Morgue Fart, the doctor told me as we came around the bend one day, putting the final touch on *How We Die*.

If the message of *How We Die* was "Live a good life, because you're not going to have much control over your ending, which is not likely to be pretty," that seemed to me like very cold comfort. Even my father, who rarely made observations about anything, had remarked one day, "Old age is hell." Earl liked to say, with a laugh, "Don't ever get old!" But that's what had happened to him—and watching Earl as he sat there in his chair asleep was to feel, as I walked home, grateful that I hadn't arrived at that point. One knew that at some point one would—and that it would be more difficult if one lived alone. But that was that. My unmarried uncle had been on his way to play golf one day when he stepped outside his apartment in Sarasota and saw a group of women putting his neighbor into a car, and when told they were taking her to an assisted-living place in Bradenton he replied, "I've been wondering about that myself," upon which one of the women said, "Get in." That he did, and the next day he was moving in himself. In other words, there would come a day when someone would inform you that you could no longer live on your own. At a certain point in life it becomes clear that the restaurant is closing; the oxygen in the coal mine is running out; the ship is about to set sail, and you'd better see the steward about getting a deck chair and a table in the dining room.

Perhaps that was why the slightest contact with young people had started to give me such pleasure. I was always happiest when I saw my neighbors' twentysomething son coming down the road with his father and mother. He was part of the generation that had inspired the term "snowflake," so sensitive that he wore a bandana tied around his nose because even in the street, he claimed, he could smell the smoke from the cigarettes his neighbors puffed in their living rooms. And even though he always walked ahead of us, as if he didn't want to be part of an age cohort not his own, eventually he'd turn around and make comments mocking the things we'd said. That was the note that cheered me: the senseless confidence, the insolence of youth. There was nothing more fun than the brief exchanges I had with cashiers and bag boys at the grocery store. The reason was simple: they were not afraid. There was no reason to be at their age. But by the time Earl began falling asleep in the middle of movies I was beginning to be obsessed with the fact that the future did not look promising. After my mother died I felt suddenly vulnerable. I was afraid of trees falling down, I was afraid the lawn mower wouldn't start, I was afraid I'd get sick, I was afraid when the airplane hit turbulence that it was going down, I was afraid to open the mail or check the answering machine. Everything seemed menacing and redolent of death, even the rusted rowboat that had been sitting on the neighbor's lawn like a dead turtle for forty years, as if someone still might take it out onto the lake.

"There is no wealth but life," said Ruskin. But life had

become something fragile, unpredictable, and dangerous to me, a series of small things that could blow up in one's face. Unable to bring myself to have someone cut down the live oaks outside my bathroom window whose roots would surely invade the septic tank, I found it equally impossible to look at my face in the mirror while shaving, because that made clear what I was—a fearful person living alone. Something was out there, stalking me, some accident with disastrous consequences waiting to happen. I was entering a new and unchartered territory, which was why I woke up so often in the dark and began thinking immediately about whatever small thing had triggered my anxiety. Sleep, I'd discovered, is, when you're young, an express train; when you're old it's a local. For no reason I'd wake up when daylight was just coming into the room, as if I had to be up for something important, though I had no obligations whatsoever; and the rest of the day I was so drowsy that simply by lying down to read I would cross the line that divides sleep from waking. In other words, I'd started to take naps. I had reduced the universe to my room, my bed, my books. I could no longer deny what I was: an old man who liked to pee in his flower bed. The town was full of us, living as quietly in our houses as snakes in a hole, waiting to die, although after Earl stopped picking blueberries I still felt I had a margin of safety that Earl did not, if only because of the numbers. Friends of mine who were five, ten years younger seemed rich in a way I wasn't. They made me think of the only honest birthday card I've ever received, which said, on the front, "I'm always happy on your birthday," and inside, "Because you're older than me!"

There were few old people in the films Earl and I watched,

although most of the performers were dead, the stars of half a century ago. I'd look them up in the encyclopedia at the base of the chair in which I sat and read their credits. About actors and their roles Earl had firm opinions, though he was never argumentative or insistent; he knew what he thought and did not care if you agreed. There were movies he liked that I did not and vice versa. *La Dolce Vita*, for instance, held so little interest for him that he let me take it home when we were done watching the DVD. Most of the time I let Earl lead the way. Out of politeness I'd watch a film in which I had no interest but whose pleasures he wished to share, the same way I'd listen to him describe with pride an antique he'd purchased years ago, or the career of a singer whose rendition of a Schubert song he wanted me to hear.

Earl loved movies even more than I did, and I loved them a lot. He loved movies with dogs and ghosts, movies made from books I had never heard of that had been bestsellers in their day but were now forgotten, movies he had seen growing up. He even liked to watch cartoons. "I'm in my second childhood," he joked when I discovered him doing this one day, embarrassed enough to blush, though there was no reason to. My father had watched cartoons before he died, which I'd considered a sign he was no longer taking anything seriously, or at least no longer participating in the world's affairs. Earl's favorite TV show was something called *Martha the Wonder Dog*, in which a dog was able to talk after eating a bowl of alphabet soup. He had other, more adolescent enthusiasms: several DVDs of *Gunsmoke*, all 152 episodes of *Robin Hood*, the complete *Flash Gordon*, and the entire run of *Hogan's Heroes*. He watched *Hogan's Heroes* over and over again, often playing an episode before the movie because he wanted me to see some bit actor he found handsome. He ordered so much through the mail that sometimes while going through the piles of new arrivals he'd realize he had ordered two copies of the same film. But he never regretted the ones he'd chosen, not even when they turned out to be stinkers, and there were, surprisingly, plenty of those.

I had no idea Hollywood had turned out so much product until I started going down to Earl's. But then the movie industry was just that: part of the whole manufacturing mania that had transformed the planet into one that was on its way to becoming uninhabitable. And for what? Many of the films he'd ordered were movies in which famous actors had appeared that were simply no good—Stanwyck, say, in *The Bride Walks Out*. In fact, the more I went there the more astonished I was at how many movies Hollywood had made with big stars that I had never heard of. Some Earl had seen as a young man in a theater in South Florida when they first came out. Others he bought because he liked the cast. Only once did he order by mistake a movie he didn't want, a film about a boxer who had beaten his opponent to death in a fight in front of the television cameras and a live audience, a famous incident neither one of us had heard of and neither one of us wanted to watch. But that was the only thing he threw out unseen. Eventually the DVDs he meant to watch were stacked so high that he'd added to the original goal of his retirement—to read all the books in his dining room— another burden.

So there we sat, watching cavalry charges on celluloid while the cockroaches' corpses piled up in the room behind us, a room we did not have to take account of because one could just shut the door. The bathroom had a shower, a bathtub, two oval sinks, a large counter, a tiled floor, and lights that still worked. It would have been so much simpler for him to use it rather than have to go back to the one off the hallway to his bedroom. But it was, for some reason, like the guest cottage, never even thought of. Only the cockroaches used it, in such numbers that I began to wonder if there was some communication among them that had led them to this room—because I never encountered one anywhere else, though once when Earl had fallen asleep while watching a film the thought did cross my mind that one of the creatures might very well crawl up his arm and he would never know it.

In *How We Die* it says there are three stages at which people kick the bucket—mid-sixties, early eighties, and early nineties—and if you pass one threshold you continue to the next. Earl seemed to have passed the first with no problem. True, he'd had trouble with his prostate, but after that was removed, he seemed fine. His hearing loss was isolating, but then he spent most of the day alone and could turn up the volume on the radio or television as loud as he wanted, which was fine with me because by that time I was losing my hearing as well.

Though we were at very different stages of life—twenty years is a lifetime to someone with just a few years left—Earl and I had several things in common: we both were gay, lived in the same town, loved books and movies, and were going deaf. It was the perfect friendship: we were together when we wanted to be and otherwise independent. We were Gertrude and Belle. There was not the slightest hint of sexual attraction between us. Once in a photograph I saw how handsome he had been when young, but even then he was not someone to whom I'd have been drawn. As a young man he'd had a face so hopeful and idealistic he looked like an English choirboy. Nor was our type the same. Often when I went on and on about someone at the boat ramp he would listen and then observe, in a mock-southern accent, "Well, I'm glad you like him, but he just don't 'peal to me." And that was that. We were different enough to interest one another and sufficiently similar to laugh at the same things.

So it was nice to walk back when the film was over through the dark and empty streets to my own bedroom, its loneliness lessened by the visit, not to mention our communion with Hollywood, Broadway, or the Berlin Philharmonic. Living in separate houses we could keep to ourselves; our routines were our own, our lives private—the difference was that Earl was so much closer to death than I was, at least on the actuarial tables.

I thought of death as the motel my father would go into when we stopped on our drive out west to see if the room would be acceptable: that is, something the older person would have to do. That your father will die before you is a given—part of the scheme of things. And after my own died Earl was the buffer between me and death. Earl was the man who'd have to go into the motel to check the room, a person I was observing for the slightest signs of decline, though the signs of what lay ahead were invisible for the longest time and when they first appeared they were so minor I did not recognize them for what they were.

The first change in Earl's habits he mentioned after we'd finished watching *Elmer Gantry* one evening—when he said he'd stopped going to church on Sunday because he could no longer hear the sermon. Instead he watched a service in

Jacksonville on television that he could turn up as loud as he wanted to. "*Im*pression without *Ex*pression leads to *De*pression!" was the preacher's mantra, which was what Earl and I used to say when we called one another up after we'd just had our groceries bagged by a particularly appealing bag boy at Food Lion.

But the biggest change was that all three of Earl's dogs died within the space of one year and had to be buried in his backyard by a man Earl had met at the boat ramp. When he had the dogs Earl had taken a walk twice a day. But after the dogs died there was no reason to go out. What does he have to live for now, I wondered; why even leave the house? When the dogs were alive they would rush to the kitchen door and make a fuss over me, smelling every inch of my trouser cuffs to learn where I'd been. I could scarcely believe it when they all expired, one after the other, in the space of a year. It was even more chilling when Earl told me he did not want to acquire another for fear he might die before the dog, and that when he changed his mind and tried to adopt one from the shelter, they told him he was too old.

Next, our favorite blueberry farm closed. The couple who owned it had experimented with some organic fertilizer that ruined their bushes—about the same time a pecan grove near Madison had to shut after the owner sprayed his trees with excrement—so we started going to another farm near Earleton. The woman who owned it had just had a stroke and her speech was so slurred that she had to write down on a pad the charge when it came time to pay for what we'd picked, which led Earl to say, "I feel so sorry for her," as we drove away—since his own troubles were nothing compared to hers—until the following month when he went to the doctor with a sore throat that would not go away.

The first diagnosis was cancer of the tonsils, which they later changed to cancer of the lymph nodes, and after a few of those had been removed they said he was cured. Indeed, a week after the chemotherapy and radiation Earl looked the same. But then the effects of the latter began to show. He lost so much weight and had so little energy that when we went to pick blueberries the following June all he could do was take a chair and sit down under the roof of the open shed where we brought our berries to be weighed by the woman who'd had a stroke; and when I returned to the shed after picking and saw him sitting there with his hands clasped on his cane, he looked for the first time like one of those old people driven places by their children so they can be out and about, and when I apologized for taking so long, he claimed he had enjoyed the chance to just sit there and watch.

There is something about Florida that disguises the passage of Time, if only because the seasons don't change as dramatically as they do up north, though in North Florida the trees lose their leaves in the fall and spring. Or it may be that there is something timeless about rural life. But the fact that I had to pick blueberries without Earl after that was a big change, and when I asked if I could bring some back for him, he told me he could not even taste blueberries anymore. The radiation had affected his taste buds; he could hardly manufacture enough saliva to chew food. Then, a few weeks after the chemotherapy and radiation had weakened his immune system, he came down with shingles, and the shingles damaged the nerve endings in his shoulders so badly that he was left with persistent pain, and the only way he could relieve that pain was to lie down in bed. And so began his new life.

When informed that he had cancer of the tonsils Earl immediately thought that he was being punished by God for giving blow jobs, but he had stopped going to the boat ramp long before he was diagnosed with cancer, after the police clamped down on the gatherings there. When the boat ramp was put off-limits I worried that we would have nothing to talk about, but it turned out we still had books, movies, music, and the news. Earl didn't listen to *All Things Considered*, but he read a great deal. His favorite magazine, *Reader's Digest*, seemed to have shrunk as much as he had after radiation, but whenever I stopped by I'd find him reading it on a stool in his kitchen, or poring over book and movie catalogs as he sipped tea and listened to classical music on the public radio station, until the public radio station changed from classical music to all-talk because the audience for classical music, like that of *Reader's Digest*, had shrunk, and Earl began listening to a gospel station because, he said, he didn't want to listen to "gasbags on NPR arguing about the stuff they broadcast just to make us all feel guilty."

Even when Earl was well I'd disliked opening the door to his kitchen if he wasn't sitting inside on a stool reading, but now that was what I had to do because many days he was too ill to sit at the counter. He was at the opposite end of the house, watching TV or listening to opera in the music room, where he could not hear my knock, which meant there was nothing to do but let myself in without an invitation. The house was one long enfilade of rooms, so that when you looked in through the screen door at the kitchen you could see the doorway to the music room at the opposite end. But now the vacancy and silence were eerie. The first day I got the courage to walk into his bedroom I discovered him lying in bed with a towel draped over his forehead reading the Bible. He had decided to work his way through the whole book again, he said, starting with Genesis—though, I did not say, it seemed to me that the relevant book at that point was the book of Job.

Earl never quoted anything from the latter book; all he said about the vicissitudes of his new situation was the usual joke: "Don't *ever* get old!" But he was now eighty-four, which may have explained the fact that the radio in the kitchen was turned to a station that played nothing but gospel music. And he was noticeably weakened. He was so weak that the first time I found him in bed in the middle of the day not long after his chemotherapy all I could think was: He's not getting better, and that can only mean one thing—the cancer is back. Cancer was no different from the Virginia creeper in my hedge or the grapevines that had taken over my yard or the four-o'clocks pushing up between the bricks of Earl's patio that his handyman pulled out to give to me, their roots wrapped in Spanish moss. They were merely examples of the same phenomenon: growth—the thing that was killing Florida as well. It was no longer a question of moving into an assisted-living establishment like the one Earl had narrowed his search down to in Lake City. It was now a matter of staying home as long as he could. Dying is like a game of musical chairs, I thought as I walked home that day; when the music stops you have to sit down wherever you are.

Clark told me that I was upset by Earl's decline because the problem of how a homosexual living alone was going to die was the fate I saw for myself—an accusation I could not deny. What's the universal concern that parents express when told their child is gay? "You'll be all alone when you're old!" And not only homosexuals. I'd just finished a biography of the English novelist Nancy Mitford, whose sister, the Duchess of Devonshire, said when she came to Paris to help her sibling during her last illness, "The trouble with Nancy is that she doesn't come first in anyone's life." There are a lot of people who don't come first in anyone's life, I thought when I read that, and Earl and I were two of them. We were what a friend in Boston told me the hospitals call people for whom there is no one waiting when they return home: "problem placements." "You have to let people in your life," Clark said. "*Some*one has to pick you up after your colonoscopy!" Another old friend, a man who now lived in Quebec, wrote in a letter: "This brings us to our own demise. What worries me most: To lose my autonomy if I live to be eighty-five or ninety or go blind? To no longer be able to drive my car, do my groceries, prepare my meals, take care of my cat? I do not see myself living in a residence for the elderly. Do you? I was counting on my younger brother, five years younger than me, to liquidate everything after my death, but life is playing tricks on us. Last year, he had a sentence worse than death: precocious dementia. He who jogged every day; who, like you, watched his diet and his weight and kept his adolescent look at seventy-five. Do you keep in touch with your sister? Do you have a close friend who would accompany you in case of serious illness? I don't. Do you resemble me? Do you expect life to make decisions for you?"

Wonderful warning, all of this, and wonderful friends: the problem was, they were scattered all over the North

American continent. That must be one reason I had begun to have a recurring nightmare in which I found myself standing in front of a door I knew I had to open and walk through, though I did not know what I would find on the other side: a room full of familiar faces, or nothing. Either way the dream was so bleak that when I woke up at three in the morning it was a relief to remember that I'd just read, in a biography of Cary Grant, that he'd said dying was simply like going into another room.

I wasn't the only person living by himself on my street—though I might as well have been, the neighbors were so invisible. It was only when the postman came by in his little jeep that people popped out of their cubbyholes. The postman, a young man so full of energy you'd see him pumping his right arm in the air as he drove by listening to music through his earbuds, was so cheerful that talking to him was a lift; some mornings I'd look over at the cluster of mailboxes across the street and see his jeep immobilized by one of my neighbors, who just wanted someone to talk to, and I'd have to give up waiting for my turn and go back to the house. I wondered how he got the mail delivered. My neighbors were such isolates I wondered if I should consider going back to church—something I'd been happy to leave behind as soon as I grew up—not for reasons of faith, but for the company, the line of people in which when I was a teenager we used to wait to shake the priest's hand on our way out. Surely that was one of the functions churches served in small towns: a network of parishioners who would help one another when they got sick, though I had no idea how often that really happened. Whatever the reality, instead of going to Mass I kept bicycling right past the church parking lot on Sunday mornings. I'd not gone to church for so long I didn't even know who the priest was anymore. It couldn't still be Father Rick, the University of Florida football fan who'd grown up in Gainesville, whom I still thought of when I bicycled on weeknights past the little house behind the church in which the priest lived. Father Rick was surely long gone, and so was his successor, a priest from the Philippines who had been discovered sending money back to his wife and children in Manila. I had no idea who was in the lighted rooms of the little house I bicycled past at night, because instead of going to Mass I was going to Earl's to watch movies—*Roman Holiday*, *Some Like It Hot*, *The Awful Truth*, *Whatever Happened to Baby Jane?*, even, one night, *I Want to Live!*

Whatever the reason for my interest in Earl's illness, whenever I telephoned him and the phone rang a long time I was now sure he was dead. Instead, he told me that he let the phone ring because it was usually someone calling on behalf of the Children's Wish Network, the state police, or some veterans' organization, calls that, he said, were simply a pestilence that had been left out of the book of Job. But once the invitations to watch *Masterpiece Theatre* with him on Sunday evening stopped, there was nothing to do but telephone—though I refrained from calling every day to ask how he felt, since I knew it must be an effort for him to get up from his bed or chair and walk to the little table in the hallway on which the phone sat, and when I did call to inquire the answer was always "About the same." So all I could do was look down the slope when I passed his house on my nightly walk to see which lights were on—they were the only other proof that he was still breathing.

There was always one comfort besides the lights in Earl's windows when I got back from my walks, and that was that I could return to the porch and watch porn on my laptop. No matter how lonely—lonely enough to consider going back to church—I always knew that at the end of my voyeuristic somnambulation through the dark and sleepy town I could go home to a handsome doctor who, after examining his young patients, would end up screwing them on the examination table, or a policeman doing the same to the thief just arrested, or a nude masseur climbing onto his prone client in an apartment somewhere in Buenos Aires. I had tried to get Earl to buy a computer. "You can do genealogical research!" I told him. "You can read the ads on craigslist from all the guys who are in the closet!"—but he was stubborn. He'd grown up learning one form of technology; he was not about to learn another. But what difference did it make? If I had the comfort of *Say Uncle* waiting for me when I got home from my nightly walk, Earl had *Gunga Din*. All that mattered to me was that he was watching something behind the lighted windows of his house when I walked by.

Before her accident my mother had liked seeing the lighted windows of a neighbor across the street whose habit of watching television past midnight made her feel she had company when she stayed up late doing the same after my father went to bed at seven. That's how I felt when I saw the lights at Earl's. If Earl's lights were on, I was not alone; there was no reason to be afraid of the dark, of the town, of death itself—even though there weren't many lamps on. The long, low house halfway down the slope was never brightly lighted, because, like most people, Earl used only a few rooms, but the lamp in the front hall was always on when he watched television and that was all I needed. That meant he was well enough to sit up and see a show. And because his front door was flanked on both sides with vertical rows of small glass squares, if I walked down his lawn I could even see, across the front hall, over his shoulder, what he was watching.

On nights when the lamp on the hall table was off, there was only a pale, anemic light that fell at a slant into the hallway from his bedroom—a light that not only looked sickly but reminded me that one day the house would be entirely dark. Everything, surely, was going in that direction. When I stopped by during the day I could see how gaunt his face and arms were, and the way the flesh beneath his chin hung down in folds. The pain of the damaged nerve ends in his neck and shoulders was so keen that he now greeted me with his right arm bent at the elbow, his hand pressing down on the shoulder that hurt, which gave him a strange ceremonial aspect, like the figure of an ancient Roman on a tomb. Pressing his shoulder eased the pain, he explained, though squeezing it too hard increased it, and then the only real relief was to lie down and not move. A strange bargain, I thought, like the one God had made with my mother: I will let you live, as long as you remain perfectly still. You can watch but not participate.

Even lying down, Earl said, he could not reach for the sheet or turn his head an inch without reigniting the nerve ends. But he refused to take medication because he did not want to become dependent on narcotics, and when he changed his mind, he'd forget to take his medication, double the dose to make up for the lapse, and then become so dizzy he couldn't walk. Once when the doctor tried a new opiate while I was away Earl took so much that he lay in bed for three days before the handyman discovered him and took him to the hospital. "I thought I was dying," he said when I got back, "but the thought didn't frighten me."

I found this inexplicable—though my father had not been afraid of death, either, so far as I could tell. My father and Earl reminded me of each other in many ways. Both men had made a living as accountants. Both men had grown up on or near farms. Both men were extremely self-reliant, courteous, good-natured, and slightly formal. Both men had big hands with square fingernails. And both men had driven me to, and picked me up at, the airport. And since I'd done very little for my father—he'd died so quickly, through sheer force of will, it seemed—I must have wanted to help Earl when he got sick, because I'd not been able to assist my progenitor very much, which, after all, may be life's chief irony—that when people express tenderness and kindness to someone it's often because of somebody else. Love and kindness have a lineage their recipients know nothing about.

So when Earl got sick I thought I'd be able to drive him to the doctor and back, to shop for groceries, to roll his garbage cans up to the road on Sunday night, to do his laundry. But each time I offered to do any of these things he said it had been taken care of by the handyman he'd used over the years to repair things around his house, whereupon I realized that Earl, like my father, except for the day I helped him walk from the table on the porch to his bed after he had his stroke, was not going to be dependent on me in any way, a courtesy for which I was grateful, if truth be known. Clark said it was because Earl did not want to return me to the position I'd been in when my mother was alive. Whatever the reason, it became clear that our relationship was not going to change. Earl was still the person on whom I relied for a phone call every few days asking me over to his house to see a movie, something that made life in that town more bearable. Otherwise, I told myself, I'd be driving over to the agricultural fair in Green Cove Springs to see the contest in which people dress their pet rabbits in little hats.

Before the radiation—a radiation he claimed had affected his mental powers—Earl had always given the movie we were about to see careful thought, hoping to show me something I might never have seen or even considered watching. But now he would just wave his hand at a stack of DVDs when I asked what we should watch and say, "You choose," a command I found, for some reason, as demoralizing as my father's letting me make decisions about his health care the last ten days of his life—a power he granted not because, as I thought at the time, there is a mysterious surrender of authority from old age to youth hard-wired in humanity, but because, I realized in retrospect, he had decided to die as quickly as he could, no matter what I did, the same way he'd decided when it was time to mow the lawn.

I suspect Earl had decided that he'd die at a certain age, the way we all conceive of a life span for ourselves, most often based on how long our parents lived, although Ray, a man we'd met at the boat ramp who belonged to the Church of the Nazarene, told Earl that the date of his death was the Lord's to choose and not his. Either way, there was no point in dwelling on it. Of course, there were things like blueberry-picking that Earl could no longer do, and when I wanted to go north I had to make arrangements with a car service now that he could no longer drive me to the Gainesville airport. But he was not to be pitied. Even when I stopped by at three in the afternoon he'd sit me down and play a favorite aria, or give me something before I left, a book or a cake he couldn't eat because his taste buds were not restored. In other words, he was still the host. Even the new bakery I had discovered in a town six miles away was of no use; I could not bring him any key lime pie or chocolate cake because sweet things still did not taste right. Movies were the only pleasure. Like the closed door of the bathroom off the music room that hundreds of roaches had chosen as a place to die, the films obscured reality. They were so effective that when the handyman came into the music room to ask Earl something, he had to speak several times; we were both so engrossed in what we were watching that after he left I'd wonder if he'd recognized us for what we were: two homosexuals in love with Irene Dunne. One never knows how large a frame of reference an individual has.

But as for helping Earl in any way, this was clearly not going to happen. He was too formal, too dignified, too independent, too proud, too courteous. Or was it simply a case of how little any of us want to be dependent on someone, even, or especially, our family or friends? Whatever the reason, I eventually had to accept the fact that the handyman was doing what Earl needed, and he was being paid to do it. There was no point in bothering Earl. And since I felt sure that getting up to answer the telephone must be painful for him I went to his house rather than call. He had never come to mine very much. One year he'd driven over for Thanksgiving dinner, a pleasant meal that only accentuated our shared loneliness, since there is a delicate undercurrent beneath get-togethers among singles on holidays that mingles the comfort of having a friend to relieve your isolation with the realization that the two of you have nobody else.

That first year of Earl's decline I thought I was his only visitor besides the woman next door who brought him an occasional meal. But that was not the case. One afternoon when Earl offered me a piece of carrot cake I asked, "Where'd you get this?" and he said, "Ray brought it." Ray had been a chef in New Jersey for years, but now as a member of the Church of the Nazarene he checked up on widows, invalids, and people in his congregation who lived alone in the woods. Ray was coming by every week, I learned, to bring Earl a hot lunch. And Ray was visiting another person with shingles, Earl said, a woman who'd had them around her eyes and had lost half her vision, which made him feel fortunate; sometimes shingles blinds people, he said, sometimes it destroys their hearing. Earl's shingles had attacked his shoulders and neck, but he still had his eyesight. It was hard to imagine what he would have done without that. His eyes were everything. He would read for hours even before he had his breakfast, read some more during the day, and then watch movies or TV at night.

When I asked Earl what he was reading it was usually a book about the Civil War. He had more books about the Civil War than anyone I knew; it still seemed to be a current event to him. He left me speechless one day when he said that if the South had won the war, the southern economy would have recovered much faster than it had. What a hypothetical, I thought—aside from that, Mrs. Lincoln, how did you like the play? But I didn't argue the point. He was southern, I was northern; he Protestant, I Catholic; he in his eighties, I in my sixties. All we had in common regarding our health was that we were both going deaf. Watching *Miss Marple*, neither one of us could understand half the dialogue no matter how loud he turned the volume up. Worse, the BBC was orchestrating shows like *Little Dorrit* with soundtracks so Wagnerian that every scene, no matter how unimportant, was accompanied by deafening orchestration that made it impossible to hear what anyone was saying. "Did you get any of that?" I'd shout, and Earl would shake his head.

Sometimes he was asleep by the time Jessica Fletcher revealed the killer on *Murder, She Wrote*. Torn between a desire to wake him up so that he could go to bed and the reluctance to disturb someone's slumber, I looked over at this man with his chin on his chest, his glasses fallen down his nose, and felt what my mother must have all those years when my father had gone to bed at seven o'clock, leaving her to sit up alone in front of the TV the rest of the night: deserted. But then my father had always kept different hours in order to have time to himself. Going to bed at seven meant rising at four, so he could sit with his coffee and copy of *Barron's* and think. The doctor I took walks with rose at 3:00 a.m., because he'd gotten into the habit when he was working in Jacksonville at the hospital and needed the extra time to review his patients' charts. Now he got up to make lasagna. Earl watched movies late into the night, which meant he would put on another after I said goodbye. I had no idea when he got up.

As for Jessica Fletcher's explanation of the murder, it made no difference; we both agreed the explanation was always so convoluted she might just as well have read a page from the Beirut phone directory.

It discomfited me, however, on those evenings when he dozed, to leave without saying goodbye, since I assumed he would feel embarrassed when he woke and found me gone; but whenever he called the next day to apologize for falling asleep he sounded, as I've already noted, so pleasant and calm that I realized it didn't bother him at all. He was someplace I could not locate—old age or illness—possessed of some serene indifference, some strange calm that gave him a perspective I did not have but which had made this part of life endurable. Earl got up every morning and went to bed every night with pain. Yet he remained good-humored. In fact, illness had eliminated the not-infrequent outbursts of temper I had witnessed before he got cancer. He had in the old days astonished me sometimes with the fury that items in the news induced in him. But now he was what they call "mellow": an equilibrium I attributed to some hope instilled in him by temperament, loving parents, or religion.

He had stopped going to church because he could not hear the sermons, but he still listened to them on the radio or watched services on TV. Yet he never spoke of his beliefs, nor did he connect his recovery with faith. Indeed, he spoke of his survival only once, and then it was the afternoon he showed me a picture of his doctor in an advertisement in *The Gainesville Sun*, a physician from Brazil who, he said, had told him, "We are going to see you through this. There's a very high rate of cure for this kind of cancer—eighty-seven percent." When I said he must have been relieved to hear those words, he replied that he had not felt any particular relief at all. "I guess I'm just stupid," he said. "All I thought was: Well, I'm sick, so fix it!"

But, like Humpty Dumpty, he'd not been fixed entirely. He had three doctors: his general practitioner, a doctor in charge of his radiation and chemotherapy, and a doctor treating his pain. The general practitioner was a handsome man whom I held to account for not having insisted Earl get the shingles vaccine long before he came down with them. The doctor treating his pain was an Egyptian who had tried different things, a salve one applied externally, pills one swallowed, and finally acupuncture, but none of them worked. That left the physical therapists in a white stucco building uptown, but when those sessions were over, he felt no different. So he was stuck with a medicine that relieved the pain to varying degrees, though the pain never went entirely away, which was why when I saw him now he seemed to be receiving me in some ceremonial fashion with his right hand placed on his shoulder.

The movies he showed were rarely Roman—those costume epics starring Victor Mature that Groucho Marx was referring to when he said he refused to go to movies in which the men's tits were bigger than the women's. Though Earl did show *Demetrius and the Gladiators*, *Quo Vadis*, *The Silver Chalice*, and *Ben-Hur*, most of the movies we watched were set in the thirties—black-and-white comedies that featured white pianos, Art Deco lobbies, shimmering gowns, and penthouses in New York, movies like *The Awful Truth*, *My Man Godfrey*, and *Holiday*. The *Thin Man* series we watched repeatedly, especially for that scene in which Myrna Loy turns to her butler at the dinner where all the suspects are assembled and says, "Would you serve the nuts?" and then, after a pause, "I mean, would you serve the guests the nuts?" Ditto the scene in *Beat the Devil* in which Robert Morley describes with undulating movements of his hands the way his ship sank as his Arab interlocutors look on suspiciously through dark glasses. And the moment in *I Was a Male War Bride* when Ann Sheridan goes off on the motorcycle, leaving Cary Grant sitting in the sidecar someone forgot to attach, Deanna Durbin singing "Spring Will Be a Little Late This Year" in *Christmas Holiday*, Rosalind Russell trying to connect calls on the telephone switchboard in *Auntie Mame*, Marilyn Monroe and Jane Russell doing "We're Just Two Little Girls from Little Rock" in *Gentlemen Prefer Blondes*, or the moment in *Letter to Three Wives* when Linda Darnell, after her sister suggests she add a necklace to the V-neck sweater she is wearing on a date, delivers the immortal line "What I got don't need beads." And there was always Fred and Ginger dancing to "Let Yourself Go" in *Follow the Fleet*—even though when I glanced over at Earl to share my delight, this man asleep on the other side of a chair heaped with DVDs looked, snoozing with his chin on his chest, more and more like a giant pelican.

The cliché that homosexuals are such aesthetes that images of old age tend to horrify them is not entirely untrue; how else do we explain the age segregation in gay bars? Of course, youth is granted a prestige, in erotic matters, among people of every sexual orientation. I was by now used to watching the heads of young men coming toward me on the sidewalk in Washington look away so quickly that all I could think of was Linda Blair's head spinning in *The Exorcist*—a movie that defines DC in more ways than one. The sight of Earl in old age was more like a Rembrandt in that room full of self-portraits at the National Gallery. This was due partly to the light coming from behind, the fluorescent tube above the bookcase crammed with opera records, and partly to the fact that he seemed to have assumed an entirely new shape. The figure slumped in the chair beside mine seemed to have been reduced to three elements: belly, hands, and glasses. Every part of his body had collapsed except his stomach. His stomach and head were normal size, but his arms and legs were gaunt. The sun-browned hands, with their thick, square fingers, were so covered with age spots they reminded me of my father's when he'd get skin tears every time he worked in the yard, and permanent purple patches where the blood vessels had burst just beneath the skin. The skin, after all, is an organ—the largest organ in the body—that fails, like all the others.

Looking back I must admit I didn't really help Earl die—or even keep a very good watch. Had I done that, I'd not have left Florida when he began to decline, since there was no telling what would happen when I was gone. Each time I told myself I could go away because he had reached a sort of plateau on which he wasn't getting any worse; but then I'd learn he had fallen while I was away, discovered by the handyman after several hours, or even days, lying on the floor. More than once he lay there in the hall for several days unattended—a literal enactment of that ad I used to make fun of in my twenties: "Help! I've fallen and I can't get up!"—though in this case I imagined cockroaches crawling on his helpless form. But that didn't seem to bother him. Indeed, he took everything in stride with a sangfroid I envied, since one reason I was drawn to Earl is that he was simply calmer than I was—things didn't frighten him the way they did me.

My friend Patrick, on the other hand, seemed to enjoy scaring me with scenarios of our future, though he was a decade younger than myself; as much as we laughed, I could never quite dispel the feeling of depression I had after one of his visits. The reason was simple: he wanted me to face something I didn't want to. He'd moved his own mother into a residence for people over sixty-five a few years before she died, and said she'd been so relieved by what she'd been resisting for years that she wished she'd moved there sooner. Patrick had grown up in Gainesville, and now that he'd retired as a photographer for *National Geographic* in Washington, he'd let his hair grow long, so that he once again looked like the student activist he'd been at the University of Florida. In Gainesville he lived in a high-rise condominium on Twenty-Third Avenue whose apartments were in separate towers, reached by individual stairwells—one of the older condos in the heart of town, near a ravine off Hogtown Creek that was heavily forested, not far from the house in which he'd grown up. Climbing the stairs to the fifth floor, I could feel the chill not only of the surrounding woods on the smooth concrete stairs and walls, but also of the older Gainesville that had been superseded by the town's westward expansion. His apartment overlooked a swimming pool and parking lot, and though the base of the open stairwell I climbed was pleasantly landscaped with a fishpond and palms, by the time I reached the fifth floor, turned right, and walked down a shadowed hallway to his apartment, the chill, even on summer days, was always palpable.

The man who lived across the hallway from him had been living with his mother elsewhere in town until she died at ninety-eight, after which he'd sold their house and moved into Patrick's building. The Carleton seemed to be one of the stops along the royal road to death, part of an Underground Railway by which people reached rigor mortis. Patrick told me about several men who'd lived, for example, in my town or on a lake nearby, until they decided to move into Gainesville to be closer to their friends and doctors; then after a few years they'd moved to the Village, an adult assisted-living facility on the west side of Gainesville he wanted me to investigate. The process was incremental—though not everyone observed the increments. A man from my town who'd moved to Patrick's building, for instance, a gay man I'd never met, had decided to move out of the Carleton not long after buying a condo there to live with his older sister, but soon after moving in with her he drove over one morning to a public park on the northwest side of town and shot himself in the mouth. "They found him slumped on the ground with his back against the wall of the men's room," Patrick said, in a way that left me uncertain whether to laugh or to cry.

Patrick thought that I should skip the Carleton and move directly to the Village. "The apartments are really nice," he said; "you can either eat in the dining room or have the meal brought to your room, there are gated grounds for your walks, and every morning when you awake you press a button to let the staff know you're still alive." I didn't tell him that in the back of my mind I'd already narrowed things down to an assisted-living place in Fort Lauderdale that was popular with gay men—unless I was saved by the other fantasy. Two of my friends had found husbands in the men's room at Tropics. There was after all a tradition of pair-bonding down there: the older man of means who agrees to leave his estate to the young man who'll stay with him to the end. Fort Lauderdale, for gay men, was what Israel is for the Jews. Knowing Fort Lauderdale was there I could postpone the move to South Florida as long as I wanted, until, that is, I had to be carried off the plane.

Patrick was not so sanguine. He warned me there might come a time when the Village would refuse to take me—like the kennel's denying Earl a dog because he was too old. That was the problem: one had to make one's move while one still could, like a fashion designer drawing his fall line in spring. But then Patrick was by nature impatient; he'd inherited that quality from his mother. His mother had not wanted to spend any more time as an old woman than she had to; before the last operation on her spine she'd told him, "I don't care if I come out of this or not," and when she had to be moved to hospice after the operation, while waiting for the paramedics to arrive she'd asked, "How long is this going to take?," which Patrick answered with "Twenty minutes," thinking she meant her transfer to the new facility, when in fact, after she died there two nights later, he realized she'd meant exiting the planet.

To continue with this gloomy subject: the man who lived across the hall from Patrick was a recluse, he said, like Boo Radley, from *To Kill a Mockingbird*. The man did nothing but read the books that lined the shelves in his living room. On the headboard of his bed was one of those little lamps on a moveable arm with a single bulb that could be pointed exactly to the page he was reading—"like the one you have," Patrick said. Perhaps that's why I began to feel a double chill whenever I reached Patrick's, once I learned the recluse was across the hallway, reading, as I knocked on Patrick's door. Even so, I was not prepared for his telling me one day, after he and I had both returned from a trip, that the recluse had died while he was away—while reading a book on his sofa—and the body had not been discovered for almost a week, which meant that the corpse was so decomposed that not only had an odor worked its way into the concrete floor, which had to be scraped to get rid of the smell, but they'd had to run an ozone machine for a week to clear the air. And now no one knew whom to notify about the man's demise. His neighbor had once told Patrick that he had no relatives left save for a cousin he'd last seen when he was nine, and he had no idea where she lived now. So his entire estate was probably going to go to the state of Florida.

"But why did they have to *scrape* the concrete floor?" I had to ask.

"Because of the fluids," Patrick said in his calm, almost inaudible voice. "We're full of fluids. And when we die we leak."

"Leak how?"

"I guess through your asshole and nostrils and mouth. Whatever the process, his bodily fluids soaked into the concrete."

"I thought concrete was impermeable."

"Guess again," said Patrick.

"So all they found was—"

"A puddle," said Patrick. "A puddle and a book."

That day, I was so unsettled by the thought of the recluse on his sofa leaving behind nothing but bodily fluids—not to mention the twinkle in Patrick's eye when he told me—that

I stopped dropping in on my friend after visiting the gym in Gainesville, because I never knew how he was going to depress me next. Earl on the other hand seemed unfazed by the prospect of extinction. The cousin from Gainesville with whom he had gone to estate sales had died shortly before Earl's diagnosis, his brother from South Florida was ill, and the friends from his years studying in Indiana or teaching in South Florida were dying off as well. But though these losses must have affected him—his cousin and brother, at least—he never said so. In fact, the night Earl got up to answer the phone in the foyer while we were watching a movie and learned that a man with whom he'd taught at the University of Miami, an old friend who'd moved to California years ago, had just died, he simply apologized for the interruption when he returned to the music room and clicked the remote control, and we went right back to watching *Sorry, Wrong Number.*

The story of the recluse, however, seemed a cautionary tale. When a man who'd lived across the street from me during the Iraq War, a widower, was dying of prostate cancer, I'd envied the fact that he was never alone; his driveway was always full of cars, whether it was hospice, or his son and daughter-in-law and grandchildren, or the neighbor down the street with whom he'd been having a romance, or the cleaning woman. Earl and I however were alone. It is a fact seldom observed that after a certain age a single man is a creature no one has any place for; my attempts to become friendly with the doctor and his wife down the street, or the woman across the park with whom I liked to talk about gardening problems, or the beekeeper at the little gym in town who was my partner in our high-interval class, were all pleasant enough. But I remained that unclassifiable thing—an old man living by himself, an old man watching porn on my laptop on the back porch while the widow next door played croquet with her guests just beyond the hedge, an old man pressing the Mute button so that the sounds of the men on my screen reaching orgasms—orgasms that took so long to achieve that watching them was like waiting for a bus—would not be heard, much less the standard dialogue of porn films, which seems to consist of only two words: "fuck" and "yeah."

The trouble with watching porn is that it tinctures real life. Walking uptown to the post office I took a shortcut via an alley in which a man my age seemed to be living by himself, but there was always a skateboarder or two hanging around outside his cottage, most often a handsome young man with curly black hair seated at the outdoor table, stirring a cup of coffee when I walked by, who raised suspicions. In Earl's case, however, it was not a handsome young skateboarder who was going to row him across the river Styx; it was the handyman.

The handyman was a husky man in his mid-fifties—neither plain nor handsome—whose appearance was strangely bifurcated; at the top he looked like an angel by Giotto—a thick, curly mop of dirty blond hair pulled back into a pony-tail, and two beautiful blue eyes edged with thick eyelashes. His arms and chest were normal sized. But at his waist he ballooned into a man with an enormous ass and thick legs. He looked like a bowling pin; there was no relationship between his upper and his lower halves. I never understood it. He was a man who had grown up in town but had had a falling-out with his father, a retired steel executive who so disapproved of his son's refusal to finish college that he wrote him out of his will. Yet there seemed no rancor or bitterness on the handyman's part over what had happened; he was so easygoing he did not seem to mind that his sister got the house while he was living in a trailer in the woods outside of town. His wife and son were both in poor health, Earl informed me—his wife had migraines; his divorced son had been injured in an accident while working as a guide for rich people who went to South Florida to hunt wild boar and was now in a wheelchair. But the handyman was always cheerful, whistling in the carport as he hammered and sawed, or painted the house or trimmed the hedge, or took Earl to the doctor, or did his laundry at the mall uptown until he persuaded Earl to buy a new washer and dryer.

Whether they assigned a dollar value to each task or whether Earl would write a check and tell him to work it off I never knew. But there were other forms of remuneration. Each time the handyman drove Earl to the doctor, for instance, they would stop in Madison on the way home and Earl would treat him to lunch or dinner. And he let the handyman use his car whenever the handyman could not trust his truck to take his son to the doctor. The handyman's son, who had moved back home after his divorce, had gone through three operations and had to be taken to the university every week for physical therapy. He also had a six-year-old daughter on whom the handyman doted, a little girl who seemed the bright spot in the family.

When widows say they will leave town if anything happens to their handyman it's meant as a joke, but it's not really. For the person living alone a handyman amounts to a kind of spouse; the broken toilet, light switch, stuck door, leaky faucet, window that won't close, rarely get fixed unless you call the plumber or electrician, who will charge a hundred dollars just for walking through the door. And a plumber won't drive you to the doctor. So now that the handyman's chores had morphed into taking care of Earl, he was no longer just a handyman; he was the person who, Earl did not have to say, would keep him from having to move to a nursing home.

Clark, who'd hired the handyman years ago, said that he had done good work, but when it was over he came back one day to ask if he could borrow two hundred dollars because it was his wife's birthday and the woman in Gainesville who was going to pay him that day had had to leave town suddenly for a funeral. He even offered to leave some big piece of machinery behind as collateral, but Clark told him that would not be necessary and loaned him the money. The handyman never came back, and Clark was so disgusted when he realized the handyman had never had any intention of repaying the loan that he never spoke to him again. The right thing would have been to remind him of the money, I suggested, which the handyman might well have simply forgotten; but Clark said that was not likely and anyway it was the responsibility of the person who received the loan, not the person who made it, to bring the topic up, which Clark was too embarrassed to do, which only made him detest the handyman more, since Clark was already ridden with guilt for being rich enough to hire people to work for him, and his own innate timidity prevented him from asking the handyman to pay him back. Then there was Mrs. Hadid, the mother of a friend of mine, who'd hired the handyman and claimed he'd stolen something from her garage—a story I could not evaluate, since Mrs. Hadid was so paranoid she had accused her brother-in-law, who lived next door to her, of stealing the oranges on her trees.

Mrs. Hadid said that the handyman had stiffed one of his former employers by overcharging him for the new toilets he installed in his house, toilets that were so shoddy (though he charged him plenty) that the man had had to cut up his bowel movements with a knife before flushing to make sure they would not stop the toilet up. This seemed a bit much even for Mrs. Hadid. But she stood her ground, and my plumber confirmed the story. As people age, he said, they tend to take pain medication, which hardens their stools, which clog the pipes.

My plumber was a man of sterling character, and I decided it was best to think that the handyman was not dishonest, especially since the main thing was that he was now taking care of Earl. Besides, he seemed to be such a friendly fellow I could not imagine him defrauding someone like that. The handyman seemed to me kind by nature, a man who'd decided that life in this small town beat trying to make it in the big cold world beyond its borders. If anything, he seemed like a hippie, a sixties leftover who'd made mistakes, a man who'd grown up in this community of eleven hundred (ten thousand, if you considered the surrounding woods full of houses and mobile homes) but never made it out, the way almost every other child raised here had, and was now preoccupied with his family's troubles. The only bright spot in the latter was the handyman's six-year-old granddaughter: a sprite with blond hair, blue eyes, and tiny fingernails and teeth whom I met one day when she was kneeling on the floor beside Earl's bed, working her scissors back and forth as she cut pictures out of an old *National Geographic*, proudly showing him each photograph when she had finished.

There was something so lovely about the sight of a man at the end of his life lying with eyes closed on what was probably his deathbed while a fresh young creature just starting hers knelt beside him making cutouts that, after the handyman had taken his granddaughter home, the first thing I said to Earl was, "What a *cute* little girl!," whereupon he lifted the towel from his forehead and said, "*Cute*? I couldn't *wait* for her to get out! She breaks things! She doesn't mean to, but she does. And I cannot hear a *word* she's saying!"

So much for sentimental images of old age. That evening I ran into the handyman and his granddaughters in the grocery store. The handyman was hoisting the little girl up and down in the middle of the cereal aisle, each time making her laugh harder, a sight so charming I started down the aisle to greet them till the handyman saw me coming and his face froze—at which point I turned and fled into the canned vegetables. He's obviously horrified, I thought as I pretended to search for diced tomatoes; he considers you pathetic because you are an old man with no grandchildren of your own. He doesn't want you to have anything to do with his little darling because he sees you as what you are—a childless poof.

The paranoia of the homosexual in a small town never disappears and observes no boundaries. The smallest thing can set it off. Whenever a handyman, a tree trimmer, a plumber, or the man who handled my air conditioner failed to return my call, I was sure it was because he'd learned I was gay, and there was no way to tell if this was paranoid.

Living alone one has no one to bounce such thoughts off of—no way to know if one is imagining things. One is torn between the hope that the plumber or electrician who shows up will be a paragon of amiable masculinity and the fear that he will be quite the opposite. At some point during the visit, I believed, it was inevitable that whoever had come to my home to fix something would wonder why I lived alone. So I'd either go off and spend the hours the hired person was in the house elsewhere, or worry when I did stay home that I'd been too friendly, too accommodating. The way one is treated by the electrician can determine one's mood for the rest of the day. It has something to do with our fathers, Clark said.

I accepted the handyman simply because he was necessary—the only thing keeping Earl out of a nursing home. And there was something else. The handyman had a prestige in my eyes simply because he could fix a leak, a lamp, or a lawn mower, and he'd sired a child who'd given him a granddaughter. When the handyman came into the music room even Earl changed; he'd drop whatever we'd been talking about and turn immediately to John to give him his full attention. Perhaps that was why I resented it the first time I saw him in Earl's Buick. Earl's Buick was a cinnamon-colored sedan covered with hundreds of small dents created by a hailstorm during which it had sat outside at a dealer's up north—pockmarks that had qualified Earl for a discount when he bought it in Gainesville. The car looked as if it had acne. But it agreed with Earl—the LeSabre was dignified and substantial—which meant the handyman looked like an imposter every time I saw him pull into the carport in the driver's seat. Get out, I wanted to say, that doesn't belong to you! Instead, I stopped asking Earl where the car was, since the answer was always "John had to take his son to the doctor."

No doubt it was because we were watching so many movies that I began to think of three classics each time I found John working at Earl's in the evening when I dropped in. One was *Gaslight*, in which Charles Boyer tries to convince Ingrid Bergman that she is mad so that he may gain control of her fortune; another was *Sunset Boulevard*, in which Erich von Stroheim plays a butler who is all that stands between an aging actress and reality; and the third was *Rebecca*, in which the housekeeper, Mrs. Danvers, psychologically tortures the just-married mistress of a country house in England. The handyman had a habit of coming back after supper in his own battered truck to Earl's house to work, I suspect to escape his own family. This meant that occasionally when we were watching a movie I would turn to Earl to say something and see him standing in the doorway behind Earl's high-backed chair—just like Mrs. Danvers, though I doubt the handyman saw any connection between himself and that movie. I did not know if the handyman knew anything about movies. What was clear was that he had a family to support; and Earl needed a caretaker. That was why, I assumed, Earl gave him yard work when there was nothing else to do—even though Earl already paid a Pentecostal minister and his son to mow the lawn.

Earl once laughed when I asked him what the solution to old age was and said, "Servants!" He certainly had no hesitation about hiring people to work for him. His yard was a perfect example. The lake we lived on had once been one large continuous body of water but had separated into a series of separate smaller lakes that had all receded from what used to be the shoreline. What had once been a broad expanse of water stretching to a faraway shore was now a prairie broken up by small ponds between which grass and wildflowers were growing. The part of the lake I lived on had remained the same size because it was spring fed. But the lake in front of Earl's house—the Big Lake—had receded so far that the back lawn now sloped down to what amounted to a prairie. His back lawn seemed to be dying as well, bleached by the same relentless drought that was burning everything else up. The back lawn was now mostly sand, with patches of grass, a few live oaks, and one incongruous yellow rosebush of which Earl for some reason disapproved; at least he told me he was not going to fertilize it. On the east a grove of old camellias planted by the previous owner ran the length of the yard from the sidewalk to the south side of the house, a grove that looked, after Earl had the handyman clear it of ferns and undergrowth, stark and bare; as did the whole yard after the handyman cut back, almost to the roots, the hedge of azaleas that ran along the sidewalk, a hedge I decided had no more of a chance of recovery than Earl. What I couldn't decide was whether Earl was destroying his yard because he wanted everything neat or because he wanted to give the handyman work so that he could stay out of a nursing home. Either way, it seemed like one more miserable consequence of old age.

The handyman usually had a little radio playing on the fender of his truck when I would arrive for the evening film. He seemed to like staying late, puttering around in the fluorescent light. He always seemed glad to see me. We would talk about the weather, or the lake, and then I'd go inside, where I'd find Earl in the music room and ask him how he felt.

For the longest time I could not decide whether Earl was dying or not. Even now, looking back, I can't say how long it took for Earl to decline—a year, two years, three? When the American novelist Howard Sturgis lay on his deathbed he was cared for so solicitously by his life partner that at one point Sturgis had to remind him, "A watched pot never boils"—surely one of the wittiest comments ever made while dying, unless you consider what the socialite Drue Heinz said when nearing the end—"They won't even let you take a book"—or the emperor Vespasian, who remarked on his deathbed, "I think I am turning into a god." Earl was the pot I was watching, the woman who could not take a book with her, the emperor who was turning into a god. But there was only confusion on my part about what exactly was happening—because I did not know if he was getting better or worse. I never knew when I walked across the lake bed to his house what state I would find him in when I entered the house: a corpse, or a man watching *Martha the Wonder Dog*.

There was a man my age, a retired painter of dioramas at the natural history museum in Gainesville, who walked his dog on the lake bed and would commiserate with me about the heat when he stopped to wipe his forehead with a handkerchief, and then proceed inevitably to talk about his dead wife. At first I was given to believe she'd died only a year ago, but one day he told me it had been three, and the next time five. Whatever the date, he could not refer to her without having to lower his head as if the blow was still fresh. The man's sole companion was a beautiful husky with one blue and one brown eye. The dog was so well behaved that I was commenting on her deportment one day as we stood chatting on the lake bed when the widower interrupted me with an excited cry, and I looked down in the direction of his gaze and saw what seemed to be little ladybugs pushing miniature logs across the grass. "Dung beetles!" he said when I inquired.

"But what are they dragging?" I said.

"Dog shit!" he cried. "It's pure energy! Pure energy!"

That's what dying is, I thought, unless you're lucky enough to stop breathing while asleep: pushing a dog turd a hundred times your size across the grass. In reality, when I got to Earl's house that day he was sitting in the den watching a movie in pressed slacks, striped polo shirt, and baseball cap, as if obeying that admonition of one's mother that you wear clean underwear because you never know when you might be hit by a bus. But for whom was he dressing? What was the reason for the expensive polo shirt, the jeans and baseball cap? I didn't ask—though wearing a cap in your own house really makes no sense, unless your head is cold—or you are waiting to be picked up by someone.

That someone, I felt sure, was Death. But Death was taking so long to come that the more the handyman took over Earl's life, the more I began to walk past his house on the lake bed without stopping by or even glancing up at it. Walking on the lake bed I was alive; sitting in Earl's music room I was in a sick room. For years it was demoralizing to watch the lakes go down, but now the drought had gone on so long that something unexpected had happened: the dry lake bed had become more beautiful than the lake. The forest that had grown up near the peninsula on which I lived was full of trees that brought me to a stop as I was hiking through it—to admire a magnolia growing unencumbered in the middle of a meadow, gigantic pines whose grove filtered the light differently from hour to hour, a grove so dense that sometimes I lay down on the carpet of russet needles to stare up at the canopy. Of course, there was always the hope that I'd encounter someone on the path. I'd already met a corrections officer trying out a motorbike before he gave it to his son, a guard at a women's prison near Ocala who worked out at the little gym in town. I'd met a park ranger searching for people who'd been firing guns, and a young man who looked like a young Donny Osmond dragging a portable platform he intended to install in a clearing in the forest so he could shoot deer with his crossbow. Then there was the man who photographed birds from his golf cart while his little Chihuahua barked hysterically at me.

The birds were everywhere. Walking along the water's edge I'd hear a noise, look up, and see a blue heron flapping its wings as it rose laboriously from its perch and flew out across the lake, like someone I'd ejected from a comfortable chair. There were egrets and hawks and bald eagles, blackbirds and wood ducks and sandhill cranes, a flock of turkeys, and shadows on the ground that made me look up in the sky to see buzzards circulating on currents of air. The lake bed was so full of life that when I went to visit Earl there was a sense of deflation, a diminution of spirit, the moment I turned up the slope to his house beside a pipe through which he'd once drawn water from the lake—now high, dry, and corroded, like old age itself. The minute I turned up the slope to Earl's house I had to prepare myself for what I found when I entered, which is why sometimes I did not turn up the slope at all; I just walked to town and back on my errands—because, as F. Scott Fitzgerald said, there is no difference so profound as that between the sick and the well.

Still, it made me glad the morning Earl called and asked if I wanted to come over that evening and watch *The Killers*. It wasn't a movie I particularly wanted to see, but then he had shown me many films I didn't want to watch that turned out to be worthwhile. Half an hour before I was to leave, however, the phone rang. It was the handyman telling me that Earl had asked him to call me to say he was feeling too sick to show the movie.

It wasn't that Earl was in danger, he said; it was just the nausea he got from time to time that sent him to bed if he did not quash it in time by eating raw ginger. What bothered me about the phone call was the fact that the handyman had delivered the news. It was like getting a call from Bette Davis in *Whatever Happened to Baby Jane?* So, I thought, the handyman is now the go-between in matters related to Earl's health. He thinks he's going to usher Earl into the next life—he's waiting for him to die too.

The next day when I called Earl his enunciation was so slurred I was certain that he'd had a stroke and was choosing to ignore it the way my father had by refusing to give me the name of his doctor. But you cannot ignore a stroke. Indeed, by the time my father was moved from the nursing home to the hospital just a week after his cerebral incident, gangrene had established itself on his right leg. Everyone said it was just as well that he was not "all there" after the amputation, since he could not have accepted the loss. It was just as well he was delirious the last time I saw him, helplessly trying to remove the catheter from his penis. He died without ever knowing that he had lost his leg, the way Mrs. McAfee never knew her husband had totaled her Oldsmobile.

How fortunate we are that people die in hospitals, where we do not have to watch it happen, from which we can conveniently be away at the final moment. So why, I wondered while hiking across the prairie to see Earl, wasn't the lake bed littered with corpses? Why did I not come upon dead rabbits, raccoons, mice, snakes, cats, and birds? The turkey buzzards circling overhead—"nature's undertakers"—couldn't alone explain the absence of bones. Occasionally I'd come upon a cluster of feathers on the ground, or a baby raccoon, its jaw open as if to bite whatever had killed it, and one day I found the skeleton of a water moccasin. But that was so rare that I could only marvel how remarkable it was that animals died so discreetly, out of sight, without the hospital rooms and funerals with which we treat the dead. A man I'd met at the boat ramp, a man I'd been having sex with for so many years I called him the Regular, had simply buried Earl's dogs in Earl's backyard, the way I'd buried a feral cat I'd found stiff as a board on my lawn one day. They'd died without hospitals, nursing or funeral homes, cemeteries or crematoria.

My mother had provided me with a lesson in this matter that only confirmed all this. Her first year in the nursing home she'd come down with pneumonia—which nurses call "the old person's friend," I learned after I took her home and made sure she recovered, thereby giving her eight more years of life as a quadriplegic. Alas, these things become clear only in retrospect, like the evening I overheard the nurses talking about people who won't let their family members go. If only our public schools provided eighth-graders a course in Death, along with Sex Education.

This time, convinced that Earl's slurred voice meant that he'd indeed had a stroke, I decided that I too would ignore it—simply to avoid "heroic" medicine with its technology and end-of-life interventions. By calling no one the handyman and I would be letting Earl die at home—the gift I'd refused my father; I would, in collusion with the handyman, allow Earl to expire in his own bed. And then, a few nights later, proud of correcting a wrong I'd done my parents, I was walking by Earl's house and saw the light of his television through the front door, went down the slope, peered through the glass squares, and saw him watching a cooking show, and when I tapped on the window, he got up and let me in, and we sat down and watched a handsome chef in New Orleans make brisket of beef with black-eyed peas. Earl hadn't had a stroke at all, I learned; he'd just taken too much of a new pain medicine. In fact, the handyman had driven him to Starke that day for a doctor's appointment and after that he'd stopped by a friend's.

I'd not known Earl had a friend in Lake City, or that the handyman was driving him around to visit acquaintances of his in other towns, including the man I had been having sex with for twenty years, a man Earl had met before I did. But I was so relieved to see Earl his old self that I forgot about my recent concern that he'd had a cerebral accident. Instead, I told him how good-looking his new eyeglasses were. "Oh, they're just an old pair I found in a drawer," he said. "I think they make me look funny. But the new ones keep sliding down my nose, because the contours of your face change, you know, as you age." And then he added, "But I no longer care how I look."

Whether or not Earl cared about his appearance, I had to admit, whenever I got there, that his house had never looked better. The handyman had made the whole place shipshape. The dead fronds on the sago palms were gone, the grove of camellias had been cleared of underbrush, the bed of hydrangeas was a deep blue because of the sulfate the handyman had added to the soil, the circular flower bed had been planted with blueberry bushes, the house itself had a new coat of paint, the patio was free of weeds, the unused porch was cleaned up, and the kitchen counter had been cleared of the tremendous pile of papers Earl had always complained of but had been unable to go through. The odd thing was that the clean, gleaming countertop seemed to me sad. A mess of papers means someone's living there; a clean room means you're ready to go.

But I didn't say this. Instead, I said, "You know, your house has never looked better," and he replied, "Yes, John has done a wonderful job." Then he paused on his way to the DVD player, turned to me with the disc in hand, like a man about to present an award, and said, "You know, without John I would never have been able to stay here," which reminded me of my own mother's request that I let her come home when she realized she was starting to die, a favor I could not grant at the time and therefore ignored. Like my parents, like everyone, I thought, Earl simply wants to die in his own bed.

And then Earl pressed Play on the DVD player, which summoned up an English film about a prize-winning cow on one of the Channel Islands the Nazis had occupied, a movie we watched in such peace and quiet that when I looked over at Earl I saw that he was sound asleep. Then when the movie ended I continued sitting there in the strange silence—strange because it was as if Earl, merely asleep, had actually died—and looked around at all the records and books he loved. Sitting there while Earl dozed in his chair I could examine everything in the room; I could leap forward in time to the moment when all this would be dispersed—the contents of this room that had brought me so much pleasure, the pleasure of being asked down for a movie. Nothing could have better illustrated the old adage that when a man dies a library dies with him than Earl's music room. Yet everything in there would be of no interest to anyone once Earl expired. And then, when I'd had enough of that, for such reflections can only go on so long, I got up and took my usual walk through town; and the next morning I left for Washington in a hired car whose driver, listening to the conservative radio station, told me that President Obama was too soft on foreign affairs and that we should drop a nuclear bomb on countries like Iran because that had always worked in the past, though I told him we had done it in only one country, Japan.

The men I knew in Washington who were facing old age had taken measures more extreme than Earl's accelerating acquisition of DVDs. One friend, a curator who'd worked for the National Gallery, had met a security guard from Bratislava, a handsome weight lifter for whom he'd moved to Slovakia, and made him the sole beneficiary of his estate. Another—a theater director who had retired to Fort Lauderdale—had left his penthouse apartment on the beach for a town south of Lake Okeechobee because his young boyfriend wanted to raise horses there; so now, like Eva Gabor in *Green Acres*, this veteran of Broadway was singing Sondheim to the colts he was feeding in the middle of the Florida scrub. At least Earl was not trying to mitigate the prospect of death with one last love affair. There was certainly nothing erotic in his relationship with the handyman—that overweight carpenter with a big butt and ponytail—though I continued to think there were elements of *Rebecca*, if not *Gaslight*, in the relationship, if only because the moment the handyman came into the music room with the dinner tray Earl's demeanor always changed. Sometimes he sounded like the chatelaine of a manor house in one of those shows the BBC produced with the ease of a popcorn-maker, planning a dinner party with the head cook, other times like Joan Crawford asking her sister for a favor in *Whatever Happened to Baby Jane?*

But there was nothing I could object to; the handyman was allowing Earl to keep the life he'd led—and he could drive me to the Gainesville airport, where I'd rent a car to drive to Jacksonville, and get on a nonstop flight on JetBlue that took me to Washington, where I could take the Metro to Dupont Circle and arrive at the baths in time for Nude Yoga. In Washington I was doing research for a man who'd written several books about the architectural history of the nation's capital. His most famous volume was simply called *Vanished Mansions*. The historian was confined to bed at the age of eighty-eight, writing what we both assumed would be his last book. I'd go around town taking photographs for him, or look for letters and diaries in the Library of Congress that he needed, and then I'd bicycle up Connecticut Avenue to one of those big old historic apartment buildings that were not only his main subject but the place in which he lived, among bullet mirrors and Colonial furniture. He was far worse off than Earl; by that time he was using supplemental oxygen as he collated text and photographs on a pile of pillows.

There was one mansion in particular with which he was obsessed: the Hay-Adams house, a Romanesque masterpiece designed by H. H. Richardson. It was there that the historian Henry Adams had lived. The house had been torn down in the 1920s to make way for what is now the Hay-Adams Hotel. Henry Adams had had a stroke one day, but unlike my father he'd recovered and lived several more years, during which time he'd been taken care of by a young woman named Aileen Tone, who would play medieval chansons for him on the piano. My employer, the bed-bound historian of Washington's vanished mansions, was himself facing an imminent departure, but the only reference he made to that final deadline came one day when he looked up at me from the pile of Xeroxes I'd brought in my knapsack and said, "You know, there's a wonderful line in one of Adams's letters that goes, 'All I want to do at this point is leave this earth without any fuss.'"

"And did he?" I said.

"Yes," he said. "He died in his bed—Aileen Tone went upstairs to get him when he didn't come down for breakfast and discovered the body."

"I don't really like the idea of my body being discovered," I said after a moment's attempt to imagine that scene.

"But you won't be conscious," he said.

"I know," I said, "but the thought still bothers me."

"Because you're worried how you'll look?"

"Because I'll be so defenseless," I said. "And yes, I suppose because I'm worried how I'll look."

"Perhaps," he said, "you're too vain to die."

"Lots of luck with that," Patrick replied when I repeated the remark.

I never made any attempt to get together with Patrick even when we happened to be in DC at the same time. Nor did I call Earl or anyone else in Florida. It was as if I didn't live there, as if Florida did not exist, though sometimes when the weather in DC was especially beautiful—a soft, mellow autumn day when the leaves were fluttering down onto the parked cars, and the whole city seemed to be crumbling in the golden sunshine—I would look in the newspaper and see that North Florida was having much the same weather and imagine the house sitting empty at the end of the driveway on a late October afternoon. I could see the leaves and branches broken off by storms scattered across the cracked asphalt, and the plants in the yard that bloom only in autumn (cassia, goldenrod), the leaves of the grapevines turning yellow, the pine cone lilies going to seed. And I would pick up the phone and call my number just to make the phone ring in the empty house.

The idea, I think, was that if I left the house alone long enough, it would die; its meaning would leak out through those jalousie windows that never closed properly, and when I finally returned the house would be devoid of meaning.

Time, after all, is the only cure for grief. On those autumn afternoons in DC, sitting at the window above the gingko trees whose yellow leaves had covered the hoods of the parked cars down in the street, I would think of the house in Florida slowly dying while I was up north. But that didn't happen.

So I continued to go back to Washington. On one trip I went to the National Gallery to see the reconstruction of an ancient tomb that had just been discovered on the Upper Nile; the exhibit was accompanied by a film running continuously in a little theater adjacent to the display. The subject of the film was Egyptian beliefs about the afterlife. The most perilous thing after the death of a pharaoh, according to the film, were the first six hours, in which the pharaoh had to pass a series of tests in order to reach the afterlife, where he could enjoy all those possessions that had been buried with him in the tomb; and the fourth hour was the most crucial because that was when the scorpion-god Anubis tried to stop him from reaching the Underworld. How wonderfully the Egyptians had dealt with death, I thought as I was flying back, and how little attention we give it in this culture. Earl did not have to worry about Anubis—indeed, I'd not seen a scorpion in my garage in years, much less a scorpion-god—but it was still a relief to drop in on him a few days after getting back and see him reading in his chair when I walked in.

In keeping with his admirable reserve Earl never asked when I returned from Washington what I'd seen and done while I was there, whereas when I got back to Florida I was soon saying, "Were you not feeling well yesterday? Your light was out last night when I walked by, and the car was gone," and he'd confuse me by saying he'd driven over to the St. Johns River the previous evening to watch the full moon rise, or he'd gone to Blue Water Bay, a restaurant in Madison, to eat fried onion rings—answers that hardly satisfied my notion of decline and death. Old age, of course, has a sort of posthumous quality in which one is still alive but barely part of human society, like the unmarried women of a certain age who retired to the *beguinhof* in the old part of Amsterdam. Who cares, I thought, if you drive over to the St. Johns to see the moon? Nobody's watching. You can do what you want on a whim. But such forays were the exception. Now that Earl no longer did his own grocery shopping he had become more house-bound; when the car was gone it was usually because the handyman had borrowed the Buick to take his wife or son to the doctor, or driven Earl to some appointment. Eventually, for both reasons, the car was gone almost all the time.

The surrender of the pockmarked LeSabre was understandable, but I was a bit startled when Earl told me that he had given John his wallet as well so he could shop for him. The only transaction for which Earl had to be present now, he said in a tone that conveyed relief, was the cashing of his pension check at the bank.

In Tennessee Williams's *The Milk Train Doesn't Stop Here Anymore* a handsome young vagabond nicknamed the Angel of Death keeps rich women company as they are dying in their villas off the coast of Italy. The play became a movie that starred Elizabeth Taylor and Richard Burton, which was the problem, Earl and I agreed: Taylor was far too beautiful to be playing an old woman at death's door, and Richard Burton was too old to play a young man. Gloria Swanson, on the other hand, was completely believable in *Sunset Boulevard* as an aged movie star whose sole connection to the outer world is her faithful butler, played by Erich von Stroheim. And so was Bergman in *Gaslight*, when Charles Boyer tricks her into thinking she is going mad so that he can commit her to an institution and gain control of her fortune. Even I, having reached my sixties, knew from personal experience that every day in Florida old people's phones ring with some version of Charles Boyer on the other end of the line, introducing one scam or another—a back brace you'd better buy or Medicare will think you're not trying to remain healthy was the most recent one I'd had to listen to until I found myself screaming at the woman on the other end of the line.

Sunset Boulevard seemed to apply because Earl had a sort of butler now; *Gaslight* because Earl was trusting the handyman with his bank account; *The Milk Train Doesn't Stop Here Anymore* because the handyman was not unlike a vagabond who'd appeared out of nowhere to usher Earl to Death's door. Of course, the handyman, with his big butt, Levi's cutoffs, ponytail, and bandana, was no Richard Burton. But the situation seemed to me even more suspicious when Ray told me that John had driven Earl over to see his stockbroker in Palatka because John thought Earl needed to have more cash in his checking account.

Even so I found myself chatting with the handyman in the carport more and more when I visited Earl, because he was right there when I entered the house via the kitchen door. He was still living in the world, the world from which Earl had more or less withdrawn, and there were things we could talk about. In fact, he was the only person with whom I could remember things that had disappeared from town long ago, like the drive-in movie theater, the old post office, the water tank at the intersection. He could remember things that had occurred when my parents were still alive, since he had been living here since the age of seven, when his parents moved down. He had even gone to school with the woman who'd grown up in the house next to mine—the house she visited only on occasional weekends, now that her father was installed in the same nursing home in which my mother was. The handyman remembered people I did. He knew what businesses had occupied certain buildings before they failed—inevitable, in this town, which seemed hostile to any inducement to spend money—and far more about town politics. He had the gossip that a loafer, a gadabout, would have collected by hanging out at the courthouse in a southern novel, if we'd had a courthouse. There were even times when I felt, while discussing a family we'd both known that had moved away, that the handyman and I were soul mates. He seemed to regard the town the way I did—as a place from which change was banished. Everyone else I'd known when I was an adolescent had moved away the first chance he or she got. We had stayed.

Looking at him I wondered what on earth could have kept both of us in the same town, but I never broached the subject—because I had a queasy feeling that the answer would not have been flattering. Instead, we chatted in the carport about the mayoral race, the skateboarders who hung around the public beach, the fate of a building that had been vacated by the techie who fixed computers, the rumor that a new supermarket was coming to town.

The more we talked the chattier the handyman became, as if he, like me, had nobody else to share his thoughts with. He was so full of opinions once we began to talk that often I was unable to get away. The vehemence of his comments on local and national politics formed a strange contrast to his otherwise benign demeanor. He said he'd already argued with Earl about abortion (something I assumed Earl was against), which made me wonder how many other areas of disagreement there might be between them. He harbored, among other things, a resentment of people who had pets but didn't care for them, people who let their dogs out without leashes, and people who had kids they didn't want, so the kids turned out to be "trash." But then he would surprise me by a comment. For instance, the skateboarders who liked to congregate in the parking lot of the public beach looked to me so depressed and sullen that when I remarked to the handyman that they all seemed to be unhappy loners, he said, "But they comfort each other."

The handyman went on to say that people who thought they were escaping Jacksonville had brought the problems of that city with them. He said the United States was now in decline because everyone was a hyphenated American. That the handyman thought in terms of history surprised me. But then I never knew what he'd say about a given issue. Earl, for instance, thought Edward Snowden should be put in jail, but the handyman complained to me that people who were criticizing Edward Snowden for breaking the law had forgotten that "segregation used to be legal!" At the same time he disapproved of the owner of the LA Clippers having to sell the team for making observations about Black people. "Political correctness has gone way too far!" The handyman had an opinion about everything. But I got so tired of listening that before long I hesitated when going into the house to even ask, "How's Earl doing?"

I had to inquire, however, because he knew more about Earl's condition than I did, since he was the one who took Earl to the doctors and learned all sorts of things that way. For instance, he told me one day that people with post-shingles nerve damage are more prone to commit suicide, though Earl told me that as well a few days later. I'd never heard this before, but when I said that was probably because there was so little discussion of anything having to do with death in the media, the handyman said, "For a simple reason—the dead can't buy anything." About people he was even more cynical; one day when I paused in the carport to tell him that while walking in the woods that had grown up on the dry lake bed, I'd turned back because I'd heard gunshots, he said, "I'm waiting for the state of Florida to give hunters permission to shoot people. Someone has to cull the herd!"

Eventually it seemed safer to just ask about Earl—even if it bothered me when we began talking about Earl as if he were a patient of ours. Earl at least was something to talk about, whereas when I finally reached the subject of our conversation in the music room, I was often reduced to the weather. There was little life in Earl's life; he was simply watching films and reading books, though when I remarked to the handyman one day that Earl was one of those people who truly do not mind living alone, he said, "You should see his long-distance bill!"

I didn't even get calls anymore unless it was a request for a donation to a fund for veterans, firefighters, people with cancer, or a political party, or an invitation to buy a burial plot. I'd stopped answering the calls that came at dinner-time and forgot to check the answering machine. Young men in faraway countries tried to frighten me by breaking into the porn film I was watching to say my computer was in danger unless I called a certain number immediately. But mostly days went by without seeing or talking to another human being. Earl's house was Grand Central compared to mine—people dropping in with cakes and pies, not to mention the handyman's almost constant presence. Mine was deserted. I was so used to there being no one around that it was a shock when the little dogs of one of the daughters who checked on the house next door started yapping at me when I walked past on my way to the woods. Their screened ve-randa had once overlooked the lake but now looked out on a wall of turkey oaks. The veranda itself held nothing but piles of wicker furniture in which no one had sat for years. It re-minded me of a production of *The Cherry Orchard* I'd seen years ago in New York, only Irene Worth was not coming onstage to deliver her opening line ("The nursery!")—there was just the silence of spiders spinning webs. And on the other side of that house was one in which nobody had lived for several years because, we'd been told, it was part of a dis-puted divorce settlement. The screen on its front porch was ripped and sagging to the ground; there were dead branches on the lawn; the driveway looked like the set for *Hush . . . Hush, Sweet Charlotte*.

On the west side of my house was a man who'd been bat-tling cancer for a long time, so that each time I saw a cluster of cars in his driveway I assumed it was because the moment for which the family was gathering had come. But no, it was just the grandkids visiting. The two little boys would play ball outside, sometimes with their father, sometimes with their mother, laughing and racing around with the dog. Occasionally I saw the man's wife outside raking leaves. One day we were talking in the street when her husband came out the front door. I had not seen him in five years and did not know what to say, till, seeing the astonished expression on my face, she finally blurted, "*Talk* to him!" But what does one say to the dying—"How's it going?" Visiting Earl was easy in comparison; we could always watch a movie.

The technology of movies was changing so rapidly that the store uptown that rented DVDs went out of business, though not before I went up on its last day and bought the only three that appealed to me: *Breakfast at Tiffany's, Best in Show,* and *De-Lovely.* But watching them by myself seemed sad, like drinking alone. So I continued to wait for Earl to call. Weeks went by when he did not. Nor did I drop in. I'd be walking home across the lake bed from the post office with every intention of visiting, and then, because the day was beautiful, or I had some magazine in hand with a story that I couldn't wait to read, I'd keep on going rather than make a detour to his house. Other days I'd wake up conscious that a visit was overdue, but one thing led to another and as I went to bed that evening I'd say to myself: Tomorrow you must visit Earl.

You'd think that the dying stink, the way people stay away; at least that's what a friend of mine told me when his lover was dying of AIDS in Green Cove Springs. I wanted to visit Earl, but his silence left me with only one option: dropping in spontaneously. This meant entering his house like a burglar, which was how I felt when the kitchen doorknob would not turn. I took the locked door as an indication that

Earl didn't want my visit, so I turned away and went home. Later I learned he'd forgotten to unlock it when he got up that morning.

Most of the time, however, the door was open. After tiptoeing down the length of the house I'd find him lying on his bed with a towel across his forehead, or sitting upright in his winged chair with his back to the blinds that hid the view of what remained of the lake. My father had played solitaire on our porch with his back to that view too, drumming the fingers of his right hand against the table in an abyss of boredom as he contemplated his next move; Earl had as little interest in the vista. But he always seemed glad to see me. I was surprising him, as my mother had begged me to surprise her, something I never did for fear it would expand my visiting schedule, since it's hard to take a concession away once you've given it. With Earl it was much easier; he had no claim on me. I could go whenever I wanted; he would, like my mother, always be there. And leaving Earl was easier than leaving her. My mother's pillow I'd spend considerable time adjusting, because however I left her was how she would remain; Earl could at least move.

One day while I was walking across the lake bed a dog that appeared out of nowhere began following me. So I turned back in the direction from which it had come and walked over to the other side of what had been the lake and went up and down the street, hoping someone would recognize the animal. But no one was about. A breeze was blowing, there were butterflies and a peaceful feeling, but the street was so deserted it was as if everyone was dead, so I walked back across the lake bed, certain that Earl would know what to do, because no one knew more about dogs than he, and when I entered the bedroom I found him lying on his bed in black tennis shoes, black gloves, and a black cap, looking like the cat burglars in *To Catch a Thief*—a sight so odd all I could ask was, "Why are you wearing gloves?"

"Because my hands are cold," he replied. He said the doctor had put him on a new pain medicine two nights ago, and that the side effects were so awful he'd been vomiting. But when I told him about the dog he sat up immediately, like a mummy in a horror film, picked up his cane, and walked out to look at her. She was lying on the brick patio, patiently waiting for us, and remained in that position while we admired her narrow waist, curious yellow eyes, and intelligent face, so intelligent I could not see how Earl could resist. But after telling him what had happened—that I'd searched for her house—he said, in a voice that seemed to contain a certain impatience: "She's lost."

"So what should I do," I said, "call the animal shelter?"

"No," he said. "Keep her!"

"But I can't," I said. "I can't have a dog—I want to be free to come and go."

"But she likes you," he said. "And a dog will give you responsibility and keep you company."

He thinks you're lonely, I reflected with astonishment as I walked home that afternoon—a bit insulted, if truth be known. So much for my plan to relieve his loneliness.

But shortly after this another dog came into Earl's life. One of the physical therapists he'd worked with uptown told him that the father of a friend had been diagnosed with inoperable cancer and had killed himself with a shotgun in his backyard. So the friend's daughter brought the dead man's dog to Earl, and she was sitting by his chair when I walked in one afternoon: a big black Labrador, so old that her muzzle and the tip of her tail were already white, a dog with bad breath and arthritis, but a dog that already would not leave his side.

So now Earl had the responsibility and companionship he'd urged on me: a dog to feed and take for walks, though he couldn't take her very far, which was just as well, since all the dog wanted to do was eat the grass that grew by the carport. The physical therapist had been there the previous Saturday to see how the dog was doing, and Earl could not have been more pleased.

The man I was seeing every few months for sex was the physical therapist's boyfriend; he and Earl had met a year before I met him. Their sexual encounters had evolved into friendship. My visits to the Regular were still carnal. He lived in a little house in the forest with the physical therapist. At first I was not invited there; instead, we had sex in the woods, beside a canal connected to a lake, in clouds of mosquitoes, in abandoned canoes, on deserted docks, in gazebos at public beaches when no one was there. Then it moved to the BarcaLounger in his cottage. It was *Love in the Afternoon*—though always tense because I was waiting for his girlfriend to walk in. But that never happened. I became the person he could call to dispel his loneliness. All I had to do when I picked up the phone was hear his deep voice say, "Whatcha doin'?" for saliva to begin flooding my mouth. I never told Earl that I'd just been to see the Regular, because I did not want to incite envy or jealousy on his part, even though he'd stopped having sex with him quite a while ago. But whenever Earl told me that Bob and his girlfriend had stopped by to visit I would feel a secret thrill at the mention of his name.

The Regular did not watch movies—whenever I'd open the door to his little cottage I'd find him sitting in the recliner with an open beer on the table watching something on television that involved cars and trucks colliding with one another. There were two recliners in the living room, separated by an end table, in which I assumed the Regular and his girlfriend spent their evenings sitting there like copilots in the cockpit of a jet flying into the gigantic TV screen on the opposite wall. Because I didn't have cable I never recognized any of the shows the Regular was watching, but that didn't matter. As soon as I arrived he would offer me a joint and within five or ten minutes I'd find myself kneeling in front of his recliner while he watched cars smash into each other above my bobbing head. Then when it was over he'd ask me to drive him to the store—to buy cigarettes and beer—because, since getting a DUI, he had been grounded. And after that I'd return him with his six-pack to the little cottage in the woods and then drive back home, listening to NPR.

The Regular was twenty years younger than I, which meant that, accustomed to the premium gay men put on youth, I could scarcely believe that he wanted to see me at all, but then I realized my being older was a positive quality in his eyes, just as Earl's having twenty years on me was; we were all providing something for one another that only an older person can.

Why I never told Earl I was seeing the Regular I didn't know, but there was a peculiar pleasure if Earl mentioned having gone to see Bob when I dropped by for a movie. It gave me, I suppose, a sense of superiority, the one the comparatively young feel over the old. I felt stronger than Earl—still in the midst of life; as Helen Gurley Brown said, it's having sex that separates the women from the girls. The feeling was especially keen when I went to see a movie at Earl's after driving back from the Regular's. Is this not the room of a shut-in, I'd wonder when I entered the music room; isn't the air stale and way too warm? Is it not creepy the way the vertical blinds at the end of the room are always closed, blocking out the view of the lake; is there not something pathetic about the fact that the lamp is always on, something unhealthy about indoor life—and something obviously obsessive about this constantly growing pile of movies? I never knew how many shows Earl had watched already when I arrived in the evening; sometimes he'd refer to a film he'd seen that afternoon, which he'd liked so much he wanted to run it again for me—the way the Regular would sometimes remark, when I arrived for sex, that he'd already masturbated twice that morning.

The town to which Earl and my father retired was not one of those artificial communities created for people in the last stage of life with which Florida is associated. But it had its share of the elderly. It was good to be reminded by the Regular of another stage of life, especially when I stopped off at the post office on my way home from his shack. The people moving slowly toward the post office on walkers when I went to get the mail induced both pity and admiration; pity for their condition, admiration for their determination to keep going. That was what Bess had meant for me and my mother when we'd gone on Sunday to visit her. Bess was leading, in her eighties, a life so sedentary she might as well have been paralyzed too, though real life makes a mockery of such a simile. But the fact that Bess was always there playing solitaire on her TV table in a muumuu and a wig had been something that gave stability to our lives; one could no more imagine her dying than one could Queen Elizabeth—till she sat up in bed one morning while her maid washed her face, gasped, and at the age of ninety-two gave up the ghost.

By the time Earl turned eighty-six even his garbage was shrinking, I noticed when I opened the bin outside his kitchen door to toss the litter I'd picked up while walking across the lake bed. The garbage bin contained so little, no matter what day of the week it was, that I had no trouble finding space for the beer cans, beer bottles, Mylar party balloons, and McDonald's wrappers people had tossed on the ground. When he was feeling well Earl had always spent his mornings seated on one of the kitchen stools going through papers, having tea, and listening to the radio. But since he now had to lie on his bed to relieve the pain, the kitchen was empty when I peered through the glass pane in the Dutch door to the kitchen, and the silence was, you might say, that of the grave. If the door was locked, I'd feel rebuked; if it was open, I'd slip inside and then walk down to his bedroom through that long series of pine-paneled rooms with the olive-green carpet from which chunks were missing, never sure what I was walking to.

I began hoping the handyman would be working in the carport when I got there, replacing the wooden ceiling with aluminum, or trying out shades of paint on the wall, since Earl had decided to have his house painted as well to make it more attractive when he put it on the market, which was the only way I could make myself have anything repaired: pretend I was fixing the house up for sale. Earl had decided to paint his yellow; a good choice, I thought, till Clark remarked that only a homosexual in a small town would choose that color.

The desire to remain in one's house, no matter what the color, made the idea of selling the place a fiction; the only real reason I could think of for the paint job was that Earl needed to keep the handyman occupied so that he would stay with him. Whatever the reason, he had succeeded. He had been able to stay in his own house—a desire so fundamental to living things that whenever I'd find a cockroach I couldn't kill, and use a broom to push it outside, and watch it scuttle away, I'd think: A moment ago you were an indoor cockroach, you had a home, with all its rooms and protection and familiarity. Now you're an outdoor cockroach who has to fend for itself.

Because Earl could no longer drive me to the Gainesville airport, where I could rent a car, and because I felt ridiculous sitting in the back seat of a black town car while someone in uniform drove me to Jacksonville for more than the cost of the plane ticket, I started driving myself to the airport. I'd mention to Earl when the movie was done that I was going up north for a few weeks, he'd wish me a good trip, and the next morning I'd leave town. At the airport I'd leave my car in an outdoor parking lot, where it was waiting for me when I returned, sometimes with a dead battery, once with a snake's nest in the air-conditioning system, and drive home by retracing the route that I had long ago driven with my father. I never stayed away more than a month, given the fact that the car was sitting outdoors and the mail had to be picked up and the lawn mown. And once I was back I let a few days go by before visiting Earl, in part because I did not want to appear clinging, and in part because I assumed he could not have changed much in four weeks. And indeed, he was still home watching movies. But one evening after returning, I noticed on my nightly walk that the lights in his house had assumed a different pattern. Instead of the glow around the front door, produced by the lamp in the foyer, there was only a strange blue light emanating at a slant from the hallway to his bedroom. At first I thought it must be the screen of some gigantic new TV he'd finally installed in front of his bed, but the next evening when I walked down to peer inside I realized that what I thought was a TV screen was merely a patch of wall illumined by a lamp with, evidently, a blue bulb. The explanation came a few days later when I dropped in and was shown the new coat of paint the handyman had put on his bedroom walls—a pale blue-green that made the room more cheerful. He had even fixed up the little alcove between the bedroom and the sliding glass doors that looked out on the lake, an alcove just big enough for a high-backed chair, table, and lamp, and had hung all the paintings of dogs that Earl had been keeping in a storeroom across the hall. It was something a decorator might do, using the client's own possessions, bringing his treasures out of storage. The light, Earl explained, came from the lamp in which he'd inserted a blue bulb, the old-fashioned kind, because the new longer-lasting ones, with their twisting white coils, made him dizzy.

When I walked over to the alcove and looked at the chair and shelves of books, all I could think was: What a perfect place to die, with a book and a dog at your feet! But all I said was: "So this is where you read."

"When I can stay awake," he laughed.

A nice way to be sent off, I thought, in a cozy alcove of one's bedroom—to fall asleep on an autumn evening reading with your dog at your feet. But it was sentimental to imagine Earl departing this earth that way, I reflected as I walked home. He might very well die while reading about the Civil War in his high-backed chair with the dog at his feet—and he might not. There was no way of knowing; he was not going to let me in on the process. I had found another version of my father: a man who kept his distance.

I always let a few days go by without making any contact with Earl after I returned from Washington to maintain the illusion that we had no claim on one another, that there was no reason I should report to him that I was back. Yet he was one of the things that made it possible for me to live in both places: knowing that he'd be there when I returned. In Washington I had friends with whom I could take walks, see movies, and go to restaurants. There were museums and lectures and bike trails and concerts, and other people on the sidewalk. In Florida there was never anybody when I took my walk. One day in a bookstore in DC I found myself in an aisle of travel books, and I took down a Fodor's guide to Florida to see what it had to say about the town Earl and I lived in. There was no reason to think it would be mentioned at all; the only time the town had ever made the news was the second year after we moved there, when a sinkhole opened up in Lake of the Palms, and that sinkhole had been eclipsed the following week by one in Orlando that swallowed up an entire Mercedes-Benz dealership. But, to my surprise, the town was in Fodor's, though all it said was that it was in the "lake-and-hill" country of Florida, and the only thing it mentioned under Attractions was the state park six miles out of town.

That was why I always glanced at Earl's house when I took my walk at night to reassure myself that he was watching television: had I written the entry in Fodor's, Earl would have been the main attraction. So it disturbed me, the week I was shown the bedroom the handyman had redecorated, that the people in the films Earl was watching when I walked down to the front door and peered through the vertical panes of glass were all Nazis. Maybe that's what everybody wants to see when they're reaching the end, I thought, the collapse of the entire world. Perhaps that's what death is, as far as the person dying is concerned: a supreme insult to the ego, a narcissistic wound beyond compare—Hitler in his bunker. "If I must die, you're all coming with me!" must be what young men who shoot up malls, movie theaters, kindergartens, and nightclubs and then turn the gun on themselves think as well. But the next day the Nazis gave way to soldiers in nineteenth-century uniforms and a man I finally realized was Napoleon, and then to Winston Churchill. He was watching great men, the way I devoured biographies, which are, in a way, just long obituaries, to see what people who had done something with their lives had accomplished. And then Churchill was replaced by Hercule Poirot.

Hercule Poirot had been, like *Miss Marple*, something Earl had always invited me over to see, but that wasn't what made me feel left out the evenings I peered through the little panes of glass. It was the stillness of the figure sitting there, the way his body was slumped in the chair, that made me realize Earl was so done in by age and illness that I couldn't really expect him to call. He exuded even with his back to me a broken-down quality. Earl was collapsing, like a star; he was going to fall silent, like a satellite so far out in space its signals can no longer reach the earth. He was traveling to another planet. And the person communicating with him was not some NASA technician in Houston; it was the handyman. They were the ones making this trip together; their symbiosis was complete. When I ran into Ray one day at the post office he told me that Earl had floated the idea of leaving his house to the handyman, though Ray didn't think he would. "I think he's dangling the possibility—the way you hold a treat out to a dog—so John won't leave him." Whatever the explanation, it was Earl and the handyman now; I was, no matter how much Earl meant to me, essentially irrelevant.

And that explained the fact that each day I walked by the house I noticed some new improvement the handyman had made; there was even a new outdoor barbecue grill, something I was sure Earl had never wanted and certainly would never use. It was like the scene in *Zorba the Greek* when Lila Kedrova dies and all the women in black robes descend on her little house and strip it bare, like vultures. Earl's house was waxing as he was waning. There could be only one reason: the handyman was improving the house because he expected to inherit it. My own I continued to let deteriorate. The white paint on the exterior was turning green; there was mildew on the garage, and patches on the house itself where shade had enabled algae to grow. The yard was so full of volunteers—ferns, camphor trees, floral Ardisia, grapevines, cherry laurels, Spanish bayonet, cabbage palms—that they were taking over. In the morning I'd sit on the porch and watch the light enter the garden and then walk out into the yard to examine its contents like a nurse checking on her patients. The real chores—the mildew, the leak in the garage roof, the warped screens, the dripping faucets, the windows that did not close—I ignored.

On one of my sister's visits she made a remark one day that distinguished between "cleaning" and "deep cleaning"—the latter, I gathered, even in her own experience, was rare, but was the only thing she really respected. As the years passed I assumed she knew what was happening to the house in Florida—but when she and my brother-in-law began wintering near Fort Myers, and would stop by on their drive down because it was difficult to find motels that would accept a dog, she'd refrain from showing her feelings about the place, simply, I sensed, because it was too deep a subject to go into. "Just hire someone," she said as she got in the car to continue her journey one year, "and pay them two hundred dollars to really clean the place."

When I went north at Christmas I entered a house that was so pleasant that after she and her husband went to bed, I'd stay downstairs just to watch the fire burning down beside the Christmas tree, alone with the ghosts of our family. My sister's house was filled with possessions too, but they were things she'd acquired; the only remnants of the past were a few figurines in the dining room and some Delft plates on the wall above the television—until Christmas Day, when she, her husband, their children and their spouses, a cousin of my brother-in-law who had Tourette's syndrome, and various other orphans like myself gathered for a dinner that entailed the most revered heirloom of all.

At some point on the morning of December 24, my sister would say, "Would you do me a favor, please, and get the silver," whereupon I'd go downstairs into a chilly basement room crowded with the weight-lifting equipment her two sons had used when they were teenagers and pull out, from a stack of luggage, a small red leather carrying case that had once contained my mother's cosmetics.

The case, like the suitcases next to it, was still festooned with the luggage tags that the shipping line on which we'd returned every two years from the Caribbean when I was growing up had attached, each one bearing the passenger's name and cabin number. The luggage tags would plunge me into a vat of depression. Oh for those days, I'd think, when we were traveling by ship to this country of which I'd dreamed from afar! And then, feeling lonely in the chilly room with nothing but nostalgia for company, I'd rouse myself and take the case that now contained twelve place settings by Georg Jensen up the stairs into the dining room, where my sister waited, as she did every year, to examine the silverware nestled in layers separated by pieces of dark brown cloth.

These were things my sister used but once a year: finger bowls, cheese knives, strange tongs, and little silver saltcellars with filigreed rims and basins of midnight blue. The two of us would sit there examining each piece, mumbling, every now and then, "What do you suppose *this* is for?" We're like refugees, I'd think, who've had to flee their homes in a time of war, carrying with them only the most precious things, the family treasure that has been handed down from one generation to another; and then I'd set the table.

When the meal was over on Christmas Day the kids washed the dishes while the grown-ups (though by that time "the kids" were married with children of their own; I should say the elderly) remained at the table finishing the wine and pecan pie, and the next day, when I went downstairs for breakfast, the first thing my sister said to me was always, "We've got to count the silver." The reason was not any criminal proclivity on the part of the guests, but the dishwasher and the garbage disposal the "kids" had used the night before, down which all sorts of things could disappear. And so once more we went through the Georg Jensen in which her children had no interest until each fork, knife, tong, saltcellar, and tiny spoon was laid out and counted, and only then was it all put back into the carrying case and taken downstairs for yet another year. And that was the moment when I bonded most with my sister; survivors of a family, of a place, that no longer existed—because after the refinery for which our father had worked had been sold to another company, the community built to house its workers had literally been torn down.

After their dog died, my sister and brother-in-law began flying to Florida every January, which meant they stopped spending a night in the town that she always thought had been my parents' greatest mistake; they flew right over it on their way to a golf course east of Fort Myers, and I became the brother who lived alone in a house with the nagging guilt that lies beneath so many gay men's psyches over not having continued the family line, even on a planet with eight billion people. My sister, so rebellious when growing up, had been the one to do that, though she too had strayed from the Church, and when she said one day apropos of something I forget that she'd been thinking she would like a Catholic funeral, I said, "Then you'd better pick a parish now, and start going to Mass."

Sometimes even when it was very cold I would take a walk around my sister's neighborhood. She no more knew her neighbors than I did, including the dentist who lived just across a hedge in her backyard all by himself, a man I never saw in all the years I went there. There was a genuine recluse next door who'd inherited the house from his parents, though that was not quite the story—after his mother died, his father had been revealed to have a mistress, and he abandoned the house to his censorious son, who now lived in his old room in the basement, and whom I never saw either. When I took my walk through the cul-de-sac behind her house, lined with houses in various faux styles—Georgian, Colonial, Mount Vernon—most were bright with Christmas lights, though not a soul was to be seen. The ones that were dark belonged to people who were retired, my sister said, their kids long ago moved away; the parents were playing golf in either Florida or Arizona. Down the street in front of my sister's house was a lovely cemetery set on the slope of a hill from which I could survey the countryside where George Washington had been stationed when Fort Pitt was the western frontier, a landscape of dark hills now sparkling with the lights of shopping malls, outlet stores, and office buildings. How few years, I'd think, it had taken the country to go from the young George Washington to Home Depot and Cinemax, but there it all was, glowing in the night as I walked slowly around the cemetery on a road that circled the gravestones, some of which I'd stop to read, during the day at least, to see the dates they had lived. Often around Christmas relatives and descendants would drive in and leave flowers on the graves, and then, after a few moments of contemplation, drive away. There was even a separate cemetery in the back that I discovered by accident one day composed entirely of Jewish grave markers, taller, more somber, more ancient-looking than the rest, if only because of the different lettering.

The room I slept in at my sister's was adjacent to the one in which our mother had tripped on the rug during the night and broken her neck, a spare bedroom where we now stored and wrapped the Christmas presents, and in it was a framed photograph of my parents taken the day the savings and loan in Florida opened, but just the two of them. Sometimes when there was no one upstairs I'd sit down on the bed and talk to the photograph and bring my parents up to date on what had happened to their children and grandchildren since the previous year: breast implants, graduation, things like that. It was slightly eerie but deeply satisfying. In Florida I never spoke to them, perhaps because we had to live together in the same house, but in the spare bedroom, the one in which we wrapped the Christmas presents, I found it perfectly normal for the three of us to have a chat.

After Christmas I took the bus back to Washington, and then a week later I returned to Florida. One year on the flight back to Jacksonville I sat beside a beautiful young woman with a shaved head who told me she'd just completed cancer treatment; her husband was driving down to Florida and would meet her in the Jacksonville airport. As we talked I kept thinking of the husband, thirty-nine thousand feet beneath us, driving to get to the airport before our plane landed, but when we got to Jacksonville I never saw the reunion. She walked away without even saying goodbye—one of those strange American experiences in which people divulge the most intimate things to perfect strangers and then vanish back into their lives—and though I looked for them in the terminal I never saw them.

There is no feeling more vacant than walking past the people in an airport who are waiting to see their friends or relatives emerge from the corridor leading to the gates. The loneliness is exquisite. One night we arrived during a storm, and as the plane taxied to the terminal I saw through the little window an enormous passenger jet sitting empty beside the terminal, the rain streaming down its shining silver fuselage, like a beast left out in the rain, its windows all dark. It looked as dead, as forlorn, as I felt landing at that late hour, a feeling that was relieved only when I'd been dropped off at my car in the long-term parking lot, afraid the engine would not start. Then, when it did, I drove to the exit, where the woman who told me how much I owed welcomed me home—with a complimentary bottle of spring water that only reminded me of the scandalous fact that the state of Florida for some reason allows companies like Nestlé to extract from its glorious springs millions of gallons they then sell in plastic bottles that are yet another ecological disaster for the planet. In some way the woman in the booth—the person who welcomed me back to Florida—had become over the years, I sometimes thought, my best friend; though one time on my way home from Washington I walked off the plane and there was Patrick sitting in the departure lounge, reading a novel by Nancy Mitford as he waited to get on the plane I'd just exited so he could fly back to DC, because in those days JetBlue had a direct flight that departed at eight-thirty, though the year after I ran into Patrick in the terminal it dropped that connection—not even airline schedules remain the same.

When I got home, the neighborhood would be so quiet that after a few weeks in other places, I'd want to yell at all the silent houses I drove past: What are you doing in there? Eating, shitting, watching TV—writing novels?

Patrick was converting to Judaism and told me that on Yom Kippur he prayed now to be enlisted in the book of the living for another year—a beautiful way to think of life—but when I told him how neat and clean and comfortable my sister's house was compared to my own he was more down-to-earth. "The way to clean your house is simple," he said. "Pretend you're dead. Pretend you're your nephew when he walks into your bedroom a week after you die, and looks around at the books and papers and heaps of sweaters and then goes into the closet and finds the cardboard box full of letters from dead friends and the plastic garbage bag with the back issues of *Mandate* and *Honcho*. That's what he'll have to deal with, if *you* don't. So just pretend you're dead and get rid of everything."

But I couldn't; that would have disturbed the fine patina of memory.

I never knew what Earl did on Christmas after his cousin died. Perhaps he had the woman who lived next door over for eggnog. But now, because of the handyman, his house looked spic-and-span—whereas I continued to find frogs in the hall and help them hop outside, or when they were trapped in a dust ball—unable to move—carry them out to the back porch, rinse them with a glass of water, pull the wet dust off their bodies, and watch them hop off into the hedge.

Or I'd sit on the porch watching the lizards that clung to the porch screens lying in wait for insects I couldn't see, their red throat sacs ballooning each time they swallowed one. And I continued to go once a week to the nursery to buy more plants that would provide either food for butterflies or leaves on which they could lay their eggs, like Earl ordering more DVDs.

At least Earl's leaving a neat house after he dies, I thought when I saw the results of the handyman's diligence. I was not. When I woke up in the middle of the night, scratching my ankles till they bled because the chiggers I'd picked up in the yard were sucking my blood, I'd think: You are simply going to be surprised one day, as your father was while doing his taxes, by a stroke—a stroke that will let you know that your time is up, like the angel announcing a child to the Blessed Virgin. There will be no time to arrange your affairs or clean up your mess, or get rid of the garbage bag filled with porn magazines in your closet; you'll simply have to go. But who will take you to the hospital? At this point all I wanted was a driver and I couldn't even find that. "Why can't you go to Venice by yourself?" Earl asked when I voiced this fantasy one evening after watching *Summertime*. "Because," I said, "no matter how nice your day, there comes that awful moment when you have to go to dinner, when you want someone to talk to about what you saw and did, but instead you're sitting by yourself at a table in a corner the restaurant uses for people who eat by themselves with your guidebook propped up against the saltshaker. The reason I envy people who are married is that they have someone to travel with."

I had entered the stage of life when no one knew where I

was, when friends had begun asking me for my sister's phone number so they could call her if I didn't answer the phone, though my sister didn't know where I was either, since I went back and forth when I wanted between Washington and Florida. I had achieved the bliss, the nightmare, of total independence. I hope he collapsed in a public place, was all I could think when Earl told me one evening that an old friend with whom he'd taught school had just died of a heart attack in Arizona. When I went to see Earl I'd open the kitchen door, tiptoe down to the opposite end of the house, and, not seeing him anywhere, conclude that what Henry James may have called "the great, the distinguished thing" had finally happened. And then one afternoon in late July I walked into the bedroom and found what I'd been waiting for all these months—Earl's corpse. Eyes closed, face gaunt, he looked just like a knight lying on a stone sepulcher in a medieval church I'd visited in Lisbon. An expression of such refined forbearance was on his face that I was sure he had died in pain, at which point his eyes opened, his head turned slightly, and I heard him say, in a perfectly pleasant voice, "Well, how do you do?" And I sat down in the chair beside the bed and learned that he was simply having one of his "bad days" because he hadn't eaten the gingerroot in time.

The next day I was even asked down for a movie, and when I walked in, the handyman was in the kitchen preparing two attractive Mexican-tiled trays with tomato soup and crackers so we could eat dinner while we watched, and once I was seated in the music room he walked in with our suppers on the trays, and, like two nine-year-olds whose parent is waiting on them as a treat during a sleepover, we unfolded our napkins and began to watch *I Was a Male War Bride*.

Earl had finally stopped making those little drives he once had to visit friends, though Ray still dropped in once a week with a dessert or hot meal; the slice of pecan pie I ate was often courtesy of the Church of the Nazarene. Ray I'd have liked to talk to at length about Earl but our visits rarely coincided. All I saw when I drove through town in the evening after a trip to the grocery store was the handyman standing on the sidewalk reading a folded newspaper under a streetlight, absorbing more evidence for his judgmental views while the dog sniffed the hedges. But Earl was invisible. He was merely the flash of a TV screen in a dark house I passed on my nightly stroll, or the figure in a chair when I walked down the slope and peered in through the front door to see what he was watching.

The feeling I had when I saw Earl watching television without me—as hurt as a spurned lover—was no more rational than the one I had whenever I saw that his car was missing, as if I should have been informed that he was going somewhere. But there was nothing to do but accept the new status quo: Earl was withdrawing, the way old people do, if they are lucky enough to remain in their own homes rather than in a wheelchair in front of a television in some nursing home. When I complained to Patrick that Earl had stopped calling, stopped going out, stopped asking me over, he fixed me with his enigmatic stare and said, "He's dying," as if I were an idiot not to recognize that fundamental fact. But I knew better. By the end of July, however, it was just a movie on Saturday night, if he was feeling well enough, and on those occasions we hardly conversed before or after. I couldn't think of anything to talk about, and he seemed to have no interest in anything but the movie we were about to see. Nothing seemed to matter to him. One day, when I asked what the best time to visit was, he waved one of his gaunt hands freckled with age spots and said, "Oh, just come whenever you want."

But the house was always dark now—or so I thought, till one evening while walking home from the post office I saw through the camellia bushes that the two windows on the east side of the music room were aglow, though the lamp on the hall table was off. He's hiding from me, I concluded, the way I hid every Halloween when I drew the curtains to make trick-or-treaters think there was nobody home.

That Earl was happy to watch movies without me felt like rejection. If you're not going to die, I thought, then you should at least ask me over. But by the end of July, when I thought he must be near death because the house had been dark five nights in a row and I called to ask how he felt, I heard him reply in a voice that sounded perfectly normal that he'd driven to the grocery store that afternoon, where he urged me to go because strawberries were on sale for a dollar ninety-eight. Then, as if reminded of my existence, he asked me over for a movie the next day and served me some rich dessert I'd never have eaten on my own, and when I got there, I saw that he'd let his hair grow long and was combing it straight back from his forehead, so that he looked like a European film director, or George Sanders in *All About Eve*.

I'd been imitating George Sanders's nasal drone as the camera pans around the people at the Sarah Siddons Awards when I trudged through the soaked air and biting flies on the lake bed on my morning walk. Only Sanders saying "Eve, dear Eve . . ." I was convinced could dispel the heat in which we were trapped. A normal person would simply have gotten a DVD of the movie, but I had come to rely on Earl. Earl, at eighty-six, was the boy I had befriended when I was seven, a boy with a vast collection of comic books I'd read when I went to see him, till one day he accused me of coming by only for his deluxe edition of *Peter Pan*. But that wasn't it. I had no desire to watch *All About Eve* by myself. I had no idea how Earl could watch all the movies he did on his own, unless he was already participating in the afterlife, an afterlife in which everyone would simply be left with a TV and a stack of DVDs.

There was nobody out in the afternoon; everyone was indoors, in central air-conditioning, or under a ceiling fan—except the man the town was paying to sit in a chair at the entrance to the public beach and collect one dollar from everyone who wished to use it whom I passed on my way to the post office. At night things were more interesting. I was beginning to notice on my walks at night a handsome young man who was always in a hooded sweatshirt sitting outside the pizza restaurant on the main street when I walked back from the post office after the restaurant had closed. He seemed to be waiting for me, like the figure stalking Dirk Bogarde as he walks around the plague-ridden city in *Death in Venice*. I had no idea what he was doing there. He had a dark beard and looked like Jesus. Then one night as I was walking by he stood up and held out his hand, offering me something. I walked over and asked him what it was. "Candy," he said.

"Hard or soft?" I asked.

"Hard," he said, at which point I shook my head, thanked him, and walked on.

He must be damaged in some way, I concluded as I walked home—who else would sit by himself in a hoodie in

August outside a shut-up pizza restaurant in a small town in Florida for hours every night, and then offer a piece of candy to a passing stranger? At the same time, I felt I'd rebuffed another solitary person's friendship. Whatever the reason I let him recede in my wake, rejected and unhelped, like the only other homosexual in town when we first moved here who asked me for places to go in Greenwich Village. A few nights after that I noticed, in the little street between the pizza restaurant and the bank, a tall, bald man hanging around for no apparent reason and wondered what he was doing till the following evening I saw a little car pull up beside him and he got in. Someone ordered drugs, I decided, and came to pick them up. But after Jesus and the bald man disappeared I had the town to myself.

By day the town was another matter—I went out only for groceries or a book at the library. Sometimes I'd see Earl when I drove by standing just outside his carport letting the dog eat grass. One morning when the handyman had taken his son to the doctor Earl asked me if I would drive him over to see Mrs. Hadid, whom he'd befriended when both of them were going to the Methodist church. I'd been going over there to walk her dog, and when I arrived I usually found her watching movies too. She loved Turner Classic Movies. Wallace Beery, Bette Davis, Henry Fonda, Veronica Lake were often in her bedroom when I arrived. John Wayne was her favorite. Visiting her was a bit like visiting Earl; one never knew when one approached the house what one would find inside. If the front door was closed I had to walk around the house to peer through the sliding glass doors on the back terrace to see if she was home, since she was too hard of hearing to hear the doorbell. If she was, she'd wave to me from her bed, meaning the front door was open, and I'd go back around to the front. Sometimes I'd find her parked in her wheelchair behind the front door, which was half glass, looking out at the front walk. It was never clear whether she was waiting for someone she knew was coming or simply hoping someone might appear. However I found her, she was glad to have a visitor. First she'd apologize for not having her teeth in, and then we'd go out into the living room, where she'd have me pour each of us a glass of white wine, which she said lessened the pain and improved her hearing and eyesight, which was being compromised by macular degeneration, while the little dog, a Chihuahua she'd adopted the day I drove her over to the county pound, burrowed beneath its blanket on the couch, until I took him for a walk.

The man in charge of the nursery who hired nothing but handsome young men and made sure Mrs. Hadid's lawn was perfect told me one day, "That dog has *never* been walked!" which, if that was true, made me feel glad to liberate the animal. The irony was that Mrs. Hadid was being attended to by gay men: her hairdresser, who took her every year to the Mayor's Ball out at the town airport; the nursery manager who kept her yard up; her own son, who still worked in Washington and was paying all the bills; and me. Mrs. Hadid held the same opinion of President Obama that Earl did; they listened to the same radio shows. But she was always hospitable and a source of gossip about the town, though the people and places she talked about were all new to me, since, like her little dog, I was living, as far as the actual town was concerned, under a blanket too.

Like Earl, Mrs. Hadid provided a stark contrast with her dwelling. Her yard was immaculate—not a brown blade of grass, or leaf on a hedge—but she herself was in decline; her hip was so bad she required a walker, her eyesight was shrinking, and congestive heart failure had made it necessary for her to keep a portable oxygen supply beside her. Watching Mrs. Hadid push a laundry basket down the hall to the washing machine in her garage while connected to the oxygen tank made Earl seem in the bloom of health. But she always entertained her guests. She'd put a CD on her portable player and sing along to songs like "You'll Never Know" and "You Made Me Love You" and "I'll Be Seeing You," songs she'd performed at a bar in Jacksonville when she was in her prime; a bar whose name she'd forgotten but called the following day to supply, when her Senior Moment was over. She'd met Earl at the Methodist church. She'd been very active in other organizations before the breast cancer metastasized; she'd gone to the parish hall beside the Catholic church every Tuesday for the fish fry, the American Legion for spaghetti on Thursday, and the Baptist church on Sunday to ring the hand bells. Now, however, during the day, her main company was the dead—Wallace Beery, Marie Dressler, and John Wayne.

The day I drove Earl over she insisted on performing "I'll Be Seeing You" for us before we left, and when it came time to hit the final note, she stretched her arms out with such vigor that the oxygen tubes in her nostrils fell out. That's show business, I thought as we drove away.

Earl was not bothered by all the things in the news that were upsetting Mrs. Hadid—China cheating on its currency, the alleged conspiracies of George Soros, the big Wall Street banks. Earl did tell me one evening that he was glad that Marco Rubio had voted against raising the debt ceiling but that was it. He was sitting on a stool in the kitchen when he said this, doing one of the things he enjoyed as much as Mrs. Hadid did singing old favorites: serving tea in the two ceramic mugs decorated with the figures of Adam and Eve.

At this point Earl's face was composed of two elements: a white beard and a big pair of glasses. With his long hair combed back from the forehead and the new eyeglasses, he had never appeared more distinguished. His right hand was always raised so that he could press down on the nerve ends in his neck. But he seemed in good spirits. I was the one who was losing it. I had come to resent NPR so much that I found myself screaming at the radio on the slightest pretext—every time Robert Siegel pronounced "Florida" as if the "o" were an "a," for example, or every time Michele Norris's velvet voice was too expressive, too warm, too emotional and empathetic. "You're not a Playboy bunny!" I'd scream. "This isn't a massage parlor! It's the news!" The only solution was to turn the radio off and take a walk on the lake bed.

When I took my walk at night, through town, there was never anybody out except a biracial couple who jogged in plastic sweat suits tied at the ankle and wrist to make them sweat more, a couple who were using the night for the same thing I was: camouflage. Some evenings I set out at twilight, when the sky was still a pale, pale blue above the dark silhouettes of the trees just after sundown. As the light faded, a sort of mysterious dignity descended on the town, until, when it was completely dark, it assumed another personality altogether. It was so easy to love the town in the dark, the glowing windows of the houses, the streetlight at the end of a dark tunnel of trees, the utter peace and quiet. It was a prosperous town, an example of the fact that since World War

Two Americans had been living rather high on the hog. Half the people in town had to park their vehicles on their front lawns because there was no room for them all in the garage. Trucks and campers, swimming pools, sometimes plastic, sometimes real, were strewn through the community along with the ubiquitous basketball hoops nailed to garages. Sometimes children were playing hopscotch under a streetlight. Other times young men appeared at intersections with gigantic dogs, like young princes, before vanishing in the dark. When the mosquitoes were bad, a truck would come through town spraying clouds of insecticide that kids on bicycles would bike through for the fun of it, a sight so alarming that I stopped beside the truck one evening to ask the driver if this wasn't dangerous; he assured me that the stuff he was spraying was composed almost entirely of marigolds.

These walks made something else quite clear, especially in summer: that I wasn't the only person who could not throw things out. On warm nights people would raise their garage doors, grab some folding chairs, and sit outside in their driveways to get the breeze. The veterinarian, who had the biggest house in town, a faux Georgian on three lots, with a tennis court and swimming pool in the back, liked to sit on a folding chair in the middle of his driveway with his back to the street, contemplating the contents of his garage, like a boy transfixed by the wonders of Ali Baba's cave. Most of the garage interiors looked like hardware stores, or libraries— libraries of tools. The night before garbage pickup the driveways would be lined with all sorts of stuff. Sometimes the objects left out for pickup the next day were sentimental. One night I noticed, while walking past a neighbor's, the tricycle she had put out beside her garbage bin, a tricycle

I'd seen that woman's son pedal around the park beside his mother when he was three years old. Now he was a handsome, grown-up, weight-lifting policeman who lived in Orlando with a wife and child of his own—but though he'd been gone for decades, only now had his mother been able to surrender the tricycle.

Was there any point in hanging on to anything? A friend in Washington who worked for the State Department had carried around with him for thirty years, from assignment to assignment, a stuffed puppy that his parents had put in his crib when he was a baby, because each time you're assigned to a new post the State Department ships your personal effects to you. But as he grew older he came to hate unpacking his things, because they made him look back on his life. So he decided to give the puppy to his sister for her new grandson the next time he was back home in Ohio—even though, he predicted, she would toss it in the garbage the minute his car went around the bend, which was just what happened, he later learned.

There was a box in a closet I seldom opened that contained, I discovered one day when searching for some Christmas ornaments, photographs of my father, grandfather, and mother—so beautiful when young that I never looked at them again. But I still could not throw them away. But why could I not dispose of the black garbage bag full of old porn magazines that I'd inherited from a friend who'd taken it out of the apartment of a friend of his who'd died of AIDS before his mother could discover it? And what would Earl do with his records and books, much less the paintings of dogs the handyman had brought out of storage and hung in his bedroom, or the carved boxes from India and Iran, or the sets of china he had never used? And what was the veterinarian thinking as he sat in his driveway contemplating his library of tools?

This demented attachment to things was visible on every street when I took my walk at night, the backyards that looked like a used car dealership, the motorboats, trailers, lawn mowers, gadgets of every kind sitting on the extra lot. Uptown things were more commercial. The inability to surrender possessions gave way to something more impersonal. Across the street from the bank, the Shell station was lighted up like a Broadway stage; people were dropping in at the convenience store, gassing up, using the air hose that intimidated me. But otherwise the main street was empty. The pizza parlor, which closed at eight o'clock, looked like the diner in an Edward Hopper painting. All the other businesses were shuttered save for the little Chinese restaurant that never had any customers. It was so depressing that some nights I'd continue on down the sidewalk to the next town, which was not really a town so much as a gas station, a bar, and the smallest post office I'd ever seen.

There was something liberating about walking down Highway 40 on a summer night; at least the passing cars and trucks were going somewhere. The sidewalk was so close to the road that when the big trucks went by, they created a vacuum that closed a moment later with a shudder. Between trucks it was utterly quiet. The houses between the sidewalk and the lake were set back so far from the sidewalk one could hardly see them. The last house in town had for unknown reasons a permanent installation of Christmas ornaments that made it look like a hut in the Black Forest even in August. Then came the biker bar in which someone had been beaten to death with pool cues, a bar I would not go near but which Earl had not been afraid to visit when he was feeling well, and then a long stretch of sidewalk so devoid of lights that on most nights you could see the stars, and once a month, most wonderful of all, the full moon floating over a trailer park across the highway from a little store that had once been called Timeless Treasures but was now the Pack Rat.

The Pack Rat was a monument to the fact that in small towns a person's death is observed twice—first the funeral, and then the estate sale, which can run the gamut from an auction advertised in the papers to tables outdoors with little price tags on each possession. Otherwise these objects end up in a friend's or relative's house. On the round table from Peru in our living room, for instance, a yellow vase with Chinese characters in blue had once belonged to Bess's sister, a woman with whom my parents liked to play poker, who died of a heart attack not long after they moved here while taking a bath in her house, a little stucco building uptown that was now where people went for physical therapy. There was, in fact, in houses around town, a sort of cemetery of furniture in which people were remembered not by tombstones but by a lamp or painting or bowl. The Pack Rat may have lacked the dignity of a grave marker. But it was a store where all sorts of stuff had ended up for anyone to peruse, even old postcards written by people on their honeymoon—a funeral pyre of mementos.

The building was always closed when I got there, so there was no one around to see me stopping at the window to look into the dimly lighted interior, its contents covered in dust, if one was to judge by the grimy windowpane. The Pack Rat was

full of lamps, figurines, cut glass bowls, teddy bears, paintings, TV tables, chairs, rugs, suitcases, racks of dresses, hats,
radios, televisions, fishing poles, dehumidifiers, silverware,
glasses, vases, fans, and old typewriters—all the detritus that
people leave after they die—such a heap that every time I'd
look in I could only think: You are all that stands between
your mother's things and this place, the bottles of perfume
on her bureau, the figurines and vases, the tray of butterfly
wings from Brazil arranged in a mosaic under glass.

There are two ways you can dispose of the contents of a
house, a friend from New York who came down to Gainesville to dispose of his mother's effects after she died of lung
cancer at eighty-four told me: hold an auction in which the
auctioneer takes a cut, or sell everything for a lump sum to
someone who will take it away. My friend chose to do it himself. I visited him one day when he was going through his
mother's drawers. Watching the postage stamps and Christmas cards and little name tags that said "Hello, my name
is _____" cascade like confetti from the drawer he was emp-
tying in his mother's bedroom that afternoon, it was obvious
that the most considerate thing we can do when we get old
is to clean things up so that others don't have to after we
croak. But who knows when he is doing to die? All I knew
as I walked home from the Pack Rat while the trucks roared
down the highway was that I hadn't had the fortitude to do
what my friend did with his dead mother's possessions.

By August the nights were so humid there were aureoles
around the streetlights, and the curtains were drawn in all
the air-conditioned houses, as if the town was buried in some
blizzard. Without a television or book to read there was
nothing to do but take a walk. That made the nights when I

wasn't at Earl's watching a movie a challenge. It was obvious when I walked through town at night that the reason I had every street to myself—except the occasional dog walker—was that everyone was indoors transfixed by a screen whose flickering images I could sometimes see as I passed the houses. The children I imagined at their computers, the parents watching TV, on a screen that was so much bigger than the dead one I had at home, it was almost like going to the movies. But if I didn't have a good book to read—and sometimes I hit a dry patch—there was nothing to do but walk around town.

When I could no longer bear the boredom any longer I broke my rule and called Earl to suggest we watch a movie. He'd say that he'd been meaning to call me but had forgotten, but I was certain, in the depths of my paranoia, that the reason Earl no longer called was that the handyman had told him something bad about me. From the evidence that he was now driving Earl's car it was but a short step to *Gaslight* or *Rebecca*—though when I entered the kitchen at five o'clock, all I saw was the handyman preparing the Mexican-tiled tray with Earl's supper—soup, saltines, and salad—patiently chopping up parsley and carrots, arranging the cucumber slices in a circle of sour cream and yogurt. On movie nights he served me as well.

It was odd at first, this conversion from handyman to butler—a butler of whom we were somehow afraid. The evening I asked Earl if we could watch a movie he'd just purchased, a classic German film about homosexual blackmail called *Anders als die Andern* (*Different from the Others*), he said we'd better not, because John might walk in while we were watching it. "But this is a very old German movie," I said; "I'm sure everyone will be in suits and ties, there'll be nothing that would look gay." Nevertheless, Earl suggested we watch it some afternoon when the handyman was not around. "But that's crazy," I said, "two men our age worrying about what he thinks!" But that was the case. Either we did not want to embarrass the handyman or we were worried that he would disapprove. And yet, every time I came upon him in the kitchen, his ponytail bobbing as he chopped up ingredients on the sideboard for Earl's dinner, his enormous ass covered by the absurd Levi's cutoffs, all I could think of was the maid in *La Cage aux Folles*.

I began to wonder if it was not humiliating for the handyman to be preparing our supper trays on the nights when I arrived for the movie. I know the sight embarrassed me as I walked through the kitchen. His ability to fix things lent him a certain superiority, the superiority the mechanically gifted have over those who are not. But the next time I walked in he was standing at one of the antique tables in the living room with a feather duster in hand; the reason the handyman was tidying up, I learned, was that Earl was expecting guests from New Smyrna Beach. The man he'd known since his days at the University of Florida, the one who called frequently and delivered what Earl said was "a monologue I have to sit and listen to," was vacationing with his partner on the coast and wanted to drive over to have lunch—"which might be," Earl said, "the last time we see each other, because you never can tell." The tears that glistened in Earl's eyes when he said this were the first I'd ever seen there. In the old days, when he'd been informed over the telephone of the death of a friend in California, he'd gone right back to watching a movie. But this was a friend he'd known since college and talked to or exchanged letters with at least once a week for the past thirty years. Indeed, I'd never understood, since the man and his lover had an apartment on the Upper West Side of Manhattan within walking distance of Lincoln Center, why Earl had not gone up to stay with them, if only to go to the opera for a week, but he hadn't, and now they were coming to visit him.

The guests ate lunch at a restaurant in Starke, I learned the next day, while Earl, too weak to go, stayed home—and the whole thing, I could see, had brought him down, mainly because of his premonition that they would never meet again. There is nothing as difficult as saying goodbye to someone one is not likely to ever see; nothing reminds us more of the burden, the finality, of mortality. When during the AIDS epidemic a friend called from Los Angeles to say he was dying, I'd had no idea how to end the phone call. How does one say goodbye to someone who's about to cease to exist—what words are right when you know you'll never see the person again? You can't use that old Italian standby: "Have a nice life!" But that's what Earl and his old friend from school had done, and it was a good thing they had, since his classmate entered the hospital not long after returning to Manhattan, went into a coma, and died.

The day after learning this I ran into Ray at the post office. He agreed that the death of his classmate had made Earl despondent. "And Earl's worried about his own salvation now," he added. "He's afraid that being gay will prevent him from getting to Heaven. I told him not to be concerned. I don't even know what I am," Ray said, "straight, gay, or bisexual—but God's not going to deny me Heaven because of that."

Earl's birthday, he said, had been the week before. It was characteristic of Earl not to tell me, since that would have been asking for attention. He was eighty-eight, Ray said; older than I'd thought. Ray had brought him his favorite thing: a pineapple upside-down cake. The next day I wished Earl a belated happy birthday and found myself listening to him talk about his days in Iran, which were always interesting, especially since I'd accepted the fact that my traveling days were over because the nameless dread that was taking over my life now included fear of flying. Listening to Earl describe the rose-colored flush on the mountains looming above Tehran when the plane began to descend the first time he went to Iran, I could only feel a sense of relief that I was sitting in a chair.

As we talked I could not help regretting the fact that the kitchen counter he stood beside, a counter that had always been heaped with papers, catalogs, and books, was now immaculate, as if Earl was getting ready to go somewhere. The mess had been a sign of life. Now I'd open the kitchen door and step into what looked like an empty house until, a moment later, the dog would come out of Earl's bedroom and start walking toward me with his tail wagging and his hips swaying, like Marilyn Monroe singing "We're Having a Heat Wave," though in the dog's case the reason was arthritis. After walking the length of the living room beside the dog I'd enter the bedroom and find Earl out like a light, head back, mouth open, book on his chest, feet dangling over the end of the bed, in the pose they call the Fish in yoga; and then, a moment later, I'd leave, despite the fact that people in hospitals or nursing homes always say they wish you'd wakened them so they would not have missed your visit.

One Saturday he apologized for eating cashew brittle while talking on the phone, and then invited me to come watch *The Third Man*, one of our favorite films; and when I arrived he made tea, and even went out to the cottage in which the handyman had installed a brand-new washer and dryer and put in a few clothes. There was no doubt about it: the handyman was using Earl's money to improve a house that he expected to inherit, though I could not bring myself to ask Earl if that was the case—if only because the next time I dropped in he was flat on his back, in pain. The beard was gone, which, with his rather stylish glasses, made him look like an advertising executive in New York circa 1955, or a gorgeous dragonfly with a thin carapace, easily crushed. When he stood up after I said I must be going, I could see that he now had to turn his whole body to look at me; he could not move only his head—everything had to go with it. He used his walker to leave the bedroom and go to the kitchen but insisted I stay for tea, so I perched on my favorite stool and watched him take down the two mugs adorned with the figures of Adam and Eve. He was upset that day because he could not remember words. He was grateful when I praised his hydrangeas since, he said, he'd spent two days trying to remember their name. As we waited for the water to boil he stood at the kitchen sink looking out at the distant lake in silence, and then he said, "Where did the twenty-three years go? I've been so happy in this house."

I thought of Clark's statement, years ago, as we drove off,

that Earl was "clinically depressed," a statement that now seemed to say more about Clark than Earl.

"Have you really?" I said.

"Yes," he said. "I love everything about this place—even the puddles on the patio when it rains. I stood there this morning looking through the back door at that pure, clear rainwater, so clear I could see the moss growing on the bricks beneath it. That moss is so pretty. I love the puddles after a rain in Florida, and the quiet. I'd love to stay here forever—although," he added, turning to me with a plate of cookies, "I'm not afraid to die."

I waited a moment until I could stand it no longer and then I said: "But of course you're afraid to die! Everyone in his right mind is! You're afraid to die for the same reason I'm afraid to die—because you love being alive! My brother-in-law said my mother was afraid to die, and I thought: Well, of course! Isn't everyone?"

"Was your mother religious?" Earl said.

"More so when she got old," I said. "When she was young it was all golf and cocktail parties. Toward the end all she wanted was two things—to see snow again and to come home."

"Well, that's how everyone feels," he said, "though I could do without the snow. And that's why I've decided to leave this house to John—so I can remain here till they carry me out in a bag—and so Betty will have a place to live after I'm gone."

So it's all about the dog, I thought. It always is down south.

Part of me realized that making such a bequest was

a decent thing to do—the handyman could surely use a house—but the minute Earl said it I realized that I resented the idea. Yes, the handyman had been helpful—but not that helpful, and he had been compensated for everything already. That Earl had decided to leave his house to the handyman could only have one explanation, I thought: he was helpless without him. Ray had already told me that John had made Earl drive over to his broker's in Palatka so he could transfer more of his money into his checking account. And now the handyman had evidently promised to take care of not just Earl but Earl's dog.

My own mother, before she fell, would never even tell my sister and me when she went into the hospital for any reason; she didn't want to worry us. And then she had no choice. She died with hired help, because when one comes to the end you have to find help where you can—the aide in a nursing home, the man who used to fix your screens. Often that person becomes your heir. When the baby boomers die, something called the Great Wealth Transfer is going to take place; a huge amount of money and things, accumulated during the postwar American boom, is going to change hands. In Earl's case the heir would be a fat, superannuated hippie of whom we were for some reason slightly afraid.

The next day, however, the handyman had to go to Jacksonville, so we finally got to watch the German film *Anders als de Andern*, and as if in celebration of his absence Earl did something he had not in a long time before we began. He had me listen to music—Barbara Bonney singing Schumann's "Der Nussbaum," a song that brought tears to Earl's eyes for the second time.

The movie was just what I thought it would be—everyone

in suits and ties—though the story of the blackmail of a homosexual was still infuriating, not least because we'd waited to watch it on a day when we were sure the handyman would not pop in. But when I told Earl that nothing had changed, that he and I lived like sex offenders, that we had not needed blackmail, exposure, or a trial; we had imprisoned ourselves under a sort of voluntary house arrest, he simply laughed and said: "The police aren't keeping me here. Old age is! And the older I get the more I *want* to be home. That's what happens when you get old. Your bed is best. All I need is a book to read and a pillow to rest my head on—and good old Betty," he said, reaching down to scratch the dog behind her ear.

Still, it seemed like a diminution to me that he no longer went to the boat ramp anymore; but then nobody did. People were meeting each other via the Internet. And we were too old to be hooking up with the people I saw on Grindr when Clark visited one day and we looked at all the men one mile, three miles, four miles away, advertising themselves on his iPhone as we sat under the gazebo by the bank. There was, I told Earl that evening, a secret town one could see no other way, a town that seemed to be composed largely of "panty bottoms"—men who liked to wear lace underwear—that existed only in photographs on a smart phone. But Earl was not about to acquire new technology at this point.

I had no idea whether Earl would make it to the winter— when you get old, the beginning of a new season presents a challenge: Do you want to go through this again?—though one day he remarked, when I told him I was starting to use my hearing aids, that by the time he needed them, he'd be gone. Of course he needed them already, but then the average span of time between a person's needing hearing aids and getting them, the audiologist had told me, is seven years. One day Earl said he could not remember the word for a group of people singing (chorus) or the place where they shoot things up in the air (Cape Canaveral) and I laughed, but to him I suspect it was anything but funny. Yet he still seemed to me quite sharp. One day I brought him a brochure from the Sackler Gallery in Washington that I'd picked up at an exhibit on Persian miniatures. There was a photograph on the cover of a carved image from Anatolia of Jonah and the Whale—an image, Earl pointed out, that was similar to the illustration of Jonah on the cover of his *Bible Dictionary*, which he went to his bedroom and fetched for me. Both of them showed Jonah being tossed overboard into the jaws of the whale from a little ship.

One more metaphor for our inevitable extinction, I thought as I saw the similarity—being tossed into the mouth of the whale, like a fish or insect finding itself in the stomach of a bird. What could that be like? When Earl was diagnosed I'd compared it to a game of musical chairs—when the music stops you have to sit down wherever you are. Now it seemed to me more like exiting a party. It was a case of what the architectural historian I worked for in Washington had said about Henry Adams: wanting to leave the world with as little fuss as possible. At least that was how I felt when I went to Mrs. Hadid's funeral at the Methodist church. The minister's remarks alternated among hymns played on the piano, readings from the Gospel, and reminiscences by family members. It was like a talk show. So this is what you get, I thought, after the oxygen tubes finally fall from your nostrils for good, after the hopeless struggle. Old age was like the tray hanging from the neck of a cigarette girl in one of those thirties movies Earl and I liked, I thought, a beautiful blonde who comes to your table in the nightclub, sweeps her arm across the tray, and asks if you'd like cigars or cigarettes—though in this case it was, "Arthritis? Spinal stenosis? Hearing loss? Diabetes? Parkinson's? Alzheimer's? Stroke? ALS? Dementia? Breast cancer? Congestive heart failure? Macular degeneration? Or a brain tumor?"

Soon after that the enormous water oak in Earl's front yard had to be pronounced dead—with good reason, since it looked like one of the trees on a battlefield in *Gone with the Wind*: stark, gray, and leafless. But he was not going to have it removed. "Let the person who lives here after I'm gone take care of it," he said. He had almost completed his will, he informed me as we stood at the screen door looking out on the sun-bleached excuse for a lawn. His niece was coming up in two weeks on a trip with her husband to a classic car convention in North Carolina and he was going to have her take whatever she wanted from the house. But before she got there he wanted me to tell him what I wanted. "But why?" I said.

"Because I want you to have something that will remind you of me," he said.

Ah, I thought, the cemetery of furniture.

The following day Earl presented me with something that looked like an eyeglass case but contained, I saw when I opened it, two elaborately filigreed silver spoons embossed with a pattern of leaves, tendrils, and acorns. "They were my mother's," he said, "and I'm giving them to you to show how much I think of you."

I did not know what to say.

"Your mother's," I finally said.

"My *lover's*," he said. "The one in England."

"I'm sorry," I said. "I misheard you."

The reason was not just my hearing loss; it was the unlikelihood of what he had in fact said—the word that sounded so sexual on his lips.

"The one you used to go to the theater with when you were stationed at the embassy in London?" I said.

"Yes," he said.

The spoons seemed to be Edwardian or late Victorian in design: something he'd found in London in the early fifties. Traces of the belle époque must have still remained in those West End theaters, I thought as I stood there looking at my present, when the two of them, young and handsome, went to their matinee. They'd not been able to reveal their relationship to anyone, but it was an affair that Earl had always held in fond regard, and why not? He'd been young, in London, in love. Forty years later, a veteran of dirty movie theaters in South Florida, I'd met him sitting in his car outside a men's room at the boat ramp in a town in North Central Florida. But at least once, in London, love and sex had been combined in the same person—love, sex, art, and freedom.

He was giving the spoons away, I suspected, not simply because he thought highly of me but because I was the only person in town with whom he could share their backstory. So I closed the worn brown case on this relic of another age, these spoons whose actual origins reached back even further than the plays by Terence Rattigan he and his lover had watched, and stepped out into the Florida sunshine. The next morning he told me to take a Copenhagen figurine of a boy and a dog—and a small gray cat, which turned out to be, when I looked on the bottom, Royal Doulton. Clark, who was a "picker"—someone who went around to estate sales to find overlooked gems—would always look at the shelves of my mother's figurines when he dropped by and tell me what was getting a good price now and what was no longer valued, Copenhagen being the first, he said, Royal Doulton the second. But I had no idea what I was getting when Earl gave me two bookends, glass globes with some kind of purple interior in the shape of birds, the next day. I only noticed that he'd stood longer than I'd seen him stand in some time in order to present me with these items. And when I began asking about other objects in the room—tables, lamps, boxes, figurines—he seemed in no hurry to sit down. He wanted to tell me at what auction he'd bought each item. He who despaired when he could not remember the word for a "group of people singing" had total recall in this matter.

His neighbor when he lived in South Florida, the woman who'd married into an old New England family, the neighbor whose departure for an assisted-living place had triggered his own last flight, had given him several of the tables and chairs in his living room—this room that I always walked through to meet the dog that came out of Earl's bedroom wagging its arthritic tail. They were authentic Colonial pieces. But I had no interest in them. When Queen Mary used to visit people, Earl told me, they were always afraid she'd admire something, because if she did they must insist she have it, and off it went to the palace; but I had no desire for bequests. I even bridled when Earl asked me if I wanted a tall lamp in the corner with a white fringed shade that looked even more Edwardian than the spoons; it seemed to me too much like something a homosexual of an earlier generation would like. So I said I wasn't sure. But I could not refuse his other gifts that day and by the time I left, passing the handyman on my way out, all he could say was: "Look at all that loot!"

A lot less than you'll be getting, I thought as I drove away.

Earl was stripping his house of things like the vases, bowls, and figurines that still filled my mother's house, objects that made the shelves at one end of our living room seem like an altar containing the Ark of the Covenant, because none of her grandchildren, according to my sister, wanted them. Every generation disdains the taste of its predecessor. The lamp with a Wedgwood base that Earl gave me I was not thrilled with, but after thinking its old-fashioned white shade, which looked like a wilted tulip, too Victorian, I put it on the table between my parents' beds. Now there were three people in that room. The tall lamp with the white fringed shade that I drove back to get the next afternoon seemed at first out of place at the far end of the living room, beside the small red chair that had been in my parents' bedroom before the flood. It represented some element of Earl's sensibility that I'd never shared: the part that liked auctions, Edwardian spoons, and *Tristan und Isolde*. That lamp is Earl's taste, I told myself.

Nevertheless, Earl had been metamorphosed, like something in Ovid; he was now a floor lamp. The following Wednesday he gave me a red and gold saucer and bowl, "probably Russian," that he had found in Meshed, where, he said, the staff had not really needed him the week he was there; he was only waiting to go to Tehran. He gave it to me because, he said, the handyman did not appreciate such things, nor did his wife; he wanted someone to have it who would enjoy it. He was in terrible pain because he had stood up the whole time his niece was visiting the previous day on her way north. The Egyptian doctor had sent Earl some new medicine but, Earl said, he'd stopped it, fearful of becoming addicted. That meant he was going to live with some level of discomfort for the rest of his life—a period of time not even he could predict.

His niece had taken the gold and white china that he never used, except when Don, his friend from college days, came to visit, when he only used the cups. He remembered a rattlesnake story from childhood—prompted by my telling him I thought I'd seen one on the lake bed, coiled in front of its hole in the ground—but couldn't remember the word "fang," which I had to supply.

There must have been something about this transfer of treasures that affected my subconscious, because that night I had a nightmare in which I knew that I was not alone in my house, so I got out of bed to investigate, walked down the hall, and saw a figure bent over in front of the refrigerator, peering into the lighted interior. The face was obscured by the refrigerator door, and yet I knew immediately even before it stood up that it was me—searching for something to eat—which caused me to waken, sit up in bed, and shudder.

That morning while walking home from the post office I noticed that the house opposite the library where the previous week a young woman with pierced ears and nose had held a garage sale was now for rent; she had moved out. Since I could think of little more alienating than piercing one's nose in this town I was glad she'd moved on. But I felt sorry for the house. There were houses that simply could not be lived in; they were too close to the library or main street, the interface between the public and residential. I'd seen them sit empty for long periods, and then turn over several times after someone tried to make a home of them until they finally became a business, a business that usually failed. Hers was one—as if being across the street from the public library constituted a fatal publicity.

"For Rent" and "For Sale" signs had always seemed to me sad; the first heralded the decline of a neighborhood, the second meant a family's history was coming to an end, at least in that particular place. I had only recently learned from a neighbor that the street we lived on had been downgraded by local real estate agents because it had three rentals on it. "Nobody wants to stay home anymore," the man who changed the oil in my car said when I mentioned the houses on my street for rent. "The man used to work, the woman stayed home. Now the woman wants to work. Nobody wants to stay home." I wanted every house to be permanent—like the one next to Earl's that had a sign by the sidewalk saying "God Bless the USA," or the one on the other side, which had a wooden sign on which someone had carved the family's name in German lettering, though it lost its aura of solidity when I walked by one day and saw that someone was having a garage sale in front of it with the usual junk, cheap glass vases, old chairs, and paintings.

Earl had now given me the Wedgwood lamp, the Copenhagen figurine of a little boy and a dog, the Royal Doulton figurine of a cat, a pair of filigreed silver spoons, the tall floor lamp with fringed shade, and the red and gold cup and saucer and bowl from Meshed. I told myself I should not accept one more thing but the truth was there was a merry aspect to his giving these objects away—he seemed enlivened by it, the way doing his taxes had perked up my father. And again, like my father, his closet, he said, was full of shirts.

Did I want any? Fortunately we were not the same size. But he got up to give me another tour of his antiques after I inquired about two pieces in his bedroom. He told me again about the woman who lived next door to him in the apartment building in South Florida, the woman who'd married into a prominent New England family. He showed me the fancy clock he'd been given by an older man he used to visit in the same apartment building. He told me that he was leaving the house to the handyman. I asked if he thought the handyman would choose to live in or sell it. "Whatever he decides," he said, putting his hand up to his shoulder in that Roman gesture.

His hands had become whiter, it seemed to me, the way old men's skin gets, more slender, more graceful, the skin smooth, shiny, and tight. He rippled his fingers when he talked, and then put them against his cheek and rested his face on the palm of his hand, the way Jack Benny used to—as if his fingers had risen, performed a little dance, and lain back down. And then the handyman arrived with Earl's arthritis medicine. Ah, I thought, now he's Earl's drug dealer—Earl, who refused to even use pain pills for the longest time.

The next morning NPR broadcast stories about the poor eating choices of inner-city residents, Texas politics, and a scientific study on a gene that made us attracted to certain foods—the culture's current obsessions: race, politics, and diet. But when I went to see Earl he was reading the Bible. When I went into his bedroom the next afternoon he was lying on his bed with a white T-shirt laid across his forehead, which led me to say, "You look like a Bedouin." He told me to get a chair, which I brought to the side of the bed, and asked me if I wanted the two speakers in the den. I said no. And then he got up and walked into the living room and gave me two more figurines and a brownie that Ray had left that morning. "You're making out like a bandit," the handyman said when I walked out.

Earl's largesse did nothing to alleviate my general dread, however, that free-floating anxiety that could be triggered by the smallest thing. I felt I was taking a risk by merely driving to Gainesville. Using a two-lane highway presumes that everyone coming toward you wants to live as much as you do—and is as careful as you are about driving. But even I could make mistakes. I found myself pulling out onto the road after underestimating the speed of the car coming toward me—something old people did. There would come a day when I'd not want to drive at all.

Earl on the other hand was still calmly reading the Bible in his high-backed chair the next time I stopped by. "The two parts of Isaiah don't go together," he said when I walked into his bedroom, a remark I could not respond to since I'd not read the Old Testament in a long time. I no longer went to Mass; I simply passed the old church, now a parish hall, where my mother had stood in her white cashmere coat that first Sunday of our new life in this town, and stared at the steps as if I could see her across an invisible medium called Time. One night while taking my walk I came upon a procession of people carrying a small statue while praying in Spanish as they walked toward the new church, the one with the sweeping roof, leaving me to wonder how long the customs, the Catholicism, of these Mexican and Central American immigrants would last in the oh-so-scientific United States.

The next day the Buick was gone and the kitchen counter was cleaner than I'd ever seen it. The dog came toward me with its arthritic sway. I entered the bedroom. Earl was out like a light, head back, mouth open, Bible on his chest, feet dangling over the end of the bed in their little black sneakers. I retraced my steps back to the lake bed. The lake had started to rise again after the summer rains, but it was no longer a lake; it was now a swamp full of submerged weeds and half-drowned trees that would make it hard to swim or traverse in a boat. Water lilies covered huge swaths of the cove by the public beach. The branches of submerged trees rose gray and sickly above the water. Dead trees lined the shore. Yet I knew now how beautiful swamps are, and so was the walk home; there were beads of silver water on the pine needles and the stillness that comes after a rain. That night we had a violent thunderstorm and afterward it rained lightly for a long time. Everything was soaked the next morning and when I went out into the yard I discovered that even more of the mimosa sapling I'd planted had been eaten—by the deer that were coming into the yard at night.

We had entered the season when summer's over but won't end, and the days become so sweltering, the air so motionless, that it feels as if some enormous storm you can't see is sucking all the energy out of the atmosphere: hurricane weather. We rarely got hurricanes; we were too far inland, or too far north. But we got the weather. Sometimes that meant still, sultry days; and sometimes nor'easters that gave us days of wind and rain. We'd follow the storm's track, half hoping it would come through town, because the rain from a hurricane would help the lakes, half hoping it would go somewhere else and spare us the electrical outage and downed trees. I imagined a hurricane that would blow the house down and all the things inside it. Instead the days went on, hot, still, and suffocating, the nights no different, as Earl sat in his chair reading the Bible. "Why did I stay in this town?" I said to him one day as we were lamenting the weather.

"Because it suits you," he said.

And with that he began pouring the hot water into the mugs as the fig leaves of Adam and Eve moved aside.

Looking back, how odd that remark seems to me now, when I have lost the insouciance of (relative) youth. He might just as well have said, "Because you cannot bring yourself to bury your parents" or "Because you cannot accept death," or "Because you have no other home," but he didn't—because I think he could not imagine anyone acting out of anything but self-interest. In other words, he was a calm and rational man—not a vain hysteric like myself.

A week later I left to see the Grand Canyon and when I got back the weather had cooled off. But while I was away Earl fell twice; after the first fall he lay on the floor for four hours, after the second, for twelve, and when the handyman found him the second time, he phoned 911, and Earl was taken first to Starke, where they decided he had to go to Gainesville, where he chose North Florida hospital, which is up the hill from the nursing home in which my mother had been. When he was admitted he had a urinary tract infection and was running a fever; then in the hospital he had a seizure, and they discovered a heart murmur and moved him to the cardiac unit.

Entering the cardiac unit of the hospital was like visiting NASA—the gleaming floors, the technology, and in the room a little old man wanting to exit the earth. He told me he could not swallow; that they were going to give him a feeding tube; that they were going to send him to a nursing home in Starke that was halfway between his doctor's office and the hospital; that his mouth was dry. He had been told that the McBurney Rehabilitation Center, the nursing home we'd put my mother in, no longer met the hospital's standards; and the handyman thought the one in Starke was a dump. "They're all awful," said a nurse when I inquired.

Afterward I drove a short distance to the gym in Gainesville and went to yoga. I was so depressed about Earl I thought it would clear my mind, which it did, especially when a handsome middle-aged man I'd seen there before came over and hugged me during yoga's version of the Sign of Peace and did it with a smile. Driving home I listened to the sextet from *Lucia di Lammermoor* on the tape Earl had made for me years ago. The next morning I went outside and stood by the flower bed watching the Gulf fritillaries flying over the pentas and porterweed and said to myself: "This is the day"—the first day of autumn—and then I remembered it was my mother's birthday.

On Sunday I went back to the hospital after talking to a friend in California who said that people shy away from death and I should visit Earl because we must visit the sick. He was alone, as I'd left him, eyes closed, and faintly moaning when I walked in. I went out and asked a nurse to give him more pain medication, though I could see no effect after the nurse did so. Earl kept making little moans, and the muscles on his forehead would not relax. I sat with him an hour. We had the usual trouble communicating; his mouth was so dry he could hardly speak, and I was hard of hearing. Though at one point I thought he said, "Ray is a remarkable person," I wasn't sure if I'd heard correctly or whether he'd he asked me to tell Ray that. I could only think: He identifies with Ray in some way, perhaps because of religion. Then I took his hand in mind and held it for a while.

In all the years I've known Earl we had never once embraced, or touched, or expressed any physical affection; the most I'd done when I left him in the den was put one hand on his shoulder as I walked out in a gesture of encouragement. So it was shocking that not only did he let me hold his hand, that dry, soft hand that reminded me so much of my father's, but he grasped mine as well. But that apparently is common among the dying—some last tether to the earth, some comfort as they are about to take this final trip, the one you never return from. If Hollywood had wanted to depict an old man dying, I thought, it's this face—oxygen tubes in nostrils, eyes closed, face gaunt. So far as I knew he was not eating. It occurred to me that they were letting him shut down naturally. That is one way we die: we stop eating. I did not ask any of the nurses, in large part because I did not want to hear the question "Who are you?"—the problem I'd encountered in the eighties in New York hospitals: I was not "family." What was I to Earl? The nurses could refuse me information because I was not a blood relative. I still had no idea what I meant to Earl. He had stood in for my father these past years, I thought: the same formality, self-possession, calm, and distance. But Earl was gay. And because he was gay I could talk to him in a way I could not my father.

I had no idea if Earl's sister knew he was dying, and his doctor was out of town on vacation. I could not find the handyman's phone number, and to my surprise Earl did not know it. The dog was locked up in the house; she'd barked when I tried the kitchen door. When I told Earl that Betty would be glad when he got back, he said, "If I get back."

So after all his efforts, I thought as I sat there in the perfect quiet, Earl ends up like everyone else—in Gainesville. It was like *The Death of Ivan Ilyich*, the story by Tolstoy about the man dying of cancer. Looking at Earl I began to think of the three aspects of death: the moment when you learn it's going to happen (a diagnosis), the instant it happens (unpredictable), and—most bizarre of all—the moment after: the fact that even though you die Time continues, and the World goes on. At one stroke you cease to be a subject and become an object: a person people who come into the room in which your corpse lies can talk about but who cannot answer back. Everything else evolves but you cannot witness it. You will not hear the people talking about you as you lie there like a sack of potatoes. Your doctor can request an autopsy, but you will not learn the results. You cannot, like Tom Sawyer, observe your own funeral.

There was no answer to any of these problems, and Earl, who was going through this very dilemma, seemed to have fallen asleep. So I made my exit when the room grew dark.

After leaving Earl in the awful solitude of his deathbed I got lost in the maze of doctors' offices and surgical pavilions behind North Florida hospital the way I always did. As I walked up the hill toward the hospital a helicopter landed and took off again, so quickly it was like a dragonfly that rests on a twig and then flies off. The history of everyone I knew, it seemed to me at that moment, was medical. The minute we are born the universe is out to kill us. We're under assault from the moment we breathe. We are nothing but our medical records. The first building I passed was the surgical pavilion in which I'd had a hernia repaired, and then my gallbladder removed, and then an abscess in my right cheek caused by the hook on a palm frond that had pierced the skin when I was pruning it, and then the building in which my mother had spent eleven years of her life, in which my neighbor still lived, though I did not have the nerve to visit him because I could not imagine entering that place again, or rather could imagine, which was why I'd never done so. I was now so far up the slope, on the same level with the nursing home, that I could see, through the glass of the side door where one entered after five o'clock, the hallway on which my mother had lived, at which point the opening line of *Rebecca* came to me—"Last night I dreamt I went to Manderley"— the house the nameless narrator has been taken to as a young bride by her mysterious husband. And the minute that happened I realized why I'd been so attendant on Earl's decline; it had all been to remember this.

In the movie Joan Fontaine tries the gate across the drive. I went to the side entrance of the nursing home and tried the door, and—as in Joan's dream—it was locked. So I stood there looking through the window, a window like the one beside Earl's front door that allowed me to see what he was watching on TV, only here it gave me a view of the intersection of two oh-so-familiar corridors. It seemed to me it had been carpeted when I was last here, but now the floor was bare wood. Nothing else had changed. The nurses' station, I knew, was just out of sight to the right. I could see down the hall almost to the doorway of my mother's room, the room in which her first roommate, an old woman so emaciated she looked like Granny in *The Beverly Hillbillies*, kept squawking, "Benadryl! Benadryl!" like a parrot. To the left, according to a sign on the wall, was the gym. But had there been a gym when my mother was there, or had they added a wing?

No, I told myself, there had to have been a gym—the place had opened as a rehabilitation center. My mother had been the eleventh person admitted; she'd pooped once in the Jacuzzi and they'd had to drain it. It was all coming back: the day we'd arrived and went out into the courtyard, where I had cruelly made her show us how much she could move her hand (hardly at all) to prove to everyone that the physical therapy was working, till she'd shaken her head and quietly asked me to stop. The physical therapy had done all that it could for her: not much.

I tried the door again but it was locked. It was shut as tight as it had been the day they closed the nursing home because a man who'd murdered five University of Florida co-eds, and left the first victim's head on the turntable of a record player in her apartment, was still on the loose. I couldn't remember the year. But I could recall the hot afternoon I arrived at this door for dinner with my mother and they had to let me in because this door was locked, as if the killer might break in, though his victims had all been beautiful young women—not exactly what was inside the McBurney Rehabilitation Center. Indeed, I could still remember, later that evening, an aide, a big, strapping young man with a beard, saying in a rich, scornful voice to the elderly woman he was undressing for bed as I walked by, "You ain't got nothin' *I* want!" The woman, I could only assume, had accused him of wanting her. His response had seemed to me the epigraph for the entire place. Nobody old has anything one wants, I thought as I stood there now staring into the corridor— advice, or money, perhaps, but nothing having to do with the flesh. And then another memory arose as I turned away and walked back across the parking lot, where it occurred to me that I might keep going all the way across University Avenue to stroll around the Oaks Mall—something I'd done with my mother till it became such a routine, like everything else about our lives, that we had no interest in going anymore. There're not many things more forlorn than going to a mall to look at people.

I remembered my gym as having a sexual atmosphere on Sunday nights, but there was none of that when I got there this time. The place had the tired air that comes at the end of a weekend. Yoga was quiet. I did not hang around afterward. I wanted more than anything to be home. I drove past the dirty bookstore in Orange Heights without stopping and then, once past the farm that sold fresh produce from a stand beside the highway, the beauty of the landscape, as always, calmed me down, as if all of Florida depended on this one stretch between Highway 301 and Madison remaining what it was: a ranch where cattle occasionally grazed, a vast open space surrounded by pinewoods. Of course, it would not; I'd already spotted a "For Sale" sign offering to subdivide the property. But for now it was still beautiful. The contrast between the wheat-colored pasture and the dark green of the distant trees was about to fade to dark. I thought of that line in Chekhov's journals, where he looks out the window and sees the funeral procession of someone he knows going by and thinks: I am eating breakfast, and you are going to the grave—Chekhov, who when he knew he was dying ordered a bottle of champagne, as opposed to Tolstoy, who when the end was nigh slipped out of his house at night to make one last run for it and ended up dying in a train station.

The handyman called at noon the next day to say that Earl had stopped breathing at four that morning. I had awakened around then hearing rain on the roof. Perhaps he died when it was raining, I thought as I sat on the edge of the bed. The storm was gone, the day was cool and breezy, the light was different. It was a crisp autumn day in North Florida, with the fresh, clean air that a good rain leaves behind. A breeze was blowing; the goldenrod had started to turn yellow; the banana spiders—aka golden orbs—had begun to spin their enormous gilded webs; butterflies sat on the ground when I walked out, folding and unfolding their wings, as if exhausted by summer. So this is the day after death, I thought. This is the day Earl did not witness. When I called Ray he said he had prayed with Earl, asking the Lord to take him when it was time. He said Earl wanted to die, there was nothing left for him to accomplish; that the death of Don, his oldest friend, in New York, had been a blow. Perhaps that's how we die, I thought, with our classmates, our cohort, our companions. We do everything as part of a group; we are social animals to the end.

In the Grand Canyon I'd been standing waiting in the lunch line one day when the woman beside me started to talk and I learned that this was her first trip since her husband had died, though her husband, immobilized by multiple sclerosis, had urged her, after many years of caretaking, to start traveling because there was no telling when he'd expire, and she'd taken him at his word and gone to South America. "He died when I was in Machu Picchu," she said as we filled our paper plates with hot dogs and potato salad. I had been back home when Earl died but miles away when it happened—as is so often the case nowadays.

I had been out west for only two weeks, but when I went out into the yard I could see I'd lost the impatiens growing in pots under the big live oak, though the geraniums and crossandra had survived, so evidently we'd had something of a drought, which the latter two can survive. The golden orb that had been sitting on its enormous web outside the porch door, so close to the screen that I could stand a foot away and watch it trap wasps and paralyze them, was still there, but the web was starting to fall apart. I was sure the spider was dead. On the windowpane were two strange white spheres wrapped in a white cocoon, eggs I assumed. I had watched this spider dash down to the insects it had trapped, sting them, and then slowly drag them back to another spot on the web, where they would be wrapped in filament, like mummies. I had watched this spider eat, reproduce, and die, all on its web—aging in place! And now I saw it down near the ground, still on the web, apparently alive.

The lizards on the porch screen were oblivious of my presence, a little red balloon emerging from their throats each time they tried to frighten or eat an insect. There were two frogs inside the house that I ushered outside to live some more. As I walked back across the lake bed that evening there were coreopsis in bloom, goldenrod blowing in the wind, pale purple daisies with gold centers and tall grasses nodding in the breeze, some of it with a full load of bushy oatmeal-colored feathers, another kind with pale purple-brown tassels, and still another with leaves that looked like ferns, and flowers that resembled tiny yellow buttercups. A cloud of eastern swallowtails had covered a field of milkweed. There were small golden wasps on the red berries on the holly trees. The stream that had once connected the Big Lake with the one I lived on was flowing again; there was even a little waterfall. Everything that had until now been too green, too lush, too overgrown, looked chastened by the colder air. There was even a rent in the plum-colored clouds on the horizon when I turned toward home—an opening through which the setting sun shone across the water with a brassy sheen—a real November sky. And when I got back to my house, the yard looked like an illuminated manuscript; I would not have been surprised to see a woman in a conical hat knitting under the live oak beside a unicorn.

That night it got so chilly it felt like snow, and when I walked by Earl's the following morning the grass in front of his house was so high it was as if it had been allowed to relax now that Earl was dead. The spider was still alive, however, when I got home from the post office; I saw it climbing down its tattered web, though it had apparently lost its capacity to spin more of the golden filament—half of the web had fallen down and was swaying in the wind. The next morning I went out and saw the spider on its back, on the ground, dead.

Two Loves Have I at Walgreens

One is tall and skinny with a face I associate with nineteenth-century England—at least the movie *Of Human Bondage*—a strange, angular boy with Bette Davis eyes, so tall, so skinny, he reminds me of a sand hill crane. In summer it is almost painful to see the T-shirt sagging from his bony shoulders; in winter when he wears a plaid shirt he looks much better. The other is the pharmacist at the back of the store. He looks like Edgar Allan Poe: short, slight, with small hands, little fingernails, handsome in a riverboat gambler way, with a goatee and wavy salt-and-pepper hair combed back from his high, pale forehead, and a bald spot on the top that looks like a monk's tonsure. The pharmacist has a sweet and ready smile, and eyes that often squint, which makes him seem even sweeter. His voice is soft, his manner is playful, his sense of humor teasing. He gives me my shot for shingles; we sit together behind a portable screen in a nook between the racks of diabetes medicine and the vitamins, like Alma and the doctor in *Summer and Smoke*. He explains what socks for diabetics are when I ask him how they differ from ordinary footwear, and what the purpose is of the red plastic jug he has brought out that looks big enough to contain gasoline or that awful stuff you have to drink before a colonoscopy. It's for disposal of biohazard waste, he says, like the needle he's going to use on me. I ask him why cinnamon is on the shelf as a health supplement. "It regulates sugar," he says. And he confirms the fact, when I ask, that indeed one thousand milligrams equals one gram, which means I've been eating one gram less of fish oil every day than I should.

At one point, while waiting for him to prepare my shingles shot, a week before Christmas, I realize I am alone in the store with both of them: the tall, skinny boy with dirty blond hair and Bette Davis eyes at the checkout counter in the front, and the fine-boned pharmacist in the rear of the store, so when I've had my shot, I do not want to leave. Perhaps, it occurs to me, there's another shot I can ask him for—so he will come outside his warren of shelves lined with drugs and sit down beside me in the intimate space created by the folding screen next to the items for people with diabetes. But I've had the shot for pneumonia. That's all I need. So I get up and go, and by the time I buy a candy bar, the person who checks me out is not the tall boy with Bette Davis eyes but a cheerful young woman who asks me if I want a bag, after which I glance over and see him watching our transaction, finally acknowledging me with a little nod, which I assume means that he remembers me from our previous exchanges.

These evenings at Walgreens are the bright spot of a long day spent indoors. My only interaction with another human being had been with Earl's handyman when he was replacing a portion of the carport that had rotted away because raindrops have been bouncing off the gas tank against the wall all these years. And he disappeared after he asked me for a loan and I gave him a check for two thousand dollars under the mistaken impression that he would pay it back. His face was so astonished when I gave him the check I knew I'd been foolish; he took it, and ran off to his car to cash it at the bank, and never came back. Before that he had asked me for money so he could buy his granddaughter Christmas presents. How can he sink that low, I wondered at the time; I was soon to find out.

All relationships with other human beings are fraught before Christmas. Christmas casts a spell that dissolves whatever carapace one uses to get through the rest of the year—leaving one so vulnerable one feels like a crab between shells. I dread the fact that in a week or so I will have to go north to my sister—because she insists I not spend Christmas by myself. The only time I feel relief from the impending doom is when I take my walk at night—the walk that often ends at Walgreens.

The houses I pass along the way seem more and more poignant the closer Christmas gets. Some of the yards have lights; most don't. Of the former, a few feature a crèche, others combine the scene of the Nativity with Santa Claus. One has Mickey and Minnie Mouse, though what they have to do with Christmas I don't know, unless it's to declare the household is agnostic, or Jewish. I've been altering my nightly walk to look at houses I see in the distance on streets I don't usually take, merely because I can see the glow of blue and green lights, the two most satisfying Christmas colors, no doubt because they are so melancholy.

One night the detour leads me toward the high school, where I can see, above the trees, the blaze of lights that illuminate the football field. Before I even arrive I hear the voice of the announcer identifying the players. He is mispronouncing the Hispanic names, which makes me think of the way the demographic composition of this country is changing, and how reluctant Americans are to learn a foreign language. Then I get to the fence that surrounds the football field and see that it is soccer, not football, players he is introducing, soccer players who run out onto the turf one by one and stand in a row.

A few people are sitting in the high, narrow concrete bleachers across the field. The lights are on poles above and behind them. The national anthem is played. The players disperse to opposite sides of the field, gather in a knot, cheer their own team, then take their positions. I watch a few plays as I stand at the fence, enjoying the energy and concentration in the players' faces, which takes me back to my own time playing soccer at school up in New Hampshire in temperatures much colder than these. And then I leave. The darkness swallows me up as if I were sinking back into a pond. I feel like an animal returning to its habitat as the lights from the football field fade the farther I go across a large expanse of sand and grass before reaching the first paved road, and then the lighted houses take over, these little jewel boxes, these Fabergé eggs of colored light, these over-the-top offerings of townspeople who have transformed their modest ranch houses into palaces of electricity.

The house in which Earl lived is lighted in a different pattern now. The handyman sold it to a retired judge who lives on my street. He never had any intention of living there; he just wanted the money. The person who rents it I'm told is a single man, a former deejay from Orlando who's put a sign up by the drive that says "Deplorables for Trump." Sometimes the kitchen is ablaze, other nights the little room at the far end of the house in which Earl used to store his paintings of dogs. I still don't know what the handyman did with Earl—cremated him, I presume, and scattered the ashes, probably in the flower bed with the blueberry bushes, where his dogs are buried. The handyman never asked me over for the ceremony if there was one. But presumably Earl has been disposed of. Indeed, I've been noticing lately how I walk by Earl's house without even thinking of him.

Cremation is not looked on favorably by the Catholic Church, a monk I know in Washington explained to me once—for a simple reason. The Church believes in the Resurrection, and at the Resurrection the body and soul are united. What age the body is, and exactly how the two are rejoined, I don't know; when I asked my friend, he said, "I'll have to get back to you on that one." The new occupant of Earl's house I've never even seen; nor has he put up any Christmas lights. Single people rarely do. In contrast, the house across the street has always been the most spectacular in town at Halloween and Christmas and has even more life-size figures than last year, so that now there are two manger scenes, four Santa Clauses, and one Rudolph the Red-Nosed Reindeer. According to rumor the owner of that house works for the local electrical cooperative, hence the display. Whatever the reason, his yard is nothing if not eclectic. Never has the Holy Family, even when depicted in illuminated, life-size plastic figures, been forced to share the stage with so many other cultural icons, many of them cartoons. We are a long way from Giotto. We are in a town two hours north of Disney World, walking, ten minutes later, past a cottage on a street that leads to the biggest of its several Baptist churches. The cottage's owners outlined its entire roof last year, but this Christmas they have confined themselves to the front of the house, framed in colors that inspire in me the feeling I had as a child when sitting by the Christmas tree, trying to figure out the contents of the wrapped boxes beneath its boughs.

What is it about the glow of Christmas lights? Why do these cheap bulbs look like jewels? Why do the deep blue, green, and red seem like sapphires, emeralds, and rubies? And why did the people in this house not do the sides of the house as well? I wonder for a moment if I should leave a note with that suggestion from "an appreciative passerby" at the front door, like a message from Santa Claus, but I walk on.

Next is the house of blue lights. When I was growing up people who put up lights that were all one color seemed stylish, irreligious, and sophisticated. Now the use of a single color is common, especially when it's white, but these blue bulbs, which the owners of this house have draped on their azaleas so that they form a sort of undulating wave, are so beautiful I stop and stare—long enough to realize I have forgotten the first stanza of "Stopping by Woods on a Snowy Evening." Ten minutes later I come to a house near the Women's Club that has gone totally bananas; there's a big sleigh with Santa in the front yard and a sign that says "The North Pole" and a small sleigh at the end of a driveway outlined in lights. A few doors down is a house whose occupants have hung big wooden snowflakes on strings from the branches of a pecan tree that turn and sparkle in a spotlight, so charmingly they make me wonder: Why doesn't everyone have these snowflakes hanging from their trees? People, after all, follow trends, like the white lights they string along the eaves that mimic icicles—icicles that induce a longing for real snow, real icicles.

Next is a house where snowdrops seem to be falling down the front of it, snowdrops projected on the wall by a light somewhere opposite the old Catholic church, the one they deconsecrated and turned into a hall for dinners and social events after building the new one with the upswept roof across the retention pond that is so full of frogs on summer nights it's deafening. The old Catholic church, where we went to Mass when we first moved here, is completely dark; the branches of the camphor tree not far from the steps cast spooky shadows on what used to be the front door. The front door has been locked for years; one no longer enters the church that way and walks down the aisle to witness the consecration that turns a wafer into the body of Christ. What is now the parish hall looks like a place where nothing, not even the memory of my mother, lives.

The next block is really dark, a tunnel of live oaks that grew up so close together that none of them could branch out, so that they look like trees you find near the ocean that have been stunted by the salt air. One block after that, the last block before my own, are three houses whose lights are nice but not outstanding. Across the highway the slope down to my own street is completely dark. The house nearest the highway has not been lived in for decades. A childless couple who retired from the State Department were living there when my father settled here, but for years now it's been one of those houses that nobody seems to want to live in, sell, or keep up. It's extraordinary, these empty houses; there's no rational explanation for them. The couple who lived there played bridge a lot. I can't even remember when or how they died. But I associate them with a time when the town was, like the nation itself, more, for lack of a better word, genteel.

Next door is another small house in which an obese couple lived till they sold it to a man who makes his living grinding tree stumps. He drives a truck he's outlined in so much neon that it looks like a traveling nightclub when he pulls into his driveway at night. Since moving here he has planted marigolds around the base of his live oaks and installed lights powered with solar energy, and now he's put up an inflatable Santa Claus, twelve feet high, that regards the street with the cheerful face of a goodwill ambassador; behind him is a little cadre of smaller figures, a snowman, a puppy, a white cat with whiskers, a little red cardinal with an orange beak, and a bear in a conical hat. On cold nights the stump grinder often builds, behind his house, a little fire that casts a glow up into the branches of his live oaks, which makes me think of the fires the original settlers must have built when Florida was still a frontier, populated by loners and dropouts whose descendants are still with us. The fire flickers on the roof of the dark cave of oaks that is the stump grinder's backyard, but Santa is doubly in the light: he is lighted from within, and he is so near the streetlight on the highway that he is illumined by it as well. He looks to me for some reason like the viceroy of an ancient king—although in the hands clasped together at his waist there is nothing more official than a small teddy bear.

I never know what condition Santa will be in when I walk by. Some nights Santa is standing there like Nebuchadnezzar or Ramses the Great; other nights he is flat on his back, as if he's been assaulted or mugged, and the inflatables behind him lie on the ground in little heaps of crumpled filthy plastic. When only Santa is standing, the scene resembles a St. Valentine's Day Massacre that he alone has survived. Last night when I walked by, Santa Claus was flat on his back, though still inflated, as if he'd passed out from drinking, and the little animals hadn't been inflated in some time. Tonight, however, they are all pumped up and radiant: a dazzling display that seems to be a declaration of goodwill from the street to which the stump grinder has just moved, even if he knows no one on it, though the same might be said of everyone in our neighborhood now, so little do my neighbors have contact with one another. The woman next door, for instance, has just sold her house and is moving at the end of the month, but I doubt very much that she'll say goodbye. Decades ago we'd gather in the communal park around which the houses are built and start a bonfire under the live oaks; everyone would bring a dish, sit there and eat, talk, and drink for hours, while the shadows cast by the dwindling fire flickered on the Spanish moss and the limbs of the live oaks overhead. Now I'm not even sure who lives four houses down, and one place seems to be owned by a drug dealer who keeps an outdoor floodlight on all night, and three other houses are being rented. So there won't be a Christmas party this year—there hasn't been one for decades, though the navy-blue V-neck sweater in which I used to carry my father's casserole out to the park is still in my closet in a bag of mothballs.

It is a law of human nature that the houses without Christmas decorations always outnumber by far those that have them, like the straight families who overwhelm the drag queens they come to take pictures of at the Halloween parades in New York and Provincetown. My street is particularly dark, my own house especially forbidding, though not as sinister as a house on the other side of town with a semicircular driveway outlined with live oaks that has been for sale for months now and looks, as houses in that situation do, more and more like something dying; that one is so dark it's menacing. But I haven't put up Christmas lights either, or a Christmas tree, in years. I don't even know where the lights my father used to put up are, but since I never throw anything out, they must be in the house somewhere, though I have no idea if they'd still work—especially since, when I need a Christmas card and go into the closet to find the ones my mother left behind, they're useless because the envelopes are all stuck shut.

The woman across the street from me, however, has put up a little tree in her carport, and a sort of altar to Santa Claus—a table with two candles and an image of Santa that looks for some reason not unlike the one you prepare for the priest when he comes to the house to give the dying Extreme Unction.

Her little Christmas tree is the only one I have access to. The prize on these walks, of course, is not the lights outside the houses I pass, spectacular though they may sometimes be; it's the glimpse of a Christmas tree within. There's nothing like a Christmas tree glowing in an otherwise dim living room—a sight that exudes the privacy of domestic life. A house's outdoor lights are put up for me, the passerby; the Christmas tree is for the family. In Washington almost all the lobbies of the apartment buildings and think tanks have beautiful Christmas trees, but they're so big and grand they seem impersonal. A Christmas tree inside someone's house, however, is touching. This year I've seen trees in only two houses, which makes my own house when I return all the more a rebuke, since I've not put one up either. The Spanish moss hanging from the live oak in the drive casts wavy black shadows on the white walls as I unlock the door, accentuating the vacancy within. It's like entering a haunted house. Sorry, it is a haunted house; my parents are still with me, though I can no longer even find their ashes.

If I were to put up Christmas lights—as my father did every year—I'd probably give in to the fact that this is Florida and there is no point in trying to reproduce icicles or snowflakes. Nothing's simpler or better, I've noticed on my walks, than a real palm tree whose trunk is wrapped in lights. That's Christmas in Florida. The next night I see two of these as I walk through parts of town I rarely visit, drawn by the lure of distant lights, though I always end up at Walgreens in the hope that the pharmacist who looks like Edgar Allan Poe or the boy with Bette Davis eyes will be there.

The store's website describes Walgreens as "a chain store with health and beauty aids, and mini-mart basics"—the latter, I assume, being the two aisles of groceries, most of it processed food—things designed for a long shelf life. But it doesn't go into the personal lives or habits of its employees, or even provide their names. So I have no idea what their schedules are, where they live, how far they commute, or whether or not they are moved around among different Walgreens in the area. The fellow with Bette Davis eyes is so young I presume he has chosen work over college, or is doing this part-time. Most of the clerks at Walgreens are women of various ages, but he is just starting out in life. His expression, it seems to me, has been growing increasingly despondent as Christmas nears, in contrast to the pharmacist, who remains his usual equable self. "Will you be open on Christmas Eve?" I want to ask when I walk in. But that's a creepy question—way too lonely—though that's the Christmas Eve I'd really like. To be the only customer in the store, just the cashier, the pharmacist, and me, alone with the sunglasses and vitamin pills and greeting cards and candy bars and toothpaste and shampoo, if only for fifteen minutes, would be the perfect Christmas Eve.

Because Walgreens stays open till ten, like the CVS across the street, they are the only businesses in this town one can visit at night. Not even the gas station is open—since the owner was caught scamming money off the sale of lottery tickets, which is why there are yellow plastic bags wrapped around all the nozzles of the gas tanks. Sometimes a band is practicing behind vertical blinds in the music store, and I stop and listen to the song they're trying to learn, most often one by Creedence Clearwater Revival, or I pause at the decorating shop next door that has a Christmas display in the window whose colors are white and blue, testifying to the taste of the woman who owns it. Christmas interiors belong mostly to women; it's men who put up the outdoor lights— those old sexual roles on which many have shipwrecked.

Because Walgreens is open till ten in a town that has otherwise gone to bed, the pleasure in going there is the one I used to feel when visiting after-hours clubs in lower Manhattan in the seventies, though at nine forty-five Walgreens is almost always empty. Why go that late? Because the later the hour, the less chance that I will have to compete for the clerk's attention with other customers. There probably won't be any customers. What I don't want is to find myself standing in line at the checkout with a bunch of other shoppers who preoccupy the boy with Bette Davis eyes so that he's all business when I present my item; or worse, I am palmed off on one of the women who work the other register down by cosmetics, when she sees the crunch of customers and waves the end of the line over to her counter.

Last year, I should mention, something terrible happened at the drugstore: the employees began to say "Welcome to Walgreens!" whenever I walked in. The first time this happened I stopped and asked the boy with Bette Davis eyes if he'd been ordered to do this, and when he said yes, I shook my head in commiseration. It seemed obviously an idea that someone in a marketing meeting at headquarters had come up with, and indeed it proved to be so disliked by the employees that after a short while it became a custom more honored in the breach than the observance. But it allowed me to express, the first time it happened, a sense of solidarity with the boy with Bette Davis eyes, to take his part, to show I saw it from his perspective, though he never mentioned it again, and after a while it ceased to provide a topic of conversation for us during checkout. Checkout is never a guarantee of intimacy anyway. Once while standing in line I saw him laughing with some customers his age at the register, whereupon my fantasy that he was attracted to older men crumbled to smithereens, and when it came time to pay for my candy bar I could think of nothing to say.

I suspect he merely associates me at this point in time with Lindt's Dark Chocolate 70%, Intense Orange, or Black Currant, the three candy bars I buy after a careful reading of the calorie counts and ingredients. Lindt candy bars are twenty cents cheaper at Walgreens than at the grocery store, and there is more of a variety of other brands; beneath the

Lindts are candy bars from Ghirardelli, Godiva, and even Green & Black's, my favorite, though the latter are the most expensive. When the Lindts are on sale I hand the boy with Bette Davis eyes my blue Walgreens discount card with a strange feeling of satisfaction, as if enrolling in their program makes us comrades. I never ask for a bag, because of the Pacific Garbage Patch; I walk home with the candy bar in my pocket, and the illusion that the boy with Bette Davis eyes would say yes if some night I came in my car and he needed a ride home and I offered him one, though I have no idea where he lives. The web page for Walgreens includes photographs and short biographies of the pharmacists but not of the clerks, and as for the pharmacists, only the first name and the first initial of their last name are given, so that they sound like characters in a nineteenth-century Austrian novel that opens with: "One summer day in the town of —— Stephen L. arrived in an old landau pulled by two bays belonging to the prefect of . . ." I assume the reason they conceal the last name is privacy, but what is gained by giving us the first initial of their surname? It doesn't matter. Stephen, the pharmacist who looks like Edgar Allan Poe, went to the University of Illinois, I read, and has been working for Walgreens for eleven years. The other pharmacist, whom I've seen only once, has been there two years and graduated from a pharmacy school in the Appalachians. The boy with Bette Davis eyes is not on the web page; his post is too insignificant. But it doesn't matter. The main thing I'd like to know about him is not something that would be online. Years ago while taking my nightly walk I was picked up by a battered queen who pulled off the side of the road in his old Volkswagen and flashed his headlights several times before I realized what that meant. He turned out to be a male nurse living in a cottage on the other side of the lake who burst my bubble by telling me that he often waited till closing at the grocery store and offered the bag boys rides home and had sex with them. The idea has always stayed in my mind, but I no more have the courage to suggest this to the boy with Bette Davis eyes than I have to tell my sister that I'm not coming to her house this Christmas. Maybe that's why the idea of spending the feast alone in this little town seems to me so erotic: just the three of us, the pharmacist, the boy with Bette Davis eyes, and me on Christmas Eve. Surely I'd experience a degree of despair, loneliness, and self-loathing unsurpassed at any other time. The lighted houses, the Christmas windows at the five-and-dime, the empty street, would be more expressive of the original story of the Nativity than anything I could experience in a house filled with people in the suburbs of a city up north.

I don't want to go to an airport and get on the road, I tell myself; I want to stay home and feel the anniversary of the birth of Christ get closer and closer as I watch the boy with Bette Davis eyes grow more and more despondent, and the voice in which he says "Welcome to Walgreens!" become less and less audible, especially to someone like myself with hearing loss.

I know my sister insists I come because she can't stand the idea of my being alone at Christmas, and bless her heart for that; her house, her table, are always so beautiful at Christmas I am glad I've gone. But I long to explain to her that single people get used to being alone, that it becomes normal for them, that it's the deviation from that condition that's painful. On the other hand, if I do stay here, won't

Walgreens surely be closed on Christmas Eve? It's unlikely they would keep it open for the likes of vampires like myself, and they'll certainly be closed on Christmas Day, and even if they were open I wouldn't have the nerve to make an appearance in the store at that time. I would hide from public view the closer it got to Christmas, too embarrassed to go out, not even daring to venture to the mailbox on the street to get the trickle of Christmas cards I receive each year, Christmas cards I no longer send anymore unless somebody sends me one. But still I feel that by going north I am missing some exquisite mixing of loneliness and lust. No matter. I will never know. I don't have the nerve to say that I'm not coming.

Before I leave, however, in preparation for my trip and the exposure to all those people in the airport, I must get my shot for this season's flu; it would be foolish to take an airplane ride in the middle of winter without having had one. I know I can take it at any time, on any day of the week, but I am also aware that the flu shot is my only chance to be with Edgar Allan Poe, so I must time my visit right. Of course, after the source of all my guilt and anxieties, *The New York Times*, advises me that it is a good idea to get the flu shot as early as possible, since the flu season in Australia (a harbinger of ours) has been especially bad this year, that adds a certain urgency to things. So for the past few weeks I have been going to Walgreens at various times in the hope that Edgar Allan Poe will be working when I get there. The problem is I don't know his schedule, so it's always a gamble. The first time I stopped in on a Saturday night the pharmacy was closed—it closes at six on weekends, I learned, at nine on the weeknights. The second time, on a weeknight, the Appalachian pharmacist was on duty, so I turned around and left. I didn't know my favorite pharmacist's hours but I did know what I wanted: the quiet, empty store that I usually find half an hour before closing. So I started walking up to Walgreens around eight-thirty in hopes that I would find no other customers with whom I'd have to share his attention—something that can be quite in demand when there's a line of cars outside his window, for the pharmacist, like the teller at the bank, has to work both sides: indoors and out.

One gets a flu shot, after all, only once a year, so I couldn't waste this opportunity—which is why whenever I go, I enter the store, accept with as much grace as I can muster the "Welcome to Walgreens!" from the cashier, whoever it is, and walk directly to the back of the store, past the cosmetics and the sunglasses, to see if he's on duty. When he is, I know we will share the sort of badinage, the intimacy that is possible only when you are the only customer and the store is deathly quiet. And that is why when he's not, even though I know the earlier you get your flu shot the better, I turn on my heel and walk right out of the store without even purchasing a candy bar, unless it's on sale at two for five dollars.

Whatever happens, the houses whose invisible occupants put on these wonderful shows of white or colored light soothe my spirit on the way back home. The people who have put up these lovely displays may be no more cognizant of the pleasure they give me than I am able to express my feelings about Christmas to my sister, the pharmacist, or the boy with Bette Davis eyes, but that doesn't change the fact that their efforts fill me with a sentimental warmth. It's Christmas, so most of us are walking around with feelings that can't be expressed; but as I walk along I know I have something to look forward to—my flu shot—which will be the case every year until the pharmacist's assigned, God forbid, somewhere else, or I kick the bucket. If all goes well at some point before I leave for Christmas we will be sitting in the little portable enclosure between the diabetic socks and the vitamins, making ironic comments on what we are there to do. Meanwhile life is pleasant. I have moved the tall Edwardian lamp with the fringed shade that Earl gave me onto the enclosed porch, where it has transformed the room into the loveliest part of the house, especially when I go out into the yard and look back at it, as if it's somebody else's home. One must be grateful for what one has. So if, when I get back to my street, Santa is lying not only flat on his back but completely deflated, and the little animals in his retinue have been reduced to crumpled heaps of dirty plastic under a tree on which someone has posted a sign urging passersby to "Get on the Trump Train," I can still take pleasure from my neighbor's fire flickering in the darkness under the live oaks, and the fact that the night is cold and the sky cloudless and clear, because, as Bette so wisely urged her beau, "Oh, Jerry, don't let's ask for the moon. We have the stars." Tomorrow I may even drive to the beach—something I haven't done in years. That's how you know you've been in Florida too long—you no longer go to the beach.